SWAMPED BY FEAR

CRITTER CATCHERS
BOOK 3

HANK EDWARDS

MITTEN GINGER MEDIA

CONTENTS

SUMMARY

A family emergency far from home. A list of people gone missing. A long, simmering attraction that finally reaches a boil.

When Demetrius flies to Florida to support his parents during his mother's health scare, Cody is left to manage their Critter Catcher business alone. And feel guilty he didn't go along to provide support.

Finally unable to stay away, Cody heads to Florida with Demetrius's Aunt Amelia. Demetrius is shocked they came to support him. And Cody is shocked about his powerful romantic feelings for Demetrius.

But all that will have to wait as they are tragically yanked into another monster hunt. In the Everglades. During a tropical storm. If they live through this latest challenge, Cody and Demetrius will need to have a long overdue conversation about their future.

It will change everything between them, forever.

This is a work of fiction. Names, characters, businesses, places, events and incidents are either the products of the author's imagination or used in a fictitious manner. Any resemblance to actual persons, living or dead, or actual events is purely coincidental.

First Publication, 2016

CHAPTER ONE

"Stop moving it around so much!"

Demetrius heard the words come out of his mouth and stopped what he was doing to close his eyes, waiting for the expected response. True to form, Cody did not disappoint.

"That's *not* what she said," Cody quipped.

Demetrius sighed. He looked back over his shoulder and cursed when he thumped his head against a joist. He lay flat on his stomach in a damp, claustrophobic crawlspace, sweating in the July humidity in his Critter Catchers jump suit, trying to keep his grip on the long handle of the animal loop collar through thick gloves. Cody was on his hands and knees a few feet behind him, half in and half out of the crawlspace entrance, holding a powerful lantern to light Demetrius's way.

"Hey, don't glare at me," Cody said. "You're the one who suggested Rock, Paper, Scissors to see who crawled into this hell hole."

"Hell hole?" a woman's voice exclaimed, and Demetrius and Cody winced at each other. Their client, a woman in her mid- to late-sixties with the ready-for-the-silver-screen name of Abigail Barcelona, had apparently decided to come see how their work was progressing. "This hell hole happens to be my home."

Demetrius caught a wink from Cody and watched as his handsome best friend and business partner backed out of the crawlspace. Unfortunately, Cody took the lantern with him and plunged Demetrius into nearly complete darkness. As Demetrius practiced deep breathing to keep the sudden nightmare images at bay, he listened to Cody turn up his charm to a hundred and ten percent, working Abigail Barcelona like she probably hadn't been worked since 1978. Although, based on the cougar vibe Demetrius had received from the woman the minute she'd opened the door wearing a negligee over a bustier and stockings with garters, he believed Cody may have met his match.

"Mrs. Barcelona—" he heard Cody say.

"Oh, Mr. Bower," she practically purred, "please call me Abigail."

"Abigail, of course. You may call me Cody."

"May I?"

"Absolutely," Cody said. He could just imagine the mega-watt smile Cody flashed. "What my partner and I meant by that—"

"Partner?" Abigail repeated. "I hope you don't mean domestic partner. Not that there's anything wrong with that, mind you. It's just that you're both so handsome and strong, it would be a waste not to make good use of that prime DNA."

Demetrius rolled his eyes and shifted position to alleviate pressure on his neck and shoulders as he continued to peer behind him at the small square of light that marked the outside world. He could see Cody's legs and hips where he knelt in front of Abigail on the other side of the crawlspace entrance, and Demetrius hoped he wasn't about to witness something inappropriate that would give him nightmares for the rest of his life.

"Well, that's very kind of you to say," Cody replied. "I can assure you, I'm not nearly good enough to be Demmy's domestic partner. We're just business partners."

Demetrius frowned and cocked his head at Cody's words. Cody often mock-flirted with men and had recently begun joking more stridently he'd be willing to be something more than friends. But those remarks were usually reserved for times they were alone. The last few months, however, Demetrius had noticed a change in Cody. He was more demonstrative with Demetrius these days, and it had been weeks, maybe even a couple of months, since Cody had been out on a date, which for him was quite the dry spell.

All of these things may be figments of Demetrius's imagination, brought on by the fact he'd begun having random, uninvited snippets of sex fantasies about Cody after Oliver, his boyfriend, had called him Demmy during sex. Demmy was what Cody called him, and pretty much only Cody. It had been that way for longer than Demetrius could remember. The intimacy of the moment with Oliver, coupled with Demetrius's confused feelings of late for Cody, had awakened a deeper hunger within him. His relationship with Oliver had, unsurprisingly, declined after that. Seeing as how it had been weeks since he'd talked with or received a text from Oliver, Demetrius assumed things between them were officially over.

The fantasies brought on by Oliver's use of Cody's nickname, however, lingered and seemed to be growing stronger and more numerous. They spun to life at any moment of the day or night, whether he was in Cody's presence or not. They left him feeling unsettled and, he hated to admit, aroused.

Cody was incredibly attractive and more charming than any other person Demetrius had met. But Cody was also prone to rash decisions and never seemed to be able to plan more than a week into the future. Demetrius, on the other hand, liked things mapped out so he'd know what to expect. However, no matter how carefully he scheduled things, quite often it all fell apart, especially with Cody as a business partner and best friend.

Something moved ahead of him. Demetrius snapped his head around to squint into the darkness as a chill skittered through him. They had been called by Abigail to track down the source of a scratching sound the woman had been hearing for about a week, and Demetrius lay in the dark, helpless and now just a bit scared of what else might be in here with him. They'd dealt with a couple of paranormal cases since starting the business — a wolf man at the local nursing home, and what they'd thought was a chupacabra out on the rural outskirts of town — and memories of those cases creeped up on Demetrius now.

"Cody!" Demetrius called.

"Yep, here," Cody responded. "Sorry. I'm sorry. Here's the light."

As Cody wedged his broad shoulders into the crawlspace once again, the flashlight beam jumped around. It illuminated posts, hanging insulation, and something about the size of a football that kept darting out of sight. Demetrius pushed up off the ground and tried to back up, forgetting about the low clearance and scraping his back along a joist.

"Ahhh!"

"Demmy!" Cody's voice was tainted with fear. "What is it? Are you bit? Did it bite you? What is it? I'm here."

"My back," Demetrius replied as he collapsed onto his stomach in the dirt. "Ow. My back."

"What about your back? Is something on you?"

Cody crawled onto him on his elbows like an Army private in training. Demetrius felt the reassuring, heavy weight of Cody move up his legs, his muscular chest resting on Demetrius's butt and his big hands at Demetrius's elbows.

"You okay?" Cody whispered.

"Scraped my back on the joist," Demetrius explained. He shifted beneath Cody and said over his shoulder, "Not to sound unappreciative of your concern and responsiveness, but I'm feeling more than a bit claustrophobic right now."

"Sorry about that." Cody eased back a bit, then chuckled before asking, "Did you have chili?"

"What?" Demetrius looked over his shoulder and saw Cody's face situated just above his ass. He shook his head and rolled his eyes. "I wish I had. It would be just what you deserve."

"For what? Rushing in here to your rescue?"

"How is this a rescue? You've pinned me down in here while something stalks me in this dark, dank crawlspace." When he said it, Demetrius remembered the thing he'd seen and squinted into the darkness ahead of him. He reached back a hand and whispered, "Give me the flashlight."

Cody handed off the flashlight, and Demetrius aimed it ahead of him. He slowly moved the beam from one corner to the other, then down the front of the structure until it came to rest on a bundle of dark, matted fur and small brown eyes.

"Oh," Demetrius said, relief going through him at not finding a giant rat or the fluke man from that episode of *The X-Files* he and Cody had watched the other night. Why the fuck had he thought watching that would be a good idea?

"What is that?" Cody said.

"I don't know, but it's scared. And it's not a monster."

"Thank God for that," Cody muttered.

"Here, take the flashlight back, and I'll try to get the loop collar around it."

While Cody focused the light on the tiny, trembling bundle of fur, Demetrius slowly extended the loop on the end of the long pole. He spoke in a calm, quiet tone Cody picked up on and emulated. The loop was nearly to the animal when Abigail Barcelona leaned down and shouted into the crawlspace opening.

"How's it going in there?"

Demetrius jumped, and the pole hit a floor joist with a loud *bonk* then bounced off the dirt floor, scattering dust and soil and startling the animal. It bolted for the opening, its tiny feet leaving small dust clouds in its wake.

"Look out!" Cody and Demetrius shouted together.

Abigail Barcelona let out a shriek that any horror movie scream queen would have envied as the small ball of fur burst out of the crawlspace and ran for freedom.

"What in the living hell was that thing?" Abigail said. "It was dirtier than my martini."

"You okay, Demmy?" Cody said, his low voice filled with concern.

Demetrius blew out a breath and looked over his shoulder. Cody lay with his face positioned right over his ass, and Demetrius forced the sudden sexual fantasies back into their grimy trunk inside his mind. "Yeah. I'm okay. Ready to get back outside though."

"Nothing else left in here?"

Cody shined the flashlight around the crawlspace and they confirmed no other animal had taken up residence. Demetrius waited for Cody to back out and then pushed the pole with the loop to him along the dirt. Finally, Demetrius inched back himself, wincing now and then when the movement pulled the scraped skin on his back. When he was finally out of the crawlspace, he paused to take a breath of fresh air, pulled off his gloves, and wiped sweat from his brow.

Abigail Barcelona stood nearby looking like she'd stepped right out of the early 1960s with tight white shorts and a cropped top. One hip was stuck out to the side and one leg bent as she assessed them through the dark lenses of her over-sized sunglasses. She wore a big, floppy sunhat and held a martini glass. "So what the hell was that thing?"

"Not sure." Cody got to his feet, reaching down to take Demetrius's hand and pull him up as well.

"You're not sure?" Abigail looked between them. "Aren't you supposed to be animal control experts? Shouldn't you be able to identify every animal you attempt to control?"

"Well, as you can see from here," Demetrius said with a gesture toward the opening, "the crawlspace allows in very little light."

"The bottom of the cover was loose when we started our work," Cody said. "I'll make certain it's well secured before we leave."

"The animal didn't seem hostile," Demetrius continued. "It was dirty and matted, so we couldn't really tell what it was."

"Yeah, and now it's loose in my neighborhood thanks to the two of you," Abigail said.

"Well, that's better than being trapped beneath your house," Cody offered.

Abigail made a "hmph" sound and polished off her martini with one gulp. She stood in place for a moment, slowly swirling the empty glass as she looked at them through her giant sunglasses. Without another word she turned and walked with a shimmy to the side door of her small house, her kitten-heeled sandals snapping in the warm, still air.

Cody looked at Demetrius with wide eyes. "Wow."

"I thought I was going to lose you for a minute when you backed out to give her an update," Demetrius said. He shrugged out of his Critter Catchers coveralls and sucked in a hissing breath. Damn, his back stung.

"Want me to look at it?"

"Not yet. Let's just get paid and get out of here."

"Roger that," Cody said, and he secured the crawlspace cover as Demetrius packed up their gear.

Minutes later, Abigail reappeared, smoking an unfiltered cigarette. She smiled as she held a check out to Cody, and Demetrius could see the tips of her nails were painted a light coral.

"Thanks for coming out on such short notice," Abigail said, her demeanor now completely different than a few minutes before.

"No problem at all, Mrs. Barcelona," Cody said as he accepted the check and tucked it into a pocket.

Abigail playfully swatted his chest. "I told you to call me Abigail, Cody."

"Right, sorry." Cody made a goofy face. "I forget stuff sometimes."

They bid Abigail goodbye and got in the truck, Cody in the driver's seat. With the air conditioner on high, Demetrius sighed as the sweat cooled on his skin. He leaned back and closed his eyes, the scrape on his back stinging with each bump.

"Doing okay?"

"I'm fine," Demetrius said. He raised his head and looked at Cody. The afternoon sun lit his handsome profile perfectly, illuminating light brown strands in his dark hair, which he wore shaggy enough to be wavy. He had forgotten his sunglasses at the office, so he had to squint against the sun. Demetrius was always amazed they were such good friends even though they were quite different from each other. Cody was the more gregarious, easy-going one, with a well-built, six-foot-five-inch athletic body, and a long list of ex-girl-friends. While Cody was a serial dater of women, Demetrius was gay and more of a one guy at a time kind of dater, usually with a few months in between. And he was much less tall and athletic than Cody.

"I didn't know you were good with big cats," Demetrius said, keeping his tone casual. "We should advertise that, bring in more business."

"Big cats?" Cody frowned at him before turning his attention back to the road. "What the hell are you talking about?"

"Abigail Barcelona, that cougar you had eating out of your hand back there."

Cody laughed and shook his head, shooting Demetrius a grin. "She was something, wasn't she?"

"You into older women now?"

"Demmy old friend, I'm into whoever I'm into at the moment."

"That's not avoiding an answer at all."

"That's the beauty of me," Cody said as he tapped out a drum roll on the steering wheel. "I'm a joyful enigma."

"You're an enigma all right."

Cody laughed and continued to drum on the steering wheel. "Where are we headed?"

"I told Amelia we'd stop by after the job. She needs some help around the house."

"Amelia Waugh, the woman, the myth, the legend." Cody looked at him and grinned. "Aunt Amelia's got a thing for me, too. Maybe I am good with the cougar crowd. Trajectory set."

It was Demetrius's turn to laugh. "You are crazy."

"Demmy my friend, it's my sincere belief that we're all crazy," Cody said.

"That's the most sense you've made all day." Demetrius winced as he shifted position.

"Really hurts, huh?"

"It's not too bad, but I should clean it out."

"Amelia will have something we can put on it," Cody said.

Demetrius noticed Cody had said *something we can put on it,* as if he had just assumed he would apply the ointment and secure the bandage. Just like a couple that had been in a relationship for twenty-three years. Maybe he and Cody were basically an old married couple just like Oliver had said to him one night a few weeks ago as he'd walked off in a huff after yet another argument. Demetrius and Cody argued about stupid shit, worried about paying the bills, and weren't having sex. Sounded like marriage to him.

All the fuss and none of the fun. The perfect couple.

CHAPTER TWO

Cody was at a crossroads in his life. It wasn't anything simple like which subject to major in at college, or whether he wanted to live in Parson's Hollow any longer than necessary. Nothing as cut and dried as that was rattling around inside his brain. This crossroads had more to do with his inner workings and the wellspring that truly made him who he was.

He had started to have feelings—maybe *urges* was the better word for it—about his best friend. His *male* best friend. His *gay* male best friend. And up to this point in his life, Cody had considered himself straight. Well, mostly straight. There'd been a time or two over the years when he'd felt something more for a guy than just friendship—Dirk Matson the workout king always came to mind first—and he'd kissed a couple of guys, but he'd never followed through. And he'd never mentioned these feelings to Demmy. He wasn't sure why, but Cody had always held back on that subject. He may have felt a tiny bit more than friendly for a couple of guys over the years, but he'd always ended up pursuing—and catching—women.

Maybe, however, he was due for a change in the line up. Lately, he'd noticed the attention he received from women felt less and less satisfying. Instead of looking forward to hitting a bar or two, either on his own or with a designated wingman, and maybe meeting an attractive, funny woman, Cody had found that the thrill of the hunt, so to speak, had tarnished. He was spending more evenings alone in his apartment. Or with Demmy.

They weren't doing anything unique or extravagant, mostly watching TV or movies, talking about the business, and maybe playing video games if Cody promised not to sneak up on Demmy and ambush him too often. As time had rolled on, Cody found himself anticipating spending time with Demmy more than he looked forward to going out in search of a woman to date.

Which led him back to the crossroads. All thinking these days seemed to lead him right back here. It felt like he stood on a set from that show Demmy had got him watching, *Supernatural*. On the show, one of the characters would go to a lonely crossroads with fields stretched out in a couple of directions and one or two run down buildings on the corners. In these intersections, the characters could summon a demon and strike a deal, asking for something they really, truly desired and signing over their immortal soul in return.

Cody, however, didn't believe in all of that sin and sinner and damnation stuff. Oh, it made for great storytelling in books and on TV, but he was pretty well set with where his life was going. He was a good person who didn't steal, who hadn't killed any one, and who respected and loved his parents who had retired and lived on the other side of the country. No, Cody wasn't going to burn in Hell for these feelings. But it would be a life changing decision.

"You agreed to go to Amelia's, right?"

"Sorry what?" Cody said.

"Amelia's house," Demetrius said. "You were okay with us going by her place, right?"

"Oh, Amelia? Yeah, sure. Love her. Of course. Why not?"

"Well, you just drove past her street," Demetrius said, looking out the passenger side window and turning his head to watch the intersection go past.

"Son of a. . ." Cody completed a three point turn and hooked a left onto Amelia's street. He parked in the driveway and stepped down out of the pickup, shaking his head at himself as he walked around the front of the truck to meet up with Demmy.

"How's the back feel?" Cody said.

Demmy rotated his shoulders and winced. "Tightening up. Going to need some attention to it, I'm afraid."

"Dr. Bower is at your service, my friend," Cody assured him.

"Oh, it's doctor now, is it?"

"Might be," Cody said with a grin. "I just haven't printed out the authentic online certification yet."

Demmy snorted a laugh and rang the doorbell. Moments later, the door opened, and Amelia Waugh, Demmy's mother's younger sister, smiled out at them. "Well, the two most handsome men in Parson's Hollow here to see me. How'd I get to be so lucky?"

"Luck's on our side, Amelia," Cody said as he followed Demmy into the house. "The pleasure, as always, is ours."

Amelia giggled, waved off his comments, and headed for the kitchen, her round bottom swaying within her Bermuda shorts. Her silver hair was cut in a bob that framed her wide, friendly face and bright blue eyes. Cody tried to remember a time when he hadn't seen her with a smile.

Oh, right. Last year when her friends from the senior center had been murdered by a real life, bloodthirsty wolf man. He wondered if maybe he and Demmy should go talk to the Parson's Hollow City Council about putting some emphasis on that case, bring in some tourists to boost the local economy. On second thought, he wasn't sure the type of people that news would attract would be a good fit for their small western Pennsylvania town.

"I've just started dinner, boys," Amelia said. "Stuffed peppers. Going to be another half hour most likely."

"Good, that'll give me enough time to tend to Demmy's injury," Cody said.

"Injury?" Amelia snapped her head up, face paling as she looked between them. "What injury? What happened?"

"It's nothing, Aunt Amelia," Demmy said after shooting Cody a stern look. "I just scraped my back. It's nothing to worry about. You worry too much."

Amelia shook her head and folded her arms. "Oh, hickory trees I worry too much. I practically raised you, Demetrius Barnaby Singleton, and as such I'm allowed to worry as much as I wish."

Cody just barely suppressed a laugh. Demmy's Aunt Amelia was one of his most favorite people on the planet. Instead of using traditional cuss words, Aunt Amelia relied on the names of trees to voice her displeasure, and she always seemed to have a species of tree locked and loaded, ready to go.

"I know that," Demmy said. "But, really, it's just a scrape."

"Show me," Amelia demanded.

Cody knew Demmy had no choice. Apparently, Demmy realized it, too, because he sighed then started to slowly work his T-shirt up.

"Need help?" Cody offered.

"I can manage to undress myself, thanks," Demmy said in a snappish tone.

Cody nodded and took a step back. "Okay, offer rescinded."

As Demmy inched the T-shirt up, slowly exposing his pale, flat belly covered with dark hair, then his torso, then his nipples, Cody forced himself not to stare. He did, however, allow himself glances. He'd seen Demmy without his shirt before. Hell, they'd been naked before when skinny dipping or rinsing off after a swim at the pool, but Cody had never taken the time to really look at Demmy's body. Now that he had become more in tune with this newly emerging part of himself, he had to admit he liked what he saw. He liked it a lot. More even than he liked watching Dirk Matson pump iron at the gym and peel off his sweaty T-shirt in the locker room afterwards.

While these thoughts he was having about Demmy were along the same lines as those startling and sexually charged day dreams starring Dirk Matson, there was more substance to the Demmy thoughts. The foundation for these thoughts wasn't just a physical attraction, though that was a part of it. Demmy was a fixture in his life, a constant, and Cody's thoughts seemed to turn more often toward bringing that constant fixture beyond friendship and into a physical relationship.

Demmy finally managed to pull the T-shirt off and turned his back to them. Cody knew Amelia's wince mimicked his own at the sight of Demmy's scrape.

"Well?" Demmy tried to see over his shoulder. "Is it bad? Like really gory bad?"

Cody shook his head, his gaze locked on the raw, red scrape that marred Demmy's pale skin. "No, it's not gory bad. But it does need to be cleaned up. It's just a scrape."

"Cody Duran Bower, you are telling the biggest fir tree fib right now," Amelia said and shook a finger at him. "That wound needs to be seen to by a doctor."

"Ugh, another visit to PHMH?" Demmy said. He looked at

Cody. "Can you call Zenona and send her a picture of my back and ask what she thinks?"

"Um, well, I don't know," Cody said, caught off guard by the sudden shift in urgency. "We're not... I could, but that's not really how injuries should be treated. She might not even be on duty tonight, and you know, it's not cool to talk to someone about work when they're enjoying some time off."

Demmy looked at him over his shoulder. "You broke up with her again, didn't you?"

Cody sighed. "Demmy, it's just what happens with Zenona and I."

"Cody, you take him to the hospital right now," Amelia said.

"Amelia, light of my life, I don't think he needs to go to the hospital," Cody said in a sweet-talking tone of voice. "How about I clean it out and put some ointment on it? After dinner we'll look at it again and decide at that time. I mean, you're about to stuff the peppers, and it all smells so good. It wouldn't be right to send us off to the hospital on empty stomachs. You know how long it takes to get seen by a doctor."

Amelia looked between them, and then she blew out a breath that lifted a lock of her hair and nodded. "Fine. I see your point. You take Demmy into the bathroom and clean that wound out good. He's not going to like how it feels, but it's got to be done. And soon."

"I'm on it." Cody pointed at the hollowed out peppers lined up on a baking tray. "And you get busy stuffing your meat into those peppers."

"Oh, go on with you," Amelia said and waved them off as a blush turned her cheeks pink.

Cody followed Demmy down the short hallway to the small bathroom. He closed the door behind them and switched on the light, glad he was already used to the 1950s style pink tiled walls, pink toilet, and pink bathtub.

"I always feel like I step into someone's stomach when I come in here," Demmy said. He turned to look at Cody. "Where do you want me?"

Far too many answers flooded Cody's mind, and he stared at Demmy a moment as he struggled to pluck the correct response out from the suggestive and filthy ones. "How about you sit on the edge of the tub with your feet in the tub and I'll sit on the toilet lid?"

Demmy nodded and turned his back to brace himself on the edge of the pedestal sink as he kicked off his shoes and peeled off his socks. He stepped into the tub and sat on the fuzzy pink bathmat Amelia hung over the side of the tub to dry when she finished her shower.

Cody moved Demmy's shoes and socks out of the way and looked at him in the mirror as he thoroughly washed his hands. The scrape was an angry red slash along the pale line of Demmy's spine, but it really wasn't too bad. Demmy would feel it for a couple of days, but it wouldn't keep him down. And, besides, Cody wasn't really looking at the scrape.

He studied the back of Demmy's head, noting the shape of his skull beneath the very short brown hair. After twenty-three years of friendship, it had become a familiar sight, but now Cody wondered what it would be like to wake up in the morning and see the back of Demmy's head on the pillow beside him. Would their friendship evolve and deepen if Cody made some kind of move for a more intimate relation-ship? Would Demmy be open to something like that? Cody knew Demmy had been seeing Oliver, the reporter for the *Parson's Hollow Herald*, but lately Demmy seemed to be spending less and less time with Oliver. Perhaps that fling had flung itself out, and Demmy would be open to at least considering a relationship with Cody.

"This is going to hurt, isn't it?" Demmy said.

The question surprised Cody, seeing as his mind was whirling with relationship possibilities. He had a feeling that it was, indeed, going to hurt before it started to feel normal and right and true, but he realized with a sudden flash of insight he needed it. He yearned for it, and he thought that, given time and coaxing, Demmy might as well.

"I'm not going to lie to you, Demmy," Cody said as he selected the rubbing alcohol, antibiotic ointment, and medical gauze and tape from the medicine cabinet. "It's not going to be as fun as a circus."

Demmy laughed. "You hate the circus."

"Clowns are fucking scary," Cody said, glad he had distracted him. "And I really hate seeing the lions and tigers caged up and made to do tricks like that."

"Yeah, I know what you mean," Demmy said. "Circuses were born in a different time period. People can see those animals in their natural habitats now in vivid HD right in their living rooms. There's no need for them to be caged up and have whips snapped at them and forced to jump through flaming hoops or whatever. It just seems cruel now."

Cody soaked a piece of gauze with alcohol and sat on the fuzzy pink cover of the toilet lid. "Ready?"

Demmy took a deep breath and Cody watched the muscles up and down his back tighten. He wondered if they would tighten like that if he slid his cock into Demmy's ass. He'd like to see them clench and release as he thrust in and pulled out.

"I'm ready," Demmy said after blowing out a breath.

"Me, too," Cody said quietly, touching the cold wet gauze to Demmy's back and flinching at the resulting shout of pain.

CHAPTER THREE

Demetrius knew the food was good, but the pain overrode whatever joy his taste buds might have experienced. Cody had cleaned and bandaged the scrape on his back almost an hour ago, and the pain lingered as a flickering heat, as if he sat with his back too close to a roaring fireplace.

Once he finished eating, Demetrius excused himself and stood at the sink to wash dishes.

"Oh, honey, I'll do that," Amelia said.

"Actually it feels good to stand up," Demetrius reassured her. "I'll clean up. You cooked for us, it's the least I can do."

As Amelia and Cody talked at the table about various people and events in and around Parson's Hollow, Demetrius rinsed and stacked dishes in the dishwasher and washed pots and pans by hand. The sound of their conversation and laughter was familiar and comforting, like long standing family dinners or evenings with friends.

Every now and then, he looked out the window over the sink into Amelia's small, neatly maintained backyard. The ceramic garden gnomes were in their summer positions, as Amelia called it, interspersed among the flowers and keeping watch over her vegetable garden. Dinner had been served later than usual, and the setting sun was blood red as it eased lower in the sky. The clouds turned golden, then pink, then orange, and finally red once the sun had dropped out of sight.

Demetrius's phone buzzed in his pocket, but his hands were submerged in soapy water and he let it go to voice mail, wondering who might have called since he was standing in the room with the two likeliest suspects. Things between him and Oliver were pretty much over, so he was sure it wasn't him.

He liked Oliver as a friend, and he hoped they could be civil when they saw each other in town. Unfortunately, the passion or whatever that X ingredient was that helped bind two people together just didn't seem to be there for them. He supposed Cody would be thrilled to hear things were over between them. Cody had never really liked Oliver, which had probably stemmed from the suspicion Oliver was a wolf man when they'd first met him the year before. Now that they knew Oliver was human, Cody still seemed to barely tolerate having him around. Maybe Demetrius would hold onto the Oliver news for a while longer, until he was certain there was absolutely no chance for them.

Amelia's wall phone rang, startling all of them. Demetrius looked over his shoulder toward the table to find Amelia and Cody staring at him.

"I don't get many calls on that line," Amelia said. "I use my mobile phone more these days."

"Might be a really early election robocall," Cody suggested and got out of his chair to pick up the receiver. "Yello."

Demetrius shared a snicker with Amelia then turned his attention back to the final pot he was scrubbing. Behind him, he heard Cody's tone change to something a bit more serious.

"No, this is Cody... Oh, hi Mr. Singleton—sorry, Marshall, I forgot... Yes both of them are here... Okay, um, sure, I'll put her on. Good talking with you."

Demetrius finished rinsing the pot and turned his back to the sink, drying the pot as he looked at Cody and frowned. "That's my dad?"

Cody nodded, keeping his gaze on Demetrius as he held the phone out to Amelia who was just getting up from the table. "Yeah. He asked for either of you, and I thought it would be good to start with Amelia, seeing as it's her phone."

As Amelia took the phone, Demetrius put the pot in the cupboard and pulled his mobile phone from his back pocket. Three missed calls, and all from his dad. How had he missed all three of them? He checked to see if his father had left a voice mail, but he hadn't.

"How did he sound?" Demetrius said. "Did he sound okay?"

Amelia had taken the phone into the living room, stretching the coiled cord, and Demetrius felt his gut clench and his heart jump when he heard her say, "Oh, dear. Oh, Marshall, no."

Demetrius didn't remember crossing the kitchen but found himself standing in front of Amelia in the living room, staring at her worried expression.

"What is it? Is it mom? What's happened?"

"Marshall, wait," Amelia said. "Demetrius is here and should hear this, too. I'll give him the phone and pick up the bedroom extension." She held out the receiver. "It's your mother. She's in the hospital."

Demetrius gripped the receiver and was glad to hear his voice sounded steady when he spoke. "Dad? What's going on?"

"Hello, son." His father's deep voice sounded tired and used up, as if he'd been talking a lot. "Your mother's in the hospital down here. Intensive care unit."

A chill went through Demetrius, and he gripped the doorway between the kitchen and the living room with his free hand. He looked into the kitchen and found Cody standing nearby, watching him closely.

"Intensive care?" Demetrius repeated and heard the click of Amelia picking up the extension. "What's happened?"

"They say it's her heart," his father continued. "Just like the last two times. But this time seems a little more serious."

"How much more serious?" Cody was beside him now, one big hand resting on Demetrius's shoulder, warm and comforting, grounding him.

"They're going to stabilize her and then check for blockages," Marshall Singleton said. "It most likely means some kind of surgery, probably a bypass."

"Bypass?" Amelia repeated. "Oh dear."

"I'm coming down."

"No, son," Marshall protested, but with no real energy behind the words. "You have your business up there. We're fine here."

"Dad, you're not fine down there," Demetrius shot back. "Mom's in the hospital, and you sound exhausted. You need help."

"We have our friends and neighbors to help us out."

"They're not family. They won't be able to see her in ICU. Only family can see a patient in ICU. Remember the last time?"

"Oh," Marshall said, his voice soft and quiet, already tired. "I didn't think about that."

"I'll be down there tomorrow," Demetrius said. "I just need to pack and get a flight out."

"What about your job?"

"Cody can manage any jobs that come in, don't worry about that," Demetrius said, feeling the affirming squeeze on his shoulder from Cody. "I'll text you once I have a flight, okay?"

"Okay, I'll meet you at the airport."

"No, don't worry about that," Demetrius said. "I'll use a ride share or a taxi and meet you at the hospital. Tell me what hospital and room number."

Marshall gave him the information and Demetrius repeated it, watching as Cody wrote it down on the notepad beneath the phone.

"All right, I've got it. I'll see you tomorrow, Dad. Get some rest, okay?"

"Marshall, do you want me to come down?" Amelia said.

"Not yet, Amelia. You stay put for now. Demetrius and I will let you know if we think you should come down as well."

Emotion surged up within Demetrius at his father's words. If they asked Amelia to travel down to Florida, it would be to say goodbye to her sister. That would leave only Amelia. He blinked back tears and had to fight to keep his voice steady as he said, "I love you, Dad. Tell Mom I love her, too, okay?"

Marshall's voice was tight as he replied. "We love you, too, Demetrius. And you as well, Amelia. I will see you tomorrow, son. Be safe."

Demetrius said goodbye and hung up the phone. Cody didn't say a word. He just pulled Demetrius into his arms, holding him tight and being careful not to touch the scraped area of his back. When Amelia emerged from the bedroom, sniffling and dabbing at her eyes with a tissue, Cody pulled her into the hug as well and the three of them stood in place, holding each other and trying not to cry too hard. There was time enough for that later.

CHAPTER FOUR

The plane banked and Demetrius leaned forward to see, flinching at the pull of the scraped skin on his back. It didn't feel as painful, more of a tight feeling. He was sitting between a nervous woman in a business suit who occupied the window seat and, on the aisle, a painfully thin man with a dark, wispy goatee and the glazed expression of a lifelong stoner. How the man had managed to get through security, Demetrius had no idea, but he was grateful neither of them tried to force conversation for the flight to Florida.

The blue water of the Atlantic Ocean sparkled down below, while glass and steel buildings glittered where they perched on the edge of the white sand beaches. They were descending into the gleaming jewel of Miami, the nearest airport to his parents' retirement village, East Glades Bayou. Demetrius had never really understood the name of the place. Well, not a part of the name anyway. East Glades referred to the fact that the community sat on the eastern edge of the Florida Everglades, about an hour north west of Miami. The Bayous part of the name was a mystery to Demetrius. That was more of a Louisiana term.

Oddly named community or not, his parents had moved there when he'd been finishing up his final semester of college. All of western Pennsylvania had just endured an especially brutal winter, and his parents announced their plans to permanently relocate during Demetrius's standing Sunday afternoon phone call home.

He hadn't been very surprised by it. They'd been complaining about the ice and snow in and around their small town of Parson's Hollow for years, and Demetrius was glad they'd finally decided to follow the lead of their friends and move south. Their house had sold in less than a week, and two days after his last final exam for college, he had packed up or donated everything in his childhood bedroom and moved into his current apartment.

That had been five years ago, and now, in the last clutches of July, Demetrius was flying to Miami where the temperature was a reported ninety-six with equally high humidity. Ugh.

The plane descended and soon Demetrius felt the vibration in his feet of the landing gear extending. Just before the wheels hit the runway, Demetrius closed his eyes, his hands clutched together in his lap. He didn't mind the flying part of air travel, but the take offs and landings always made him nervous. The landing was uneventful, and he snagged his carry on from the overhead compartment and followed his glaze-eyed seatmate into the terminal.

He'd only brought a carry-on bag to make traveling easier and a little bit cheaper. Now he headed down to baggage claim to check into the possibility of a rental car or, if there were none available, make use of his Uber app. When he stepped off the escalator, an older gentleman with a dramatic silver pompadour who wore a loud Hawaiian shirt over basketball shorts and dark socks with sandals caught Demetrius's eye. The outfit was a true attention getter, but the sign he held had his full name printed on it: DEMETRIUS BARNABY SINGLETON.

"Um, hi," Demetrius said with a small wave. "I'm Demetrius."

"Oh yeah?" The man looked him up and down, and then he shrugged. "Yeah, okay. You look like the photos. Come on."

"Wait, I don't... Who are you? And where would we be going?"

The man stared at him in silence for a moment, and just when Demetrius thought he should repeat himself, his driver finally replied. "I'm Hubert Potts. Marshall sent me to pick you up."

"My father sent you?"

"Yeah, your dad. He didn't want you having to rent a car or use that Usher car thing."

"Uber."

Hubert stared at him again. "They warned me you might be a bit testy." He tipped his head toward the outer doors. "Come on, I'm parked in short term parking and the clock's ticking."

Demetrius bit back a response about which of them was the more testy and followed Hubert outside. The humid air closed around him like a damp blanket taken right out of the dryer, and he let out an involuntary gasp.

"You get used to it," Hubert said over his shoulder.

"Wow, it's hard to breathe." He followed after Hubert who lumbered along the pick up points. "How long have you lived in East Glades Bayou?" he said to the back of his Hawaiian print shirt.

"Nineteen years."

Demetrius followed Hubert across lanes of traffic to a short term parking lot. The sun blazed down on them and baked the asphalt beneath their feet. Sweat ran down

Demetrius's back and sides, and he was just about to ask if it was much farther when Hubert used his remote to unlock a white Lincoln MKS and pop the trunk open. Demetrius stowed his bag inside and then slid slowly into the leather passenger seat and eased back. The interior smelled like Old Spice and Ben Gay, and a trace of coolness still lingered from Hubert having the air on as he'd driven to the airport.

Once Demetrius saw Hubert was a good and cautious driver, he spent the ride looking out his side window as they drove away from Miami toward the Florida Everglades. A morning talk radio show was turned low, but Hubert bumped up the volume as the hosts started talking about a tropical storm that had just begun taking shape out in the Atlantic.

"Tropical storm," Hubert muttered. "That could be a mess."

"Do they expect it to strengthen into a hurricane?"

Hubert shrugged. "Never know with Mother Nature. She can be a bitch or a goddess, but never both at once."

Demetrius nodded, and they both fell silent for the rest of the drive. He stifled a yawn and looked out the window again. His poor sleep and the hectic travel day was starting to catch up with him. The smooth car ride and comfortable leather seat finally did him in, and he closed his eyes.

"We're here," Hubert said, his voice bringing Demetrius up out of a deep doze.

Demetrius blinked awake and looked around. His mouth tasted like it had been stuffed with cotton, and he wiped his lips with the back of his hand. They sat in the driveway of his parents' detached condominium, a white ranch condo that looked identical to all the other homes up and down the curved street. Palm trees grew tall and regal at perfectly placed intervals, and each home brandished a different decorative flag alongside the front door. His parents' home sported a colorful flower print behind the words Happy Summer!

Hubert kept the engine running and pressed a button to pop the trunk. He gave Demetrius a long, serious look then nodded once. "Good to meet you, Demetrius. I know your dad's glad you've come down. Key's under the third flower pot."

"Why didn't you take me to the hospital?"

"Your dad wanted me to bring you here to their condo. He thought you might want to clean up before going to see your mom."

"Oh? He said that?"

Hubert nodded. "He did. Oh, and he said to text him when you got here, and he'd come and pick you up."

"Okay, I'll do that," Demetrius said. "Thank you for the ride, Mr. Potts."

"Call me Hubert."

"Hubert it is."

Demetrius shook Hubert's hand and stepped out into the crushing heat. He grabbed his bag from the trunk, closed the lid, and approached the house. He retrieved the key and let himself in, exhaling at the blissfully cool interior. Blinds at the windows were made up of wide wooden slats and had been left half open, keeping the glare of the sun to a minimum. The stillness of the condo gave Demetrius a shiver as he set his bag in the hallway.

After using the bathroom, Demetrius poked his head into each bedroom. The largest at the end of the hall included a well-appointed master bathroom accessed through a closet area, his parents' king-sized bed, their dresser and bureau, and a flat screen TV fastened to the wall. A room down the hall had two single beds with a nightstand between them and a small dresser. Demetrius set his bag at the foot of one of the beds and slowly stretched out across it on his back. He adjusted his position until he was more comfortable, staring at the white plaster ceiling as he tried to get himself acclimated to actually being in Florida.

Pulling out his phone, Demetrius called his father and listened to the ring. He was expecting it to go to voice mail when his father picked up.

"Demetrius? Are you here?"

"Hi, Dad. Yeah, I'm here at the condo. How are you? How's mom?"

"Oh, your mother's doing all right. I've just been talking to the doctor about their treatment plan for her."

"Yeah? And what's that entail?"

"Well, it's a lot to go into right now. Let me come pick you up, and we can talk about it on the way back to the hospital."

"Okay. How long will you be do you think?"

"About half an hour. I'll see you soon, son. We're both glad you're here."

"Me, too, Dad. Drive safe."

Demetrius ended the call and lay with the phone on his belly, still staring at the ceiling. He needed to sit up and start moving or else he was going to doze off again. Just as he was about to sit up, his phone buzzed, startling him, and he picked it up to check the display.

It was Cody, and Demetrius smiled at the photo he had chosen to display when Cody called. Demetrius had snapped it when he'd been sitting across from him at Margie's Diner one day during lunch. In the photo, Cody had a big smile and looked relaxed and happy and handsome. Just seeing the picture opened up a tiny ache of loneliness inside Demetrius, and he was surprised to realize he really, truly missed Cody.

Before his thoughts could swing into strange—and dangerous—territory, Demetrius accepted the call.

"Hello, you have reached the hottest level of Hell, how may I direct your call?" Demetrius said in a calm, phone support tone of voice.

Cody laughed. "So, I take it you've arrived all right."

"Yep. I arrived on time and was picked up at the airport by Hubert Potts."

"Hubert Potts?" Cody repeated. "Who's that?"

"He's a friend of my parents. Interesting dresser. He had my full name printed on a sign down in baggage claim."

"Nice touch," Cody said.

"Oh, and I corrected him when he referred to Uber as Usher, and he said he had been warned that I might be, and I quote, 'testy.'"

"Oh my," Cody said. Demetrius could perfectly visualize his friend's grin. "It sounds like you might have met your match down there, Demmy."

"Yeah, yeah," Demetrius grumbled.

"How's your back feeling?"

"It's better, thanks. Still a little touchy."

"Testy?"

"Um, no. I said touchy, smart-ass. So how are things there? Burn the office down yet?"

"No, but speaking of which, do you know if we have a fire extinguisher?"

"Funny."

"I was kinda being serious," Cody said in a quiet voice.

"And the funny has ended," Demetrius said drily. "Seriously, did we get any calls?"

"A couple. I handled them, though. A woman had lost her boyfriend's ferret inside her house while she was watching it during his business trip."

"Tell me you caught the ferret and didn't sleep with her," Demetrius said.

"Come on, Demmy, that hurts my feelings."

"Just say yes or no."

Cody sighed. "I did find the ferret, and I did *not* sleep with her. And before you ask, I did not ask her for her number, either."

"Wow, really?"

"Yes, really. I have changed, my friend. You're talking to the more mature, more responsible version of Cody Bower."

A loud beeping in the background interrupted Cody and made Demetrius sit upright.

"What is that?" Demetrius asked. "Is that the fire alarm? I was just kidding about the fire, but what's going on there?"

"Um, nothing to worry about, no fire, just a lot of... Um, just a lot of smoke. Look, everything's fine, but I have to go, okay? Give your folks my love, and I'll talk with you soon. Okay, Demmy, take care, buh bye."

Cody disconnected, and Demetrius made a sound of disgust. He sat on the edge of the bed staring at the phone in his hands. If he called Cody back, it would just go to voice-mail, so that would be a waste of time. Besides, his father was on his way to the condo to pick him up.

Demetrius would have to trust in Cody to do the right thing and instead focus on his current location and situation. Right now he needed to be present for his parents, pay attention to the doctors, and try to think of the right questions to ask.

Demetrius took a deep breath, let it out, then repeated it. He hesitated, then sent Cody a text: *Call me when you've finished putting out that fire. And don't sit at my desk and fuck with my chair settings. I like it just the way it is.*

He felt better after he'd pressed send. He stood up, put the phone in his pocket, and grabbed his shaving kit. Carrying it into the hall bathroom, he brushed his teeth, then washed his face and neck and made sure he looked halfway presentable. With that done, he sat on the microfiber sofa in the living room to wait for his father to arrive. The condo was so quiet, he could hear the ticking of the mantel clock his mother had inherited from her grandmother. Was this what he had to look forward to when he was a senior citizen? Sitting alone in a condominium listening to his life tick away?

CHAPTER FIVE

Cody coughed as he stepped back from the smoke and stench billowing out of the sink. In an effort to save a little money, he'd bought frozen mini pizzas and stored them in the mini fridge/freezer at the office. Of course, he'd had to first buy the mini fridge/freezer from Costco. And the toaster oven in which he'd left the first two pizzas during his call to Demmy. So, in hindsight, he probably hadn't saved much money when he compared it to eating out.

"No wonder Demmy's worried about leaving you alone with the business," Cody muttered.

He shut off the water he'd been running into the sink and surveyed the damage. The two mini pizzas were charcoal lumps and would have to be thrown out. The tray from the toaster oven would require a soaking, and then a severe scraping. He sighed and put his hands on his hips as he shook his head. Maybe he shouldn't be left on his own for too long. Maybe he should have accompanied Demmy to Florida and supported him during this difficult time.

"Nice odor," a man said from the kitchen doorway. "Is that a new body spray?"

Cody jumped and managed to hold back a startled shout before he turned. A tall, African American man stood in the doorway, his broad shoulders extending almost frame to frame. A soft halo of hair made him almost as tall as Cody, his big arms were crossed over his large chest, and he wore a bright smile on his handsome face.

"Jugs!" Cody stepped forward, shaking Jugs's massive hand and leaning in for a brief bro-hug accompanied by a couple of hard pats on the back for each of them.

Darnell Perramon, known by the name Jugs because of the size of his pectoral muscles, had attended Harriettville High School, the closest school to Parson's Hollow, and its biggest rival. While Cody played defense as a linebacker, Jugs had played as an offensive tackle, and the two had often gone head to head. Jugs was a few inches shorter than Cody's six foot five height, but he had a massive chest and the pecs to back up his nickname. He was handsome and outgoing and probably three times as cocky as Cody, which amounted to around seven times cockier than other men. They had always had an easy-going, casual friendship based on respect for each other's athletic and dating prowess.

"What brings you by?"

Jugs shrugged his big shoulders. "I was slumming around over here in Parson's Hollow and thought I'd stop in and see how being a business owner was treating you." Jugs glanced toward the ruins of the mini pizzas in the sink. "Pretty much the same as when you were in high school, huh?"

Cody waved him off and turned back to the sink to stuff the pizzas down the disposal. "Yeah, yeah. You think you've got it made over there in Harriettville with your fancy manager position at Furniture, Furniture, Furniture and your two bedroom apartment."

"Well, I did have it made," Jugs said with a sigh. "Until they let me go."

"What? What happened?"

"Business is dropping, so they had to make some cuts. Guess they only needed fourteen people to manage Furniture, Furniture, Furniture." Jugs shrugged. "I'm trying to see it as a business decision and nothing personal."

"Well, that sucks," Cody said. "I'm sorry to hear that. You have anything lined up yet?"

"Not yet. I've got a bit of money saved, so I'm taking my time." He stepped back into the hallway and looked down the short hall to the office space. "I like what you and your friend have set up here. Demetrius Singleton, right? Your buddy from high school?"

Cody felt a small twinge of nervousness, wondering what track the conversation was about to take. He had no idea where Jugs fell on the gay acceptance spectrum, but Cody mentally prepared himself to defend Demmy's honor. And apparently his own, with the thoughts he'd been having lately.

"That's right," Cody said. "Demmy had the idea, and I've come along for the ride."

Jugs nodded then stepped out of sight, disappearing toward the office setup. Cody followed him down the hall and into the not much wider space taken up by his and Demmy's desks pushed together to face each other, a filing cabinet, and a couple of plastic visitor's chairs, in case they ever had a visitor.

"This is a nice setup," Jugs said. "Small, but professional." He cocked an eyebrow as he looked Cody up and down, taking in his work boots, cargo shorts, and old, comfortable polo. "It's almost like you're an adult now, Bower. If you'd just learn to dress better."

"Yeah, yeah. You don't have much room to talk."

Jugs gave a quiet laugh, and his expression shifted for a moment to something so sad, so lost, Cody found himself choked up. He knew just how Jugs felt, because he'd been feeling the same way before Demmy had come up with the idea for them to start Critter Catchers. Trapped in some dead end job and not knowing where to go or how to feel happy.

Before he could respond, the phone rang and he circled the desks to sit in his chair and pick up the receiver. "Critter Catchers, this is Cody."

A woman's voice sounded as if she were edging toward hysterical panic. "Hi, yeah, um, you're animal control, right?"

"That's right, ma'am, we catch all sorts of critters. What kind of critter is giving you problems?"

Jugs pulled out Demmy's chair and sat across from Cody, smirking as he listened to his end of the conversation.

"A deer is trapped inside my yard," the woman said, her voice going up in pitch with her frustration, "and it's battering my privacy fence with its antlers. It's ruining my fence!" She took the phone away from her mouth and Cody could hear her shout, "Hear now, stop that! Stop that right now!" She came back to the phone, a little breathless. "It's very agitated, and when I've tried to shoo it out the gate, it's charged me instead. It's just frantic, and I have to get it out of my yard. Oh, my jonquils!"

"Okay, I can help you out," Cody said. "Give me your name and address, and I'll be right over."

The woman practically screamed the information to him. Cody wrote it all down, promised her he'd be right there, and hung up. He looked at Jugs and found him grinning as he sat with his elbows on the desk, chin propped in his hands.

"The master at work," Jugs said. "You got her name and address before you even got her number. Very smooth."

"Hey now, this is all professional," Cody said and grabbed his keys and wallet from a desk drawer before he stood up.

The comment from Jugs made him a little uncomfortable,

and he wasn't really sure why. Well, he pretty much knew why. He had a long-standing reputation for being the Parson's Hollow Lothario, but he had to change his ways if he was serious about pursuing something more meaningful with Demmy. All of this deep thinking and fretting was new to him, and it wasn't just the whole guy-on-guy aspect of the situation.

Cody had never really, truly been in love with anyone before, and when he allowed himself think about what he was contemplating with Demmy, Cody seemed to get more and more confused. He thought he was ready to step outside of his comfort zone, but this was going to be a major change for him, and he needed to be certain he was ready for it, not just for his sake, but for Demmy's as well.

"So, you're off then, I guess, huh?" Jugs said and got to his feet.

"Yeah, this woman, Ann Eaton, has a deer trapped in her backyard trashing her privacy fence." Cody started to turn for the door, then stopped. "Hey, you got anything going on right now?"

Jugs shook his head. "Nope."

"Want to do a ride along? We could catch up, and you could watch a master animal controller in action."

"Master animal controller, huh? We meeting someone else there?" Jugs grinned and shrugged his big shoulders. "Sure, why not? I've got nowhere to be and all the time in the world to get there."

"Okay, then, come on."

The drive to Ann Eaton's place took fifteen minutes, during which time they talked about games they'd played in high school, and Jugs brought up girls they'd both dated. Cody was not surprised to find out he and Jugs had been swimming in the same dating pool. Ever since high school, when they'd first learned of each other, the two seemed to be trading off a long list of girls, each of them dating a girl either just before or just after the other. It got to be a kind of competition, really, and one Cody liked to think he'd won.

However, some evenings, when he sat in his apartment alone, playing video games or watching shitty reality TV shows, he had his doubts. And from the sound of things on Jugs's end, he was having his doubts as well.

Ann Eaton turned out to be an attractive woman in her fifties with shoulder length blonde hair and hips that would make Cody's Grandma Felicia shout, "now she's a baby-maker!" Ann stood on her front porch, hands clutched together, eyes wide as she watched them pull up to the curb.

"Ms. Eaton?" Cody called as he walked up the driveway. A loud bang from the tall privacy fence near the back of the house brought him and Jugs up short. The driveway ended at a grassy strip in front of the fence, just beyond a side door into the house. Cody saw no garage roof above the top of the privacy fence, which explained why there was only a standard gate entry into the yard, and not a double swing gate entry to allow a car to pass through.

"As you can hear, I have a situation," Ann Eaton said. "Come inside, and you can look out the patio door."

Cody introduced Jugs as Darnell, and they followed her into a small, bright kitchen with a sliding glass door. A wrought iron patio chair had been situated on the small wooden deck outside the door, most likely to discourage the deer from smashing through the glass and into the house. Two dogs barked from a back bedroom, sounding like a smaller breed, maybe Pomeranians or some kind of terriers, the kinds of dogs Cody didn't care for. Every small dog he'd ever met had been a biter.

When he peered through the sliding door, Cody saw a twelve point buck run full tilt at Ann Eaton's privacy fence, hit the once treated and nicely painted wood and then stagger back. Dents and splinters were left in its wake, and the deer turned to charge another section with the same result.

"That damn thing is costing me thousands of dollars," Ann said with a groan.

"You tried opening the gate?" Jugs said.

Ann gave him a sour look. "Yes, I tried opening the gate. And the stupid thing avoided it and chased me back into the house. Then the school down the street let out. I didn't want it charging into a group of kids, so I closed the gate again."

"Kids are a lot of trouble, aren't they?" Jugs said, apparently trying to lighten the mood. Ann gave him a long, steady glare, and he took a step back though he towered over her by at least a foot.

"Okay, we'll see what we've got out in the truck," Cody said. "You called the right company."

"Just hurry, please." Ann flinched as the deer rammed into another portion of the fence. "Damn you!" she shouted through the patio door. "Damn you to deer Hell!"

Jugs followed Cody out to the truck and when they were out of earshot, tried to stifle his laughter as he said, "Damn you to deer Hell?"

Cody chuckled as he pulled his coveralls out of a storage compartment in the bed of his truck and stepped into them. He handed Jugs a spare pair of coveralls. "What the hell are you going to do to get that deer out of there?" Jugs said.

"I don't know yet. I'm thinking."

"Got a tranquilizer gun?"

"We're not that sophisticated," Cody said. "Or licensed. Plus those things cost money, and we just got Demmy's truck out of the shop and got our credit card balances paid down, so we're about back to enjoying food again."

Jugs furrowed his brow. "Damn, Bower. Sounds like you

and Demetrius are married or something, the way you talk about him."

Panic and frustration reared up within Cody as he turned his back to Jugs and sorted through the various implements in another storage compartment in the bed of his truck. He knew he should say it was none of Jugs's business what kind of relationship he and Demmy had, but he was quickly finding out that knowing he should say something and actually saying it were two different things.

While Cody had slowly allowed himself to think about having a sexual relationship with Demmy, he had no idea if either of them were ready yet for that kind of change. And he hadn't really, truly sat down and considered what it would mean to the people they knew, including those on the outer edges of their personal networks. So, instead of what he should say, Cody managed to cobble together something that sounded good and truthful as he assembled a net with a long handle and a long handled tool with a loop at the end he thought he might be able to slip over the deer's head and antlers.

"Well, Jugs, when you go into business with someone, it kind of becomes a marriage," Cody said handing Jugs the net. "Here, make yourself useful, unlike that homecoming game we played against each other in 2003."

"Was that the same game you let our quarterback slip past you three times to score?"

Cody shot him a dirty look. "No. That was a different game."

Jugs grinned. "I see."

"Yes, I hope you do." Cody started up the driveway once again. "Come on."

"So what's your plan?" Cody liked that Jugs sounded a little nervous, because Cody was pretty much ready to piss himself. While deer were pretty much harmless, any pissed off animal could be dangerous, especially one with bone hard weapons on its head and sharp hooves on its feet.

"I'm kind of playing things by ear," Cody said.

"Sort of like how you played football, eh?"

Cody stopped at the fence with his hand on the handle as he turned to meet Jugs's gaze. "Exactly. Which is why Parson's Hollow High beat Harriettville High in the state standings three years in a row."

"Too bad about your senior year," Jugs shot back, then nodded at the gate. "Ready?"

"Jugs my friend, I'm always ready."

Cody pushed open the gate and stepped through. He felt Jugs crowd in behind him, then heard the gate click shut. He scanned the yard, gazing over a shed in the back corner as he looked around for the deer. Before he could locate it, however, Jugs gave a shout and ran off to the left, sticking close to the fence. Cody looked right and saw the deer charging at him, head down and antlers ready for a goring. He dove out of the way and ended up flat on his stomach on the ground as the deer hit the fence and staggered back, shaking its head.

With the deer momentarily stunned, Cody scrambled to his feet and ran to the opposite corner of the yard. He'd dropped the long handled loop somewhere along the way, but Jugs was waiting in the corner and still held onto the net. Cody was glad to see Jugs's eyes were wide and his smart mouth shut tight.

"That deer is fucking pissed," Jugs said.

"Probably just got back from a date with your Mama," Cody said.

"Really? You gotta go there now? We're about to be skewered by some rageaholic deer."

Cody looked around the yard as the deer shook its head

and regained its bearings. A crazy idea flickered to life, and he mentally cursed himself for dropping the loop.

"Okay, I'm going to get its attention," Cody said.

"Uh, what? You want it to charge us?"

"Yep. We'll wait until the last second and jump out of the way. When it hits the fence, it'll knock itself silly for a minute. That's when we'll get our hands on it."

"You want to grab it?" Jugs said, his skeptical tone perfectly relaying what he thought about Cody's idea. "With our bare hands?"

"I'm going to get the loop. We're going to push it over, and I'll hog tie its feet together. Then we'll carry it to the truck and take it out to the woods."

"Really?"

Cody nodded. "Yep, really."

"Is this the kind of bullshit last minute stuff you and Demetrius do every day?"

"Pretty much." Cody stopped himself from adding, *Only we usually have a monster or two thrown into the mix every so often.* Instead, he met Jug's gaze. "Ready?"

Jugs took a deep breath and let it out. "Ready as I'll ever be."

"Here we go." Cody waved his arms overhead and shouted. "Hey, stupid deer! You've got some real anger issues. Come on over here and try to get us again. Come on, stupid!"

The deer lowered its head and charged them. Cody grabbed hold of Jugs's arm, keeping him in place until the last possible minute when he released his hold and they jumped to either side. The deer stampeded between them and hit the fence at full speed. Cody ran across the yard and grabbed the handle of the loop. He turned to see Jugs with the net tangled in the dazed deer's antlers. With a shake of its head, the deer pulled the net from Jugs's hands.

"Grab it!" Cody called.

"Ahh!" Jugs shouted as he launched himself forward. He grabbed the deer in a headlock and tried to wrestle it to the ground. The deer wasn't about to go down easily, though. It tossed its head, the handle of the net bobbing around and the antlers narrowly missing Jugs's face.

Cody ran to assist and pulled the deer's hind legs out from under it, sending both it and Jugs toppling to the ground. He fell to the grass on his knees and gathered the deer's flailing feet together beneath one arm, doing his best to avoid being kicked. Once he had all four legs held in place between his side and his arm, Cody got the loop around the deer's ankles and tightened it.

"Got it!" Cody shouted.

Jugs lingered long enough to pull the net off the antlers and then stepped back. The deer lay on its side, twisting its head around and flopping on the ground like a fish as it tried to get its feet free, but the loop held tight.

"I can't believe it worked," Jugs said and then let out a deep, rumbling laugh that got Cody going as well.

"Did you get it?" Ann called from the sliding patio door. "My dogs have to pee!"

Cody remembered the dogs and looked around, dismayed to find with all his rolling on the ground he'd gotten dog shit on his boots and coveralls. Well, at least he could take off the coveralls. Jugs appeared to have escaped the poop land mines as he sat catching his breath, a small cut on his cheek the only sign he had recently struggled with an enraged deer.

"Yeah, we got it," Cody replied. "Just need to get it out of the yard. Do you have a wheelbarrow or a cart or something?"

Ann remained inside the house as she stuck an arm out of the patio door and gestured toward the shed in the back corner that stood surprisingly unscathed. "There's a wheelbarrow in the shed. It's unlocked. You didn't kill it, did you?"

"No, it's not dead," Cody said as he got to his feet with a groan. "Just angry."

It took them longer than he'd hoped to get the deer into the wheelbarrow. It bucked and thrashed the whole way down the driveway to the truck. After several attempts to lift the writhing and kicking deer, Cody and Jugs finally managed to slide the animal into the truck bed where it lay still, apparently having worn itself out. As the deer lay staring at them with glazed eyes, they leaned on the sides of the truck to catch their breath.

"This is a fucked up way to make a buck," Jugs said, then grinned. "Make a buck. Get it? We captured a deer, we're making a buck."

Cody groaned. "A regular comedian. I'm going to get paid, get in the back."

"Wait, what?" Jugs looked at the deer then back at Cody. "Oh, hell no. I'll drive wherever you tell me to go, but I'm not riding back there to get beat on by some deer. This is your job, not mine."

"Fine. Give me a minute." Cody walked back to the front door where Ann stood with a credit card in hand.

"My fence will need to be replaced," she said, giving the deer an angry stare as Cody swiped her card through the small reader he attached to his phone.

"Insurance may cover it," he offered.

"I got video of it on my phone," she said. "That lazy ass insurance agent better cover it."

Cody wished her a good day. Trudging back to the truck, he climbed into the bed and sat with his back against the side-wall and his legs over the deer's side.

"Where to?" Jugs said through the small back window.

"Parson's Pond. Lots of woods out there."

"You're the boss."

As the deer snorted, panted, and thumped against the

truck bed beneath his legs, Cody wondered how Demmy was doing down in Florida. He hoped his mom was improving. He wished he'd gone down with him or at least taken him to the airport, rather than agreeing to let Amelia drop him off. He'd been spending so much time with Demmy lately, his absence was like a physical presence.

Jugs turned down the dirt road leading to Parson's Pond, and the truck bounced over the ruts. Cody winced and grunted along with the deer until Jugs pulled the truck off the road and on the grassy berm. Cody got out, and he and Jugs hauled the deer to the edge of the tailgate. Cody loosened the loop and the deer immediately kicked, forcing them to duck.

"Feisty little fucker, isn't he?" Jugs said.

"Cuz of your mama," Cody said as they managed to get the deer off the tailgate and onto the ground. "I told you that."

The deer swung its head back and forth, and with a buck of its hindquarters, it ran off into the trees. Cody watched the deer go and suddenly felt a kinship with it. He wanted to buck and kick free of his old life and run into something new, something better and deeper, with Demmy.

"All right man," Jugs said and clapped him on the shoulder, startling him back into the moment. "I need to get back."

"Yeah, sure," Cody said. "Let me get out of these coveralls covered in dog shit first."

"I was going to say your new body spray sucks," Jugs shot back. "But I think I already told you that."

Cody chuckled, stepped out of the coveralls, and kicked off his shoes, tossing it all into the bed of the truck. He got in the driver's seat and drove them back to the small strip mall housing the Critter Catchers office. Jugs followed him inside and sat at Cody's desk to wait as Cody washed up in the small bathroom.

When he stepped out of the bathroom drying his hands,

Cody said, "You did good on the job with me today. I appreciate the help."

Jugs nodded. "I gotta admit, it was kind of fun. Even with you covered in dog shit, which is about the sweetest thing I've seen in a while."

Cody smirked and shook his head. "Always a class act, aren't you?"

Jugs spread his arms wide. "I'm just a great big chocolate-covered Christmas gift. Open the box, baby!"

Cody laughed and pulled his wallet out of his shorts. He fished out fifty dollars and handed the cash to Jugs. "You earned this."

"Hey, Bower, you don't have to do this."

"No, seriously, Jugs. I couldn't have done it today without you. Thanks."

Jugs got up and stuffed the money in his pocket. "Well, hell, Bower, if you need help like that again, just give me a call. I can definitely help control some critters for a little bit of scratch."

"You're on, Jugs," Cody said, waving toward the door. "Now get out of here. I need to get home and get a shower, then go pay a visit to my grandma."

"You're just as all American as they come, aren't you, Bower?"

Cody shrugged and thought about Demmy. He wondered if their life together would be considered all American. Instead of bringing all that up, however, he said, "Just like apple pie, baseball, and Superman, my friend."

Jugs gave him another bro-hug and stepped out into the July heat. Cody milled around in the office for a bit before he left and locked the door behind him. He wiped sweat off his brow before he got into the truck and headed for his apartment, thinking about Demmy and wondering if it would be too much to call and check in again. Maybe tell him about the job with the deer and get him to laugh. But then again, maybe it would be better to leave that for tomorrow. Later tonight he'd go see his grandma and maybe stop by Amelia's house and check on her, too.

As he drove, Cody thought more about Demmy and caught himself whistling.

CHAPTER SIX

Sirens approached, grating against Demetrius's already stretched nerves. His father slowed and pulled the car to the curb, both of them wincing as an ambulance screamed past. As Marshall merged back into traffic, Demetrius studied his father's profile. He hadn't visited his parents in a few years, and he noted the deep creases that lined the narrow width of his father's forehead. And if Demetrius wasn't mistaken, his father's nose may have gotten larger. Dear God, was this what he had to look forward to? He'd already lost more hair than his father, who wore his swept back from his forehead in a thick white wave.

"So many ambulance runs down here," Marshall said, his deep voice sounding tired. "Those companies make a fortune off us seniors."

Demetrius squeezed his father's shoulder and gave him a quick smile. "You want me to drive, Dad?"

Marshall frowned and gripped the wheel tight. "I've been driving for almost sixty years, Demetrius. I think I can manage to get from our condo to the hospital."

"Okay, no offense. I was just offering."

Demetrius looked out his window at the retirement communities and acres and acres of swampland they slowly passed by. His father had always been a slow driver, and it made Demetrius think back to when he had been growing up in Parson's Hollow.

Because his parents were so much older than every other set of parents in town who were raising kids Demetrius's age, he had always felt like an outcast no matter where he was: at school, among his few friends, at their community pool, attending social events like picnics and county fairs, and even Cub Scout meetings. His parents had always been the oldest in attendance, their silver hair standing out among the younger and hipper parents. More often than not, someone mistook them for his grandparents, which always made Demetrius cringe even though his parents laughed it away. He sensed their awkwardness when interacting with the other parents, and not only felt embarrassed, for himself as well as them, but also somehow responsible. As if he hadn't allowed himself to be born at the right time in their lives.

It had gotten so bad, he started telling them about only select events. For the others, he tagged along with Cody and his jumble of older and younger brothers who attended events with their calm, down to earth mother or environmentally conscious father.

A few years after he and Cody had become friends, Cody had cajoled Demetrius into figuring out how old his parents had been when Demetrius had been born. Instead of just coming out and asking, Demetrius had made it a kind of investigation. He snuck into their bedroom and checked their driver licenses for their birth years, then he did the math and was surprised to discover his mother had been forty-seven years old and his father fifty when they'd had him. He remembered being stunned at those ages back then and still was to this day.

All through his life, Demetrius had heard the story of how he had been a miracle baby. Marshall and Olivia Singleton had tried to have children all throughout their twenty-five years of marriage. Each of their few pregnancies had ended in a miscarriage. They had finally put aside all hopes of having a family when, three months following their silver wedding anniversary, Olivia discovered she was pregnant yet again.

She was anxious about the pregnancy, and her doctor had cautioned her about the dangers of childbirth at her advanced age, but she took her vitamins and exercised and ate right and went to see her doctor more frequently than a younger mother would. The months went like clockwork and finally, on August 26, a stormy night in 1987, following ten hours of labor, she gave birth to their son, their precious little miracle, and they named him Demetrius Barnaby Singleton.

Demetrius came back to the present as his father turned into the parking lot of Coastal Waters Memorial Hospital, and he looked up the side of the ten-story building blazing white under the hot sun. Marshall found a spot on the fourth level of the neighboring parking structure. They walked to the exit without speaking, and Demetrius was glad to see his father eschewed the elevator to walk down the steps to the cross-walk. He was seventy-eight and still standing tall and walking well. Demetrius would hopefully inherit that from his father instead of a large nose and ears.

Once inside the hospital, Marshall waved to a number of older people they passed in the halls, greeting several of them by name. When they were alone in the elevator, Demetrius said, "A lot of your friends are here it seems."

His father's smile seemed grim. "Florida is just a way station to the grave, Demetrius. We all came down here to die."

"Jesus, Dad!" Demetrius said, surprised to find he had tears in his eyes. "That's a bleak way of looking at it."

Marshall shrugged as the elevator doors opened. "It is what it is, son. We've had a good life, and we've enjoyed living down here. What happens next is just like what happens with everybody else."

"Well let's hope it's put off a little bit, okay?" Demetrius followed his father down the hallway. "No need to rush the reaper, if you know what I mean."

"Oh, I know what you mean all right." Marshall stopped at the hydraulic doors leading to the Intensive Care Unit. "I don't want to alarm you, but your mother may look...bad to you."

"Bad? Bad how?"

But Marshall had slapped his hand on the plate to open the doors and was already power walking away. Demetrius grumbled a curse and followed his father just around the corner to the nurse's desk.

"This is Demetrius," Marshall said with a wave of his hand.

"Hi Demetrius, and you're their grandson?" the nurse said with a smile.

"I'm their son."

"Oh. I'm sorry."

"It's all right, Peggy," Marshall said with a smile. "It happens a lot. I just wanted you to know who he was since he's come down to see to us. Anything you tell me or Olivia you may also tell him."

"Well, it's very good of you to come down," Peggy said with a smile. "I will make a note that Demetrius may be updated about Olivia's condition. Let us know what we can do to keep Olivia comfortable. Her surgery is scheduled for two days from now, so any questions you have in the meantime or any items you all might need, just let us know."

"Surgery?" Demetrius said, looking between Peggy and

his father. "What surgery? When was this decided? Why wasn't I told?"

"I'm sorry," Peggy said, flustered once again. "I thought your father would have told you."

Demetrius found himself looking at his father's back as he walked off down the hall. "Yes, I would have thought so, too." He put his hands on the counter and smiled at Peggy. "Apparently, my dad isn't up to discussing this with me. Can you please give me an overview of my mother's condition?"

Peggy tapped some keys on her computer and gave him a quick update. Olivia had suffered a rather severe episode of angina. While not technically a heart attack, it was a symptom of a heart condition. After a number of tests, the doctor had discovered she had a number of blockages in her coronary arteries, so he had scheduled her for a triple bypass.

"Oh my God," Demetrius said, his voice barely above a whisper. He felt cold and a little lightheaded. How could his father not have told him about all of this? He'd mentioned the possibility of a bypass during the phone call, but why hadn't he told him on the drive over that they had decided to perform surgery?

"It's really a much more simple procedure these days," Peggy assured him. "The surgeons here do a number of them every day. She's in very good hands."

Demetrius gave her what he hoped was a genuine smile. "Thank you, Peggy. For the reassurance, the update, and for taking care of my parents."

"They're very sweet," Peggy replied. "The whole staff likes them both, and we've been taking good care of your mom. She's down the hall in room thirty-eight."

Demetrius thanked Peggy and headed down the hall, pausing outside his mother's room. He heard the low murmuring of his parents conversing and took several deep breaths, preparing himself for his mother's condition. His father had warned him his mother would look pretty bad, and Demetrius didn't want to overreact and make her feel any worse than she probably already did. When he felt ready, he fixed a big smile on his face and stepped into the room.

"Demetrius! Oh, my boy, just look at you!"

He stopped and stared, his smile falling as his expression went slack. His mother sat in a recliner pushed into the corner, her left leg crossed over her right thigh as she applied polish to her toenails. Her silver hair was cut short and worn in gentle waves that framed her tanned face. She had applied a light layer of lipstick and her blue eyes practically glittered with vitality when she saw him.

"Mom!" Demetrius managed to say. "You look great!"

"Oh, stop lying and come over here and give me a hug."

Demetrius crossed to her and leaned down. Olivia pulled him close for a strong hug and kissed both cheeks before releasing him. She smiled up at him, practically beaming.

"I thought..." Demetrius looked at his father, but Marshall sat across the room looking through a magazine. He looked back at his mother and shook his head. "Never mind. Anyway, you look really great for everything that's going on."

"Well, I do get tired easily," Olivia said. "But I thought that was the new blood pressure medication or something. Anyway, I cut back to three yoga sessions a week, and I've only gone to the track twice a week. The doctor says the blockages are most likely genetic and hereditary, so you might want to get a check up when you get back home."

"Okay, yeah, sure. Are you nervous about the surgery?"

Olivia widened her eyes. "I'm terrified! And I'm going to have a scar on my chest."

"She's going to obsess about it when she puts on her swim suit for water aerobics," Marshall said, turning the page of the magazine.

"Oh, Marshall," Olivia said before bending back to polishing her toes.

Demetrius stood at the foot of the hospital bed and looked between them. His mother sat in the recliner with her leg pulled up practically to her crotch in a show of flexibility that put him to shame, and his father sat in a plastic chair across a small table from her, looking through a magazine aimed at active geriatrics. If there wasn't the smell of antiseptic in the air, the quiet calls for doctors in the hall outside the door, and the hospital bed to his left, Demetrius might think he was standing in the living room of his parents' condo.

"So, you look well," he said, unable to get past how youthful and vibrant his mother appeared. Had she always been this way, and it had just taken Demetrius being apart from them for so many years to see it?

Olivia smiled and gestured to the bed. "Have a seat, honey. Tell us about your company. How's the critter catching going?"

Demetrius sat on the edge of the bed. "It's been, well, it's been a bit wild."

"Oh?" Marshall put down the magazine and sat with his hands folded in his lap and an expectant expression on his face. "Wild in what way?"

"Well, we've had some really unusual cases."

"Are you getting paid?" Marshall said.

"Yeah, we've been paid," Demetrius said. *When our client didn't end up dead.*

"Making enough to get by?"

"For the most part," Demetrius said.

"How's Cody?" Olivia smiled as she shook her head. "That boy is quite the Romeo. Is he still charming?"

He was surprised to feel a genuine smile at the thought of Cody. "Yeah, he's still charming. It's been kind of fun running the business with him." Demetrius left off saying that it was also a little confusing and sort of frustrating as well.

"Amelia loves when you two stop by her house," Olivia told him. "Every time I talk to her, she just raves on and on about you two."

Demetrius shifted position on the bed, a bit uncomfortable at the fact that his mother and, by extension, Aunt Amelia, made him and Cody sound like some kind of couple.

"Well, we both like to keep an eye on her."

"So, any nice men in your life?"

"God, Mom, really?"

"What? A mother can't ask about her son's love life?"

A nurse walked in with a plastic bin. "Time to donate some blood."

Marshall got to his feet. "I'll take Demetrius down and show him where the cafeteria is located."

"Oh, bring me back a fruit cup," Olivia said and looked at the nurse. "Can I have a fruit cup?"

The nurse smiled. "Save your money. I'll get you one from the cart."

"So sweet," Olivia said with a smile. "See you boys in a bit."

Demetrius and his father rode down to the first floor with a large group of people, all of them quiet as they watched the floor numbers change. When he stepped off the elevator behind his father, Demetrius stopped to look at a bulletin board covered with missing persons flyers.

"Dad? What's this all about?"

Marshall turned to look. "Oh, those are people missing from the area. Their friends and relatives post their pictures and information in the hospitals in case they're brought here or wander in. Some of them most likely have Alzheimer's."

"This is a lot of people, Dad," Demetrius said in a quiet

voice as a chill went through him. "Are there always this many?"

His father shrugged. "I guess so. A member of our pinochle group went missing six months ago."

"What? That's awful. Have they been found?"

"Not yet. We thought she might have wandered off into the Everglades and got taken by a gator. Lots of pets lost to gators around here."

"Gators?" Demetrius looked back at the flyers and counted eight people missing. "Do you think gators could have gotten all of these people?"

Marshall shrugged again. "I guess it's possible. There are a lot of gators out there in the swamps. People don't realize just how fast they can run, you know?"

"Yeah, but, would all of these people have wandered off into the Everglades?"

"The glades are big and wild, Demetrius. No one really knows what happens out there."

"You're sounding kind of creepy, Dad."

"Didn't mean to." Marshall put a hand on Demetrius's shoulder and turned him away from the bulletin board with the smiling photos. "Come on, son. I'll buy you some lunch and you can tell me about these wild nights catching critters."

Demetrius allowed his father to lead him off down the hall, but he couldn't stop thinking about the flyers posted on that bulletin board. How many other flyers were posted at different hospitals in the area? Weren't the police involved in this at all?

If he were back home in Parson's Hollow, he or Cody would go to the police station and have a talk with Lucia Durant, a sheriff's deputy and another in a long string of Cody's ex-girlfriends. She usually gave them a difficult time whenever she saw them, but Demetrius could always count on her to be honest with him. Down here in East Glades

Bayou, however, he had no connections at the police station. If he were to pay them a visit and ask what they were doing about their many missing person cases, they might take offense.

It was probably a good idea to keep a low profile for now. Besides, he had his mother's impending surgery to worry about. Demetrius put the missing persons flyers out of his mind and followed his father into the cafeteria, suddenly realizing he was pretty darn hungry.

CHAPTER SEVEN

Cody stood on the back patio of Parson's Pines Nursing and Convalescent Home of Serenity. It was early for him at 5:30 p.m., and the heat of the day was fading down to just warm. He stood with his arms crossed and legs spread, watching his grandmother Felicia sit on a bench under a shade tree. She was very animated, looking years younger than her actual age as she talked and tipped her head back in bouts of gleeful laughter. It was all very idyllic, but Cody just wished his grandmother sat with at least one other person. Instead, she sat on her own, talking to whoever might be appearing in whatever time period she was living in at that moment.

Finding her in these states made him uncomfortable. He loved seeing her happy but worried for her. Most times when she slipped into the past, she had no idea who he was, and that always left him feeling sad and alone. She was his only relative remaining in Parson's Hollow. His parents had moved out west years ago, and his four brothers had scattered to different states where they were busy with families of their own. Cody hadn't stayed in Parson's Hollow just for his grandmother, but now that she was living in the past more than the present, he was glad he'd remained close. Not wanting to confuse her right now, he hesitated to approach where she sat on her own out under the tree.

"She's asked about you."

The voice was sure but shaky, and Cody turned to find a spry-looking elderly man standing behind him. He was about a foot and a half shorter than Cody with wild wisps of white hair standing up around his nearly bald head and a retro cool *Star Wars* T-shirt.

"Asked how?" Cody said with a frown. "Like wondering why I haven't stopped by more often?"

"No, nothing like that," the man said with a shake of his head and a frown. "More like wondering when you'd come by again. She says you're her favorite grandson."

"Probably the only one she can remember," Cody said as he looked across the lawn to where his grandmother was enjoying the party inside her mind.

"Not on her lucid days," the man said. "She mentions all five of you boys by name, but gets a big smile when she talks about you."

"That's better than most of my ex-girlfriends," Cody mumbled.

"I hear that," the man agreed.

Cody grinned and stuck out his hand. "You know my name, old-timer, what's yours?"

The old man took Cody's hand and gave it a surprisingly firm shake. "Wallace Benson."

"Thanks for the talk, Wallace. I needed it today."

"Glad to help." He gestured to Felicia. "Go on out and visit with her for a while. I know she'd like it."

Cody walked out to the space beneath the tree. A grouping of chairs surrounded the bench on which Felicia sat, and he lowered himself into the one nearest her. She was in the middle of a laugh, and when he sat down, she stopped abruptly and turned to give him a long, steady look.

"Hi Grandma," he said. "How are you today?"

"This was not about you," she said. "But I'm glad to see you."

Cody cocked his head and gave her a tentative smile. "Oh? Well, I'm glad to see you, too."

"You're the only one of my grandchildren that comes to see me," Felicia said. "I still have some of my memory intact, you know."

Encouraged, Cody got up from the chair and sat beside her on the bench. He stretched his arm out around the back of the bench and touched her bony shoulder. Even with the heat of the day, she felt cool to his touch, and he considered going back inside to grab a sweater from her room.

"You know, I've always been able to tell when you're troubled, Cody Duran," she said. "And lately, you seem to be dragging trouble around behind you in a great big bag."

"You make me sound like Santa Claus or something," Cody said.

"Santa Claus with a bag full of deep thoughts maybe."

"First time anyone's accused me of having a deep thought."

"Well, I doubt that," Felicia said with a sniff. "Although you've been known to stretch the truth when it suits you."

Cody laughed and pulled her up against his side for a hug. "You don't let me get away with anything, do you?"

"Can't say as I do. Now what's on your mind?"

Cody shook his head. "Just feel like I'm at a crossroads right now, Grandma."

"Those are the most exciting places to be," she said with a smile. "It makes you decide about something one way or the other."

"It could mess up something very special," Cody said.

"So it's a romance quandary. Take it from my many decades of experience, it's very telling if you are feeling this confused and concerned about her."

Cody tried not to flinch at his grandmother's use of pronoun. "Yeah, I guess you could say that."

"Have you known her very long?"

He sighed. "Feels like forever."

"Then what's the problem?"

"What if I mess everything up? I've been known to do that on more than one occasion."

Felicia shook her head. "You need to put aside all the noise and focus on the relationship. Does it feel right? Does it feel good? But most important of all, does it make you happy and do you make each other laugh?"

Cody sat and stared at the trunk of the tree for a long moment. He thought about Demmy and all the years they'd known one another. He thought about how deeply he felt the connection between them when they were together, and how much he missed Demmy now that they were apart. Things seemed unfinished or not quite right in his life, and it left him feeling hollow and out of sorts. Was Demmy feeling this way without him around, or was he too busy trying to manage his mother's health care?

And there were hours and hours of shared laughter between them.

"It does make me happy, and we do laugh a lot," Cody finally said. When he looked at his grandmother, he saw she had tears in her eyes and felt the sting of his own. "Why are you crying, Grandma?"

"Because, my dear sweet boy," she replied and wiped away her tears. "After all the years of dating and trying to find someone to keep your interest for longer than a few weeks, you seem to have finally found the one who's meant for you."

"Yeah? Do you think so?" He wondered what his brothers and parents might have to say about it all when he brought Demmy around and introduced him as...what? His boyfriend? His lover? Hell, he didn't think he was ready for all of this yet, and he sure as fuck knew his brother Roman—the most conservative of all of the Bower boys—wasn't ready for it, either.

"I think you've been floundering for a few years now," Felicia said. "But lately I've noticed you seem to be acting more settled."

"That's funny. I don't feel settled," Cody said. "I feel more anxious than anything."

Felicia leaned in and lowered her voice. "That's love, my boy. You're in love."

"Yeah?"

She smiled. "Yeah."

Cody stared at the empty chair across from him. "I just never thought I would feel this way for...this person."

Felicia gave a quiet snort and shook her head. "No one ever expects it to happen the way it does. Sometimes it can happen like a lightning strike, and other times it's like the tiny glowing ember in a fireplace that just refuses to go out. It's love. It refuses to be defined or explained." She sighed. "It's a real bitch sometimes."

Cody laughed. He tipped back his head and laughed loud and long at the tree branches arching overhead. Behind them, he could hear a small group of residents talking and laughing as well, and he hoped he and Felicia were the subject of their conversation.

"Where did you come up with all of this stuff?" Cody said.

"Oh, honey, just because I'm in my nineties doesn't mean I don't know what's going on." After a long pause, she held up a wrinkled and bony finger and said, "Usually I don't know what's going on. Sometimes I get confused. But right now, I know perfectly well I'm talking with my grandson, Cody, who I love very much, and who I want to see happy."

"Well, Grandma, I want to be happy, too, so we've got a lot in common." He kissed her on the cheek and gave her a careful hug. "Now, let's talk about something else."

"Good, Horatio over here was getting bored with all of this talk about love and feelings," Felicia said with a wave to an empty chair and an elaborate roll of her eyes. "He's so dramatic."

CHAPTER EIGHT

A ball of sweat ran down Demetrius's side and buried itself under the waistband of his underwear. He picked up the margarita glass, also sweating, took a sip, then coughed and blinked back tears. The drink was mostly tequila, and though Demetrius needed it after the long day he'd had, it was still a bit of a shock. He had talked with nurses and doctors and more nurses and different doctors, trying to understand everything about his mother's condition as well as the risks involved in the surgery.

Not only did he need to understand and retain the information, but he had to be able to explain it to his parents and Cody and Amelia back home. And all day long, he'd been responding to text messages from Cody and Amelia who wanted to check in. Even Oliver Berridge had sent a text hoping things were well, despite the way things had fizzled out between them. Apparently word was spreading around Parson's Hollow about his mother's condition, and Demetrius wondered ruefully if Oliver was going to write a short article about it. Maybe title it something like, *Here's What's Up With...*

"How's that 'rita treating you?"

Demetrius took another sip, the tequila burning its way down his throat and bringing fresh tears to his eyes. "Just what I needed." In fact, it was easing the mild pain of the scrape on his back even as he sat there.

Eunice Potts smiled and nodded where she stood on the lanai of the condo she shared with her husband, Hubert, the slightly prickly man who had picked Demetrius up at the airport earlier that day. Had he only been in Florida less than one day? Demetrius took another sip of the margarita that tasted like a chemical fire in his throat. The warmth of the liquor seeped through him, and he blinked away more tears as he smiled at Eunice. Her shoulder length platinum blonde hair perfectly framed her tanned, youthful face, and her khaki shorts and pink polo hugged her trim body. If Demetrius had to guess, he'd say Eunice was at most sixty-five years old to Hubert's most likely late seventies or early eighties, and she was in a hell of a lot better shape than her husband.

"Spending the day inside a hospital is a real suck ass way to pass the time in Florida," Eunice said with a firm single nod, tiny hands on her hips. "Your parents are real lucky to have a son like you who flew all the way down here to help them out."

"Well, they've done so much for me," Demetrius said, shocked to hear himself already slightly slurring his "S" sounds. "It's the least I can do for them."

Hubert stuck his head out the sliding door, his silver pompadour sweeping back from his forehead, which was now wrinkled with concern. "That storm is getting stronger out in the Atlantic."

Eunice smiled over her shoulder at her husband. "We're not planning to do any sailing on the ocean, dear. We get more tropical storms than we can count down here, you know that. No need to raise the alarm yet."

He made a noncommittal grunting sound, followed up with, "I'll be back in a few minutes. I need to walk the Fosters' dogs."

"Okay. I'll keep Demetrius and Marshall company." Eunice smiled at Demetrius, and then frowned and looked toward the house. "Where is your father?"

"I'm here, I'm here." Marshall stepped through the sliding glass door. He wore white shorts with leg openings that seemed to float around his skinny thighs, a bright red short-sleeved button down shirt, and dark socks with sandals. He held a margarita glass of his own and took a sip from it as he crossed to sit beside Demetrius at the glass-topped table.

"How's your 'rita, Marshall?"

"Well, let me check and see." Marshall reached out to pick up Demetrius's drink and took a sip. His eyes widened and he blinked a few times as he stared at Demetrius. He slowly returned the drink to its place in front of Demetrius, then held his own glass out toward Eunice. "I would like to make an exchange, please."

Eunice folded her arms and gave him a steady look. "Oh, you would, would you?"

"Yes. I would like one with just as much tequila as my son's." Marshall shook the glass, making the ice cubes rattle.

"You should not have so much alcohol while you're taking blood pressure medicine," Eunice said.

"If it's not the alcohol, it will be something else, Eunice," Marshall replied, and shook his glass a little harder. "I'd like to enjoy what time I have left."

Demetrius was about to swap drinks with his father just to end the stand off between the two when Eunice let out a heavy, persecuted sigh and stomped up to the table. She snatched the glass out of Marshall's hand and strode into the house, sliding the patio door shut hard behind her.

Demetrius looked at his father for a moment, then each of

them lost control at the same time and burst into laughter. It lasted just a minute or two, but the bonding moment felt good as Demetrius had never felt very close with his father as he'd been growing up.

"She's the worrier of our group." Marshall gestured toward the patio door. "She's kind of like an exuberant Girl Scout who wants to make sure everyone else is safe and sound before seeing to herself."

"She's nice," Demetrius said. "Both Eunice and Hubert are nice."

"Hubert's a bit of a prickly pear at times, but he's a dependable friend." Marshall nodded and his eyes took on a faraway, sad quality. "They've helped me so much with your mother's health problems."

"Health problems?" Demetrius asked after another swallow of his margarita. "You make it sound like an ongoing thing. How often has Mom been to the hospital?"

"Oh, a few," Marshall said, seeming flustered now, as if he'd slipped up and said something he shouldn't. "We didn't want to worry you about those things, though."

"But I do worry about you guys," Demetrius said. "Just like you worry about me. Now I feel like I should call you more often to check in."

"No no no." Marshall waved Demetrius's statement away. "We are very proud of you and happy that you've started this new business venture. We both hope you find someone special to bring into your life soon. And we don't care about the fact that you're gay. We just want you to be with someone who loves and appreciates you for who you are."

Tears filled Demetrius's eyes, and he grabbed his glass for a hearty swallow, then said, "Dad..."

Eunice opened the patio door and stepped out, balancing a small tray supporting two margaritas. As she approached the table, Demetrius's phone buzzed in his pocket and he pulled it out to check the display.

"This is Cody," Demetrius said. "It might be work related."

Marshall nodded and sipped the fresh drink Eunice handed him. As Demetrius accepted the call and got out of his chair, he heard his father say, "Now that's a margarita!"

"Hi there, how are you?" Demetrius said, stepping inside the condo and shivering in the air conditioning.

"Hey, hi," Cody said, sounding surprised. "I didn't expect you to answer. I was prepared to leave a message."

"Dad and I are having drinks at a condo down the street from my parents' place," Demetrius said.

"Drinks to celebrate Mom being okay?"

"Well, drinks to relax us," Demetrius said. "And, boy, am I relaxed now."

"What's going on, Demmy?" Cody said, his voice soft.

"It's a lot to deal with, that's all. I mean, I just got here this morning and I'm already exhausted. I don't know how people deal with health care for an aging parent on a day-to-day basis. It's pretty overwhelming."

"I'm sorry. What can I do?"

Cody sounded so earnest and thoughtful and open to whatever Demetrius needed from him. It sent a wave of emotion through him he was powerless to hold at bay. The tequila had loosened him up, and now Cody's sincerity and understanding had knocked aside the small barriers Demetrius had erected during his day at the hospital. He tried to say that Cody was doing what needed to be done by staying at home and managing the business, but what came out was an audible gulping sound followed by a hitching breath and then a choked sob as tears spilled down his cheeks.

"Demmy? Jesus, are you crying?" Cody sounded alarmed, and Demetrius could just picture him pacing the open space in their office or perhaps the length of the living room of his apartment. "Demmy, talk to me. Tell me what you need me to do. Do you want me to come down there? I'll be there tomorrow morning. Fuck, I'll pack a bag and start driving there right now."

Demetrius took some deep breaths in an effort to get himself under control. He palmed the tears from his eyes and wished he'd brought his drink inside with him. When he felt like he could talk again, he said, "Sorry about that."

"Hey," Cody said in that gentle tone that seemed to reach right inside Demetrius's chest and wrap around his heart. "You had me worried there. I thought things were, like, really super bad down there."

"No, just kind of lonely."

"Want me to come down?"

"We can't afford to have both of us away from the business," Demetrius said.

"Hell, we can afford to be closed for a few days."

"We haven't made enough to pay the rent on the place yet this month," Demetrius told him. "And besides, I'm fine. I've just had a very strong margarita, and you know what tequila does to me."

"Makes you horny, if I remember correctly," Cody said, and Demetrius could hear the smile in his voice. "You say nice things and get pretty handsy."

"You're an ass," Demetrius muttered.

"Yep, got a fine one at that," Cody shot back. "Which you told me about the last time you had a healthy dose of tequila." He turned serious again. "I could be down there in no time, Demmy. Just give me the word. You know that."

Demetrius smiled as he thought about Cody coming down to Florida. Cody would charm all the senior women in the retirement complex and befriend all the men within an hour. And his parents loved Cody. They'd probably fed him half the dinners he'd eaten all the years they'd been friends in school, so they would enjoy seeing him, too. But the money was a concern for Demetrius. He'd always been very budget conscious, his parents instilling in him from an early age the importance of managing his money and not overspending. But with this business they'd started, he'd overextended his monetary reach, and it left him feeling unsettled and edgy.

"I know, Cody," he finally said. "But I'm okay down here, really. I'm tired from the flight down, and the first day was just a little overwhelming with all the doctors and medical decisions. She's going in for a triple bypass in a couple of days."

"A triple bypass? Shit, Demmy, that's pretty serious. Shouldn't Amelia be down there with you guys at least? I mean, she is your Mom's sister."

"No, I don't think she needs to be here," Demetrius said, trying to explain his parents' wishes while he didn't believe them himself.

"That's your folks talking," Cody said, calling him out immediately. "They've always been like that, the whole 'No, we don't want to put you through any bother. Olivia is having open heart surgery, but everything is fine!'"

Demetrius could not help laughing. "My parents do not sound like that."

"Maybe not to you, but that's because you grew up with them," Cody said. "To the rest of us, they sound just like that."

"You're crazy."

"You're crazier for being my friend."

"This is a good point."

A comfortable silence stretched between them, and within it Demetrius thought he could hear the whispers of so many things he should be saying but couldn't. Not only was Cody straight, but he was his best friend, and also completely out of Demetrius's league. Even if Cody were gay, there was no way he'd be interested in Demetrius as more than a friend. They were just too different. And Cody was way too good looking for Demetrius to even hope to land him. And, as he'd had to remind himself many times over the years, Cody was straight. End of story.

Sometimes, opposites didn't attract.

"Okay, I should get back out on the patio," Demetrius said. "Before my father gets himself plastered on margaritas."

"Keep us posted, please. I mean it."

"I will, I promise. Jobs going okay?"

"Yeah, sure," Cody said breezily. "I go to a place, I get dirty, I catch a critter, I get paid, I come back to the office. The usual."

"No crazy monsters to chase?"

"Not yet. But the week is still young."

"Yeah, true. Take care of yourself."

"You, too. Talk to you soon."

"Bye." Demetrius disconnected the call and stood for a moment in Eunice and Hubert's maritime-themed living room, smiling at the salt-water fish tank. It had been good to talk with Cody, even if it was for just a few minutes. He did miss the big lug, he had to admit.

Demetrius took a breath, let it out, then headed back out on the lanai where his father and Eunice were arguing over which grocery store had the best price for turnips.

CODY STOOD in the middle of his apartment living room holding the phone. The sound of Demmy crying had flipped a protective switch inside him he couldn't seem to deactivate. No matter what Demmy had said after he'd pulled himself together, Cody knew he and Amelia should be down there.

He scrolled through the contacts list in his phone and touched Amelia's number, listening as it rang on her end.

Amelia answered sounding slightly out of breath. "Hi Cody, have you heard anything?"

"I just talked to Demmy, and he's trying to tell me we don't need to be down there, but..."

"I want to go," Amelia said immediately. "Do you think we can get flights this late?"

"Not sure, but that's pretty pricey anyway," Cody said. "Tell me, how many miles do you have on your car?"

CHAPTER NINE

Demetrius yawned as he stood in line in the Coastal Waters Memorial Hospital cafeteria. He was getting even sleepier and starting to sweat from the heat soaking through the cardboard protectors of the two large cups of coffee he held. Both he and his father had had a tough time getting up and moving that morning. Apparently, Eunice's super duper rockin' and rollin' margaritas packed more of a punch than either one of them had realized. While his father visited with his mother in ICU, Demetrius volunteered to make a coffee run to the cafeteria.

He had a vague memory of talking with Cody the evening before, but couldn't really remember what they had discussed. As he shuffled up to the register, a bleary memory surfaced of him crying while on the phone with Cody, and he must have flinched. The woman behind the register said, "Everything all right, dear?"

Demetrius flashed a quick smile and handed over the twenty his father had given him, "Yeah, thanks." He tried unsuccessfully to tamp down the feeling of guilt about being almost thirty years old and still taking money from his father for coffee.

The quiet sounds of the hospital pinged and scuffed and squeaked around him as he made his way back to his mother's room. She was sleeping when he walked in, her face turned away from the door and toward the corner where his father had dozed off in the one comfortable chair. Demetrius took a moment to study them both, feeling as if a bubble of warmth and peace surrounded them right this very moment, shutting out the ICU and the nurses and the reality of his mother's condition. Right now it was just the three of them here together, like it had been while he'd been growing up.

He had realized at a young age his birth had to have surprised them, coming along at the time when they had most likely been mapping out how many years until they could both retire. But even though his arrival had to have put a major crimp in whatever plans they had been discussing, all of his life they'd given him everything he needed and most of what he wanted. They had never once made him feel guilty for his late arrival, only loved and cared for. When he'd realized he was gay while attending middle school, Demetrius had suffered with years of crushing guilt over being unable or unwilling to provide them with the standard daughter-in-law and grandchildren. Sure, he could adopt or find a woman willing to be a surrogate, but Demetrius knew it wouldn't be the same.

When he'd finally come out to them, they'd been quiet but supportive. They'd told him it wasn't the life they'd hoped he would lead, but they loved him and supported him and wanted him to be happy. And then they'd each hugged him and told him it was okay to be gay. They knew some very nice gay men who owned a florist shop in town and they seemed happy, and so they were sure he would be happy, too.

Now, as he stood in the doorway of his mother's hospital room, tears filled Demetrius's eyes, and he set down both coffees to grab a tissue from the box near the bed. He used the abrasive tissue to wipe his eyes and wondered why the hell hospitals couldn't spring for a softer tissue with all the money they raked in. He decided to let his parents rest and placed his father's coffee on a small table beside him before leaving the room. He stopped at the nurse's station down the hall to inquire how his mother had slept the night before and ask when the doctor would be making rounds.

"Not until three o'clock," the nurse said. "Sorry."

"Ugh, long day. Any word on a time for my mother's surgery?"

"Oh, yeah, they have her set for seven a.m. tomorrow," the nurse said, then frowned. "No one told you? I'm sure we discussed it with your father."

Demetrius sighed. "He probably thought I was there with him and heard it as well. Okay, thanks for letting me know."

With the rest of the morning and most of the afternoon stretching before him, Demetrius decided to go down to the lobby. He needed some time to think, and the cafeteria would soon get crowded and loud as more people arrived and the lunch hour approached. He returned to the room and left a note for his parents telling them to text him when they awoke, and then he took the elevator down to the first floor.

After getting turned around a few times, he finally figured out the color-coded signs and lines on the floor of the hallways and stepped out into the glass and steel lobby where he paused to look around. Half of the lobby had been built as a large interior garden, with a number of paths twisting through it and spaces set aside with benches near water features and colorful beds of flowers.

Demetrius wandered through the paths for a bit, then settled on a bench set off in a corner. From this spot, he could see the main elevators and keep an eye out for his father. After adjusting his position to keep pressure off the scrape on his back, he stared at the flowers across the path and let his mind wander.

As was happening more and more often these days, his thoughts turned to Cody. Demetrius often acted irritated or exasperated with Cody and his comments and antics, but when he was honest with himself, Cody more often than not impressed him. There was no one Cody couldn't charm. Hell, he sometimes managed to win over any of his ex-girlfriends they ran into. That list was long, too, so they were constantly encountering a new ex-girlfriend of Cody's during jobs.

Cody brought a lot of craziness along with him every place he went, and though he rolled his eyes and sighed about it, Demetrius really did enjoy it. He never knew what the day might hold, and when he was apart from Cody, like he was now, everything around him seemed staid and as if it had a little less color.

And then there was Cody's physical presence. Tall, strong, and good-looking, Demetrius could not deny a sense of pride at the fact that Cody had chosen him as his best friend. Despite the occasional erotic dream—or even daydream— Demetrius was able to keep his thoughts about Cody firmly in the friend zone. For the most part.

Thinking about Cody brought along the thought that he should call and check-in on things with Critter Catchers. But after a second thought, Demetrius decided he was too tired at that moment, so he put his head back and closed his eyes. He needed to put aside his worries. The finances would take care of themselves, or they would close up shop and find new jobs. Demetrius knew he and Cody would still be friends either way, although he'd rather keep working with Cody than meeting up for drinks with him after whatever soul-crushing desk or retail jobs had released them for the day. The past few months had provided more excitement, more danger and death, and more craziness than Demetrius had ever anticipated in his lifetime. But the fact that Cody had been beside him the entire time had made Demetrius feel safe and protected.

Though he felt calm and relaxed at that moment, Demetrius knew tomorrow would be difficult. The doctors had said the bypass surgery could take six or more hours. And then she'd have recovery time in the hospital and rehabilitation time back home which would take weeks. He'd have to arrange for someone to assist his parents at home for a while before he could even think about heading back to Parson's Hollow. Again, too many thoughts tried to crowd into the front of his brain, and he made himself take a breath and push them all aside.

He listened to the quiet sounds of the water features and soft bird songs piped in from hidden speakers and let his mind drift. A bit of meditation instruction came back to him from a CD he'd used during college to help him prep for final exams, and he latched onto it. He was a boat on a calm lake, nothing around him but silence and water. On the lake there was no vanity, no ego, no arguments. Here there was only himself and the physical space he was taking up. His problems and concerns had been left back on the shore and only rest and tranquility accompanied him in the boat.

"Demmy?"

Demetrius started and opened his eyes, blinking up, way up, at the man who stood before him. He must have dozed off during his meditation and was a little confused. He frowned as he stared up at this man. Where was he? Was he back home and had been dreaming this whole time that his mother was going to have heart surgery?

"Demmy, it's Cody." He hunkered down in front of the

bench and looked him in the eye, concern clear in his expression. "Everything okay? You all right?"

"Hi," Demetrius said, pushing himself upright on the bench as he looked around in confusion. He was still in the lobby of the Coastal Waters Memorial Hospital, sitting in the gardens with the bubbling sound of the water and the electronic bird songs. But if he was here, how was Cody crouching in front of him? "What? How?"

The warm and wonderful sight of Cody's smile made Demetrius smile in return.

"After we talked last night, I called Amelia and we drove down," Cody said. "She drove the first five hours while I slept, and then I drove the rest of the way." He widened his eyes, the dark chocolate brown so familiar and comforting. "I'm kind of tired, but I'll sleep when I'm dead, right?"

"But who's running the office?"

Cody rose to his full six foot five inches with a grunt and sat on the bench next to him. "Well, remember I told you about Jugs helping me out?"

"Yeah. But he's not trained."

Cody shrugged. "I trained him."

"In a day?"

"It was a crash course," Cody said, then put an arm around Demetrius and pulled him in close. "Sorry if I smell funky, but I just spent seventeen hours in a car driving like hell." He chuckled. "Aunt Amelia could be the next Danica Patrick."

Demetrius pushed away from Cody and glared at him. "Dammit, Cody, I told you things were fine down here. And now you've hired someone we barely know to run our business while we're both away? Come on, I trusted you to be responsible and take care of things back home, and a day later you show up down here in Florida. How is this helping us grow our business? How is this bringing in money for us to be able to live on?"

Cody's open and earnest expression shut down as Demetrius spoke. He pressed his lips tight together. When Demetrius finished, Cody looked at him and when he spoke his voice was chilled by anger. "I appreciate what you're saying, but I feel like you've stepped over a line, Demmy, and it hurts. Just so you know, I came down here to support you during a really difficult time, so I'm sorry if my concern for you and my friendship has become a bother to you. Like it or not, I think of you as my best friend first and my business partner second. Your Aunt Amelia wanted to come down, and I suggested she and I drive down in her car to save all of us the money of a last minute flight, which I would hope you could appreciate since you jumped on one to come down here yesterday. I would have appreciated hearing a thank you instead of getting bitched out for leaving someone behind to field calls and manage our business, yes for a cut of the money coming in, but also as maybe a future employee we could use to, I don't know, go on vacation ourselves one day."

Cody got to his feet and stood looking down at him, his expression and stance so closed off and defensive a tidal wave of shame and guilt swamped Demetrius.

"Cody—"

"I get that you're stressed," Cody interrupted him. "But it doesn't give you the right to be an asshole when someone does something nice for you. You could be a decent human being about how much Amelia and I put ourselves out to be down here to support you and provide what help we can."

He turned and started to walk off, but Demetrius was fully awake now and got to his feet quick, grabbing Cody's arm and pulling him back. Cody resisted, but just slightly, and that gave Demetrius hope his rant hadn't done any permanent damage to their friendship. He tugged on Cody's arm, feeling the muscle tighten beneath his fingers and wondering how it would feel to be as strong and tall as Cody even as he pulled his friend around to face him again.

"I'm sorry," Demetrius said, looking Cody in the eye as he continued to hold onto his upper arm. "Please forgive me. You surprised me, and I had just been worrying about money before you showed up."

Cody grunted and looked away a moment, then back at him. "You're always worried about money."

Demetrius nodded and grinned. "I'd have to agree with you about that." He gave Cody's arm a gentle shake. "Forgive me?"

After letting out a heavy breath, Cody pulled Demetrius in for a tight hug. "How could I stay mad at my best friend?"

Demetrius closed his eyes and lost himself in the damp heat of Cody's body and the vague funk of his travel sweat. He was glad to have Cody here now, despite his concerns about what was happening back home with their business. With Cody alongside him, Demetrius felt he could handle anything that might happen.

"Cody?" someone said from behind them, and they turned to see Marshall and Amelia standing there, both of them smiling.

"Hi, Mr. Singleton," Cody said, reaching out to shake Marshall's hand.

"Oh, stop that handshake foolishness and come here," Marshall said. He hugged him, looking ridiculously short and elderly compared to Cody. That didn't stop Marshall from thumping Cody on the back a few times before releasing him and stepping back. "And I've told you to call me Marshall. You're more like family than anyone else in Demetrius's life."

"Marshall, yes, sorry," Cody said. He glanced at Demetrius, his grin igniting a warm feeling of home inside

Demetrius's chest. Then Cody looked back at Marshall. "Can we see Mrs. Singleton...sorry, Olivia?"

Marshall frowned. "I'm sorry, son, it's family only. They're very strict about that sort of thing here."

"You take Amelia upstairs, Dad," Demetrius said. "Cody and I will head to the cafeteria."

"You sure?" Amelia said as she moved around Cody and Marshall to give Demetrius a hug.

Demetrius hugged her back, grateful she had arrived to help take some of the pressure off him. "Oh yeah, I'm sure. I'm getting hungry anyway."

Marshall and Amelia started to go, then Marshall turned back and pulled his phone from the pocket of his shorts. "Oh, I forgot. Hubert sent me a text asking if you could help him with something back at the condos."

"Oh?" Demetrius wondered what Hubert would need him for since the condo association had a maintenance crew. "Do you know what it is?"

Marshall shook his head. "No idea. I'll forward you the text and his number. Here, you can take our car since Amelia has her car here now."

Demetrius accepted the keys and pocketed them, then looked up at Cody as Marshall and Amelia turned the corner and disappeared from sight.

"Well, we can go back to my parents' condo and you can get a shower and sleep a bit if you want," Demetrius said.

Cody nodded, his expression thoughtful as he met Demetrius's gaze. "Yeah, why don't we head back there? I'm not that tired right now, though. I had a few energy drinks the last leg of the drive so I'm feeling pretty perky."

"Oh boy," Demetrius said with a groan and led the way toward the parking garage. "Try not to over perk yourself, eh?"

"I love it when you talk dirty," Cody said.

"I know you do." He punched the button for the elevator and then grinned up at Cody. "I'm glad you're here."

"Really?"

"Really. I just hope Jugs doesn't burn someone's house down."

Cody shrugged. "We're probably due for that ourselves, the luck we have."

"Good point."

The elevator arrived and they stepped into the car. As the doors slid shut, Demetrius's phone buzzed and he looked at the text from his father with Hubert's phone number and the brief message the man had sent. No clue in the message as to what Hubert wanted Demetrius's help with, and he wondered what he might be in for. Well, if Cody was going along with him, Eunice would probably fall all over herself to get Cody to drink one or two of her super duper rockin' and rollin' margaritas, and that would open the doors to anything happening. Oh boy.

CHAPTER TEN

Thoughts collided inside Cody's mind as Demetrius drove them back to his parents' condo. Each collision caused the thoughts to explode into other, smaller thoughts branching off into a wide variety of directions his brain tried to follow. Demetrius was talking about his Mom's condition and the strong drinks he'd had the night before, but Cody was only half listening. He was still pretty amped up on the energy drinks. Whenever he turned his head, his brain took a couple seconds longer to catch up.

And then there was the whole needing to talk to Demmy thing. A speech ran on a constant loop in the back of Cody's mind, like a repeating film clip in a museum. He saw himself from Demmy's point of view, looking beat up and wicked bad. How long had it been since he'd had a decent night's sleep? Shit, those missed hours seemed to be stacking up harder against him as the years piled on.

Anyway, in the film clip, he would be able to see and hear himself stumble through an admission of sorts. "Demmy, we've been friends for most of our lives, and now we're spending even more time together running a business. As you know, I've been pretty restless in my dating life, only staying with the same girl for a few weeks at most. Well, I've done a lot of soul searching about it, and I think I've figured out what's been missing." He would pause here for dramatic effect and look Demmy right in the eye. "You."

"Goddamn it, take the senior shuttle and save all our lives," Demetrius practically shouted. His exclamation pulled Cody back to the moment where Demmy was trying to avoid rear-ending a senior driver who had come to a sudden and complete stop directly in front of them. The elderly driver sat half outside of the center left turn lane, and now that all forward motion had halted, decided to switch on the left turn signal.

"You have got to be kidding me," Demmy grumbled. He waited for a break in traffic to their right before speeding around the elderly man who could barely see over the steering wheel.

"You okay over there?" Cody said.

"I'm fine," Demmy muttered. "Sorry about that."

"Perfectly understandable," Cody said. "It's like a whole state filled with Widow Monroes."

Demmy laughed, which was what Cody was going for. JoAnn Monroe, known around Parson's Hollow as the Widow Monroe, was the widow of the town's late fire chief who passed away forty years ago and held a special place in the heart of the townspeople. Currently somewhere in her nineties, she refused to quit driving. For the safety not just of the Widow Monroe but everyone in town, the sheriff had installed a revolving yellow light on top of her car. It was a warning beacon to all others, motorists and pedestrians alike, and it allowed people to keep track of where the widow was and adjust their own speeds and trajectories accordingly. Though she was annoying and a menace to public safety in general, the Widow Monroe had inadvertently saved their lives a few months ago by running down a rage and steroid fueled monster pursuing them who had once been their client, Reed Wilkes, a local farmer. All hail the Widow Monroe.

Cody looked over at Demmy, taking note of the strong line of his nose, rounded chin with its perfectly centered dimple, and a day's worth of beard. He wanted to say something reassuring about Olivia's condition and follow it up with a hint at the confusion of feelings teeming within him... but the words, so clear in his mental film clip, seemed muddled and in the wrong order when he considered saying them aloud.

Demetrius drove through a retirement village which looked like every other one they'd passed, and Cody let the moment go. If he tried to say something now, after being in the car for almost a full day and buzzed on energy drinks, he'd most assuredly fuck it up even more than he would if he were completely prepared. No, better to wait and get it at least half right than rush into it and get it all wrong.

And he was definitely not sure he wanted to risk the most important relationship outside of his family on that kind of experiment. No, he needed to think about this for a bit longer and get it right.

"Here we are," Demmy said as he pulled into the driveway of a detached ranch-style condominium.

Cody stepped out of the car and groaned at the damp heat. He looked up and down the street at the similar condos lining each side, then looked at Demmy. "How the hell do any of them get back to the right house?"

Demmy laughed and shrugged. "Your guess is as good as mine. Some of them have seasonal flags to stand out, but the association has really strict rules about making changes to the condo's appearance. Maybe it's how the association employees get their kicks?"

"Weird." Cody grabbed his duffle out of the backseat. "Okay, let me drop off my bag, drain the dragon, and wash up a bit, then we can see what this old guy needs us to do."

"Drain the dragon?" Demmy repeated as he led Cody to the front door.

"Well, it's much bigger than a lizard, so, you know, I'm not gonna short change myself," Cody said.

"I see."

"Do you?"

Demmy unlocked the door and stepped into the condo and Cody followed, sighing gratefully at the cool air conditioning. He followed Demmy down the hall to what he assumed was the guest bedroom. They stood side by side just inside the door as they looked at the two single beds, one neatly made and the other with sheets in a tangle, apparently the one Demmy had slept in the night before. A small nightstand separated them, with barely enough room on its top to support a tall lamp and a wind up alarm clock.

"Which one of us is Laverne and which is Shirley?" Cody said.

"Well, given your dating history, I'd say you should be the one with the big *L* on your chest."

Cody nodded in acceptance. "I see your point."

He dropped his bag on the neatly made bed and unzipped it. After pulling out his flip-flops, a few pairs of underwear and shorts, Cody finally found his toiletries bag. Demmy still lingered in the doorway and Cody held up his kit.

"Bathroom?"

Demmy stepped out into the hall and pointed toward the far end. "Bathroom is two doors down on the left."

Cody headed for the bathroom but stopped and turned back when Demmy called his name.

"I really am glad you drove down. Sorry I lashed out at

you. I know you did it to support me and my parents, and I appreciate it."

Cody smiled and felt something within him loosen a bit at Demmy's apology. He sounded more sincere than he had back at the hospital when Cody's anger and frustration had been so close beneath the surface of his skin.

"You're welcome, Demmy. I'm glad to be here."

After peeing for what felt like half an hour, Cody brushed his teeth, gargled with mouthwash, washed his face, and applied fresh deodorant. He felt closer to human when he stepped out of the bathroom. Demmy was not in the bedroom, and Cody took the opportunity to survey the narrow gap between their single beds. As best friends, they'd slept in the same room numerous times over the years, but with Cody's recent contemplations about their relationship, the room sharing might be awkward.

"You ready?"

Cody looked up and found Demmy standing in the doorway, keys in hand and that familiar expression of slight impatience touched with a bit of anxiety. Cody stuffed his shaving kit back into the duffel and nodded.

"I'm ready. Let's hit it."

He followed Demmy down the hall and out the door, both of them griping about the heat the minute they stepped outside. Cody walked to the passenger door of the car and was surprised when Demmy walk past the car and down into the street.

"We're not driving?" Cody called out.

"No, Hubert lives just down the street."

Cody felt his shirt already sticking to his back. "Oh? How far? Should we maybe drive down there in case we need to get the car like real quick?"

Demmy looked back at him, hands on hips. "I know the

heat is a lot to take, but everyone sweats down here, Cody. You'll get used to it, too."

"Ridiculous state," Cody muttered as he tromped down the driveway after Demmy. "No wonder it's full of old people, their blood's a lot thinner."

Cody felt as if the sun focused on them through a giant magnifying glass, and figured it was most likely pay back for all the ants he'd burned when he was young. He regretted doing it now, but it was the smallest of regrets. Right now the heat was making him so crabby, he'd set a whole colony of ants on fire if it would help ease his tension.

A few doors down from the Singleton residence, a large boat anchor rested in a flowerbed, surrounded by some kind of wonder flower that didn't seem to mind the blazing sun and heat. Demmy walked up the driveway and knocked at the door. Cody noticed a long line of sweat sticking the back of Demmy's T-shirt to his spine. He wondered whether he would be inclined to run his tongue through beads of sweat on Demmy's skin if they did ever have sex, and the confused turmoil in Cody's mind, sudden hardening of his cock, and oppressive heat nearly made him pass out. Thankfully, the door opened and an attractive woman in her mid-sixties stood there, looking cool and fresh. She smiled at Demmy, then set her eyes on Cody.

Over the years, he'd become pretty good at detecting the predatory lust in the gazes of women he met, but this woman took that lust to a whole new level. She practically dropped to all fours and let out a cougar growl. In a moment, however, she recovered herself. Running a hand through her platinum shoulder length bob, she stepped aside and allowed them to enter the deliciously cool interior.

"Thank you for coming over, Demetrius," the woman said, standing in front of Cody with her hand held out. "And who might this be?"

"This is my friend and business partner, Cody Bower," Demetrius said. "Cody, this is Eunice Potts, Hubert's wife."

Cody heard the undercurrent of warning in Demmy's tone, but Eunice either didn't hear it or didn't care. Her smile broadened, and she took another step closer. Cody reacted on instinct and leaned down to kiss the back of Eunice's hand.

"A pleasure to meet such a fresh daisy of a woman among all this humidity and heat."

"Oh, my," Eunice said. She stepped back when her husband entered the room, but she kept her gaze on Cody.

"Took you long enough," Hubert groused, and then glared at Cody. "Who's this one?"

Cody stepped forward, hand extended. "Cody Bower, sir. I'm Demmy's business partner and good friend."

"Business partner?" Hubert nodded, ignoring Cody's hand as he looked between him and Demmy. "Good. It'll probably take the two of you. You're animal control back up north, right?"

"Yes," Demmy said.

Without responding, Hubert headed for the front door, and Cody sagged a bit when he realized they were headed back out into the heat and scorching sunlight. With a tight smile and a nod at Eunice, Cody trailed after Demmy who followed Hubert out into the swampy heat.

"We run a business called Critter Catchers," Demmy explained as they headed across the street. The condos on this side of the street butted right up against a chain link fence behind which stood thick trees hung with moss.

"Good name," Hubert said over his shoulder. "Cute and catchy."

Cody was surprised to hear such a description from the gruff and seemingly just-this-side-of-miserable man. Before he or Demmy could reply, however, Hubert pulled a key ring with a number of house keys from his pocket. He sorted through the keys and selected one which opened the door of a condo with a Georgia Bulldogs flag flapping from a flag pole holder. Two small Pomeranians barked and pawed at the windows to either side of the door and Hubert groused at the animals as he pushed the door open.

"I know, I know," Hubert told the dogs. "I've got help now. You can go out into the backyard soon."

The air in the condo was almost frigid, and Cody wondered if his skull might crack at such a drastic temperature change. The Pomeranians trotted around their feet, barking and pausing now and then to paw at their legs. They seemed friendly enough, but Cody resisted the urge to reach down and pet them. From his past experience, he'd found that small dogs bit.

"That's a lot of keys," Cody said.

"Yeah, I'm the pet sitter for a good part of the village," Hubert said and gave a small shrug. "I like the animals. This condo belongs to the Underwoods. They're away visiting their grandkids in Utah. But that's beside the point. This is the problem I need help with."

He led them to a sliding door and they stood side by side, peering out at the backyard. The Pomeranians barked non-stop and pawed at the glass door, and Cody winced at the sound. He wished Hubert would just open the door and let the little rats out already. Something had to be amiss, though, so he looked around the backyard. An in-ground pool took up the majority of the backyard, save for a small patio right outside the sliding door and a strip of lawn the dogs probably wished was four times as wide. An awning extended from the back of the condo out over the patio, casting cool shade on a couple of tables and a number of chairs. An inflatable raft in the shape of an alligator floated low in the water.

"Notice anything unusual?" Hubert said.

"Nice pool," Cody said, then looked at Demmy. "Do your folks have a pool?"

"No," Demmy replied with a sigh, then he frowned and squinted, leaning in closer to the patio door. "Did I just see what I think I saw?"

Cody peered out the door again. He frowned as he looked the backyard over, trying to find something unusual. "What did you see?"

"Is that a live alligator?" Demmy said.

"What?" Cody stared at the pool float and jumped when the eye facing him blinked. "Holy shit. That's a gator!"

"You're both pretty quick," Hubert said dryly. "Yeah, it's a live gator."

"Uh," Cody started, then stopped, not really knowing what he was about to say. But Demmy had picked up his train of thought and continued for him.

"Hubert, we're not licensed to work here in Florida," Demmy said. "And especially not with alligators."

"I'll pay you five hundred dollars."

Cody lifted his eyebrows and looked back out at the gator. Ten feet long didn't seem that big when he considered the five hundred bucks.

Demmy cleared his throat. "That's a generous offer, but surely a team or a group associated with the village here handles this?"

"There's been a lot of gators in peoples' pools lately. So they're a little tied up. Until next week, actually."

"That many gators?" Cody said.

"That many gators."

"Is that a typical number of gators in pools?" Cody wondered.

"No, it's a lot higher than normal." Hubert shrugged. "Seems to be going up just like the number of missing people lately."

"Think the gators are getting the people?"

"Doesn't seem to be the case. Lot of the people are away from home when they go missing. You probably saw the notices at the hospital."

Cody shook his head, but Demmy nodded. "I did see a number of flyers. My dad said they were posted at the hospital in case the seniors had memory problems and ended up there."

"Not that many Alzheimer's patients around here," Hubert said. "They're in places with more staff and more oversight." He lifted his chin toward the pool beyond the door as the dogs continued to bark like mad. "What do you think? I'll give you eight hundred, and that's as high as I'll go."

Demmy blew out a breath and looked up at Cody. "What do you think?"

"Eight hundred bucks could help a lot," Cody said. "It's just an animal, right? And, to be honest, we've dealt with worse."

Demmy gave a tight smile. "True. Okay, let's give it a try."

CHAPTER ELEVEN

While Hubert corralled the barking Pomeranians into a back bedroom, Demetrius stood beside Cody and stared out the patio door at the alligator floating in the pool.

"Think we could lure it out of there?" Demetrius said.

"You going to cut your palm to do it?"

"Um, no."

"Me neither." Cody looked around the living room of the condo. "Think these people left a chicken in the freezer?"

"Interesting thought," Demetrius said, heading for the kitchen.

All he found in the freezer were vegetarian microwave meals and some ice cream, and the refrigerator's condiments and suspicious looking cheese slices weren't exactly alligator bait either.

"Great, the only seniors in the whole complex who eat out every day," Cody mumbled.

Hubert stepped into the kitchen and gave them a frown when he found them looking in the refrigerator. "What are you doing?"

"We were going to try and lure the alligator with a frozen chicken or something," Cody said.

"The Underwoods are vegetarians," Hubert said, his tone making it more than obvious that he thought the idea idiotic. "Come on, we're wasting time. The dogs need to wee wee, and I'm not walking them on a leash in this heat."

Hubert stomped out of the kitchen and Demetrius looked at Cody. He found him looking right back at him with a big smile. Demetrius held a finger up in Cody's face, but felt himself grinning as he whispered, "Don't you dare laugh."

"He said 'wee wee,'" Cody whispered. "Hubert the grump said 'wee wee.'"

"You keep that in, Cody," Demetrius said. "Don't even think about laughing. We need to stay focused for this."

"You two cooking me dinner in there or what?" Hubert called from the other room.

"Coming," Demetrius said, then lowered his voice. "Pull it together!"

"Why didn't you tell him we were taking a wee wee?"

Demetrius broke into a snuffling, snorting laugh and saw that Cody had tears running down his face as he lost his self-control and followed suit. Demetrius leaned his head onto Cody's shoulder, letting go of all the worries about his mom and money and life in general and simply enjoying the moment.

Cody put his arms around Demetrius and held him close. For once, Demetrius allowed Cody to support him. It felt good to give up not just his concerns about everything in his life, but also the physical strength of just standing on his own feet, even if it was just for a moment.

Their laughter faded, but Cody kept him close for a little longer. Demetrius was surprised that he wanted to linger there in Cody's strong, warm, still-slightly-damp-with-sweat-but-not-in-a-gross-way embrace.

"You two make out on jobs back home all the time?" Hubert said from the kitchen doorway.

Demetrius pushed back from Cody and felt himself blush as he stammered over words that seemed to tumble out of his mouth in a rush. "What? No! We weren't making out. We were just..." He stopped, unable to find the words to explain what had been happening between him and Cody, and not sure he understood it himself.

"I wasn't... We weren't..." Cody said at the same time Demetrius was speaking.

Hubert looked between them, then shook his head and gestured over his shoulder with his thumb. "Well, whatever it was, you're burning daylight. Let's get a move on. That gator's not going to vacate himself."

Hubert walked away and Demetrius looked at Cody.

"Sorry," Demetrius said.

Cody shook his head, but couldn't seem to look Demetrius in the eye. "What? No! Not your fault. I shouldn't have... It was just something silly that..." He blew out a breath and stepped aside, waving for Demetrius to precede him out of the kitchen. "After you."

Demetrius nodded and walked past him. Hubert waited until they were both at the patio door, then slid it open and all three stepped out under the awning. Even though they were in the shade, Demetrius instantly started to sweat, but he wasn't sure if it was mainly because of the heat or his proximity to the alligator.

"How do you want to do this?" Demetrius said.

"Carefully."

"That would make for a nice change."

"Cute."

"I thought so."

Cody looked around the pool area. "There's one of those leaf cleaner things over there by the shed. We could try to lure it to one of the pool corners and get some rope around the snout."

Demetrius nodded. "Where are we getting the rope?"

"I don't know," Cody muttered. "I'm making this up."

"Let's check out the pool equipment they have."

They walked to the other side of the pool, giving the edge a wide berth. The alligator moved its tail back and forth, spinning itself to watch them.

"That's bigger than ten feet," Demetrius said.

"Never took you for a size queen," Cody said, surprising a laugh out of Demetrius.

"Inappropriate. For many reasons."

The leaf rake leaned against the shed, and a life ring with a length of rope attached to it hung on the outer shed wall. Demetrius watched as Cody tested the rope's strength. A splash from the pool behind him made Demetrius yelp and back up against the fence as he looked at the pool. The gator had turned to float back into the deep end, keeping one eye on them as it slowly swished its tail back and forth in the water. Demetrius let out his breath and tried to step away from the fence, but his shorts caught on something. He looked down to see a gap where the wire fencing had pulled away from the steel pole, obviously where the alligator had gotten into the yard. A long, slimy looking strand of moss or seaweed had snagged on the top of the chain link fence, and Demetrius leaned in to peer at it more closely.

"Okay, I have a plan," Cody said.

"Huh?" Demetrius looked over at where Cody stood with the leaf net in one hand, and the life ring rope coiled in the other. "Oh, yeah. Okay."

"You distract it with the leaf net, and I'll lasso its snout."

"Yeah? Have you ever lassoed anything before?"

"Have you?"

Demetrius sighed. "Fine."

He took the leaf net and warily approached the deep end of the pool. The alligator turned, keeping him in sight. Cody circled around the other side of the pool, the rope held loosely in one hand. Hubert stood back in the shade under the awning.

"Hey buddy," Demetrius said as he dipped the end of the leaf net in the water and made some splashing sounds. "Let's get you out of there, okay? You've got to hate the chlorine, don't you? I bet it's messing up your eyes and burning your sinuses, isn't it?"

The alligator floated closer. Demetrius took a step back, extending his reach to keep the edge of the leaf net just above the water.

"Careful Demmy," Cody said in a calm, gentle voice.

"Yep, absolutely."

He knew alligators could move fast, but when the thing lunged at the leaf rake, as prepared as he thought he was, it still surprised him. The gator grabbed the leaf rake in its strong jaws and twisted as it dove beneath the water. Demetrius reacted without thinking and tightened his grip instead of releasing the rake. As the gator pulled the leaf rake under, it pulled Demetrius into the pool and under the water as well.

Fear flared inside him, hot and suffocating. He realized he needed to release the leaf rake and loosened his grip, then struggled up to the surface. This section of the pool was ten feet deep, so he couldn't touch the bottom. Every moment he expected to feel the alligator's jaws clamp down on his foot or leg and drag him underwater for good. Demetrius swam frantically toward the pool's edge. It seemed miles away instead of just a few feet. Cody was shouting something, but Demetrius couldn't make it out over the sound of his own gasping breath and splashing water.

Something hit him in the back of the head and Demetrius

screamed, thinking it was the alligator. But then he realized it was the life ring that Cody had thrown to him. He grabbed the ring to hold himself up and looked across the length of the pool as he reached out for the concrete edge. The alligator swam right for him, its snout creating a furrow through the water. Demetrius's heart pounded, and his breath came in short pants. He was never going to see how his mother's surgery went. He was never going to see his parents again. He was going to die with a whole list of things he had yet to do.

Cody was shouting his name over and over again, but Demetrius could not understand what he was saying. All he heard was the blood rushing in his ears and the sound of his own breathing. The alligator lifted its nose up out of the water and started to open its jaws. It was only a few feet from him now, and coming fast like a speedboat.

Demetrius pushed off from the wall, dragging the life ring along without thinking about it. The alligator missed him and hit the edge of the pool, sending a tidal wave of water out onto the deck. It thrashed its tail in anger. Demetrius did the sidestroke, heading for the shallow end of the pool as he kept the gator in sight, his left arm hooked through the life ring.

The alligator dove under the water and a sense of panic enveloped and consumed the fear inside him. The panic built on the fear, quadrupling then octupling it until it lived within him like some kind of invasive spirit, making it difficult for him to breathe. Demetrius swam faster, kicking with his feet, stretching with his right arm as he watched behind him for any sign of the alligator. It was coming up from beneath him, he knew it, but he could do nothing about it.

Something tugged on the life ring, pulling him off his course and toward the side of the pool closest to the house. At that moment he felt the swell of displaced water behind him and it pushed him even closer to the house side of the pool.

The alligator had surfaced right where he had been swimming, and if he hadn't been pulled out of the gator's path, it would have dragged him beneath the water and drowned him.

Cody crouched on the side of the pool, Hubert right behind him, both of them pulling on the rope tied to the life ring, dragging Demetrius through the water. Both men were shouting, but Demetrius still couldn't understand what they said as his heart pounded, his breath rasped in his throat, and the water sloshed around him. He touched the side of the pool and then reached up, feet kicking, stretching for the bottom but still unable to find it. How fucking deep was this pool, anyway? Then Cody had hold of his hands and lifted him out of the water and into his arms.

"I've got you," Cody said, holding him tight. "I've got you. You're safe."

Demetrius's heart pounded, and he could feel Cody's heart beating in time. They both had been frightened by his fall into the pool.

"Someone's upset he missed dinner," Hubert said from behind Cody.

"Look out!" Cody said and pulled Demetrius back from the edge of the pool.

The alligator hauled itself half out of the pool, jaws opening and closing as its claws scrabbled for purchase on the slick concrete. Demetrius found himself staring down into the gator's gullet, and when it closed its jaws briefly, reacted on instinct. He crammed the life ring onto the animal's snout and pushed as hard as he could. The ring stuck tight around the alligator's jaws, and it dropped back beneath the surface of the water, the rope trailing after it.

Cody let out a whoop of joy and pulled Demetrius up against him for a strong hug, Demetrius's back to Cody's front. Demetrius didn't even care about the sting of pressure against the scratch on his back. He clung to Cody's strong forearms as he leaned back against his strong frame, shivering even in the humid heat of the day as the adrenaline left his body.

"I thought I was dead," Demetrius said.

"I thought so, too," Cody said, hugging him a little tighter. "I need to talk to you."

"About what?"

Hubert was tracking the alligator from the far end of the pool, pointing to it and laughing as the gator tried in vain to dislodge the life ring from around its jaws.

"Everything," Cody said. "Near death changes everything."

"Let's get rid of this gator first," Demetrius said. "Then we can talk, okay?"

"Yeah." Cody released him, but kept his big hands on Demetrius's shoulders for a moment before finally letting go.

"Okay," Cody called to Hubert. "We've got it kind of contained. How do we transport it back to the swamp?"

"The Underwoods have a cart they bought from an airport auction," Hubert said, pointing to a roll up door built into the back wall of the garage. "It should manage the weight of the thing. We just need to wrangle it into the cart."

Cody looked at Demetrius and rolled his eyes. "Oh, is that all?"

"Yeah, right," Demetrius said, then looked away, wondering what Cody needed to talk about.

"It's doing it for us!" Hubert shouted, pointing at the pool.

The alligator had been spinning beneath the water, doing barrel rolls as it tried to free its jaws. The rope attached to the life ring had wound around its body, pinning its front legs against its belly and securing the gator.

"Holy shit," Cody whispered. "We're gator wranglers."

"We are not adding this to our business cards," Demetrius said.

"I'm with you on that one," Cody agreed. "One time only experience. Okay, let's get this guy out of here."

It took less time than Demetrius had expected. With the gator's jaws secured, they used the rope to pull it into the shallow end. Demetrius and Cody then got into the waist deep water and secured the alligator's legs with the rest of the rope. Hubert found a roll of duct tape in the garage, and they wrapped it around the jaws a few times before removing the life ring.

"Watch the tail," Hubert coached from the pool deck. "They can break bones with their tail."

"Yeah, I remember that from watching episodes of *Crocodile Hunter*," Cody said.

"This is an alligator," Hubert pointed out.

Cody glared up at Hubert. "Tomay-to, tomah-to."

With much grunting and swearing, Demetrius and Cody lifted it out of the water and onto the hard backed transport stretcher they found on the far side of the shed. As the gator shifted and struggled beneath them, they dodged the tail and got it belted in place.

"Good thing the Underwoods believe in being prepared for anything," Cody said as he hefted his end of the stretcher.

"This thing weighs a fucking ton!" Demetrius said. His muscles strained as they hurried the gator to where Hubert had backed the cart out of the garage's rear door and on to the deck of the pool.

They had to rest the gator's jaw on the cart while they held up the tail end of the stretcher as Hubert slowly pulled the cart back into the door, straight through the garage, and out the main roll up door onto the driveway. As Demetrius and Cody shifted the gator to perpendicular across the back compartment, Hubert closed up the garage and let the Pomeranians out to 'wee wee' on the small strip of grass.

"I could use a wee wee myself," Cody muttered.

"I don't need one. I went in the pool," Demetrius said, and they both laughed. "Hey, what did you want to talk with me about?"

Cody looked at him, really looked at him, and gave a mysterious half smile. "We'll talk later."

"Okay."

Hubert let the dogs back in the condo and returned to the cart with a towel he had dipped into the pool and wrung out. He placed the towel across the alligator's eyes and stepped back.

"What's that for?" Demetrius said.

"You going to do a mud mask next?" Cody said.

"Covering its eyes calms it down, smart-asses."

Hubert got into the cart and set off at a slow pace down the road. Demetrius continued to wonder what Cody wanted to talk about as he sat on the cramped back jump seat facing him, both of them with an arm around the gator to hold it in place. People stopped to stare and drivers swerved to give them plenty of room as Hubert cruised slowly down the street. Soon, they came to a cul-de-sac and Hubert pulled into a narrow driveway that led to a chain link gate secured with a padlock. A sign posted on the gate stated EVERGLADES NATIONAL PARK - OFFICIAL ADMITTANCE ONLY.

"You've got a key to the Everglades?" Cody said as Hubert got out of the cart.

Hubert winked. "Let's just say I found one."

He unlocked the gate and pushed it open, then climbed back into the cart and drove down a long, bumpy dirt trail. Trees grew close to either side, moss and lichen hanging from the branches down into the dark, still waters of the swamp.

The air was close and even more humid inside the trees, and bugs swarmed them almost immediately.

"Great place your folks moved to," Cody griped as he swatted several bugs in a row. "Does our health care cover malaria treatment?"

"I don't think I checked that box when I signed us up," Demetrius said.

"Did they mean to move in behind the nation's biggest swamp?"

"It's not a swamp," Hubert said over his shoulder. "It's swampish."

"Swampish?" Cody and Demetrius said together.

"Yeah," Hubert said with a wave of his hand as he kept his eyes on the trail. "Not really a true swamp, but it is a wetland. It's *swampish*, but not a swamp."

"Thanks, that clears it up perfectly," Demetrius said and exchanged a wide-eyed look with Cody.

The alligator struggled within the rope and belts keeping it in place on the stretcher, and they both tightened their grips on the board.

"I think we're far enough from the condos now," Cody said between swats.

The bugs didn't appear to be bothering Hubert, and Demetrius wondered if the old man didn't have some secret lotion he wasn't telling them about.

"Still too close," Hubert said over his shoulder. "This gator needs to not find his way back again."

They rode for another fifteen minutes, the alligator becoming more and more agitated the deeper they traveled into the Everglades. Birds called all around them, and they drove through several swarms of biting bugs that left Demetrius and Cody covered in welts.

"Enough!" Cody shouted and reached forward to grab

Hubert's shoulder. "We're getting eaten alive back here, man! Come on!"

"Okay, okay!" Hubert shouted back with a wave of his hand.

He brought the cart to a stop and they clambered out. Demetrius and Cody did quick dances to shoo away the bugs swarming them before approaching the gator. They left the towel over its eyes and lifted the stretcher from the cart, carrying it a few feet off the trail toward the dark, swampy water. The ground was soft, and they sank up to their ankles in muck.

"Oh, gross," Cody said. "It's in my shoes and my socks!"

"I know!" Demetrius said. "Me too!" He looked over his shoulder to where Hubert stood back on the trail. "This is very much a swamp!"

"It's not!" Hubert called back. "It's—"

"Yeah, yeah, we know!" Cody shouted as he floundered in the muck. "It's *swampish!*" He struggled to pull his foot free and finally said, "Here. Just set the fucking thing down here."

Demetrius was glad Cody called it, because his left foot was stuck up to his shin in muck. He was afraid he was going to lose his shoe trying to pull his foot out. They set the stretcher down with the gator's snout pointed toward the water about five feet away. Cody kept the stretcher belts fastened and slowly unwound the rope.

He swatted a few bugs but kept focused on his task as he had to pull the rope out from under the gator's belly and then untangle it from around its legs. When he had the rope completely unraveled from around the alligator, he opened his penknife and cut away the duct tape around the gator's jaws. The gator lay still, the towel over its eyes apparently still keeping it calm.

"On three, we release the belts," Cody said in a quiet voice. "And then I'll pull off the towel. One, two, three!"

Demetrius released the seatbelt style clasp on the belt near the tail at the same time Cody loosened the one near the gator's head. The animal lay still. They pulled their feet free from the muck, and Cody used a stick to flip the towel off the gator's eyes.

The alligator lay very still, just staring straight ahead as Demetrius and Cody tried to run back to the cart. Demetrius's foot became stuck about the same time Cody's did, and when he leaned down to try and pull free, he heard the scratching of the gator's claws as it scrambled off the stretcher. Instead of heading to the water, however, it turned away and hurried up the rise toward the trail. It ran between both of them without a second look, rushing past as they stood and watched it go. The alligator reached the trail and headed back toward the gate.

Cody looked at Demetrius, his expression of incredulousness mirroring just how Demetrius felt.

"Are you fucking kidding me?" Cody shouted.

"Oh my God!" Demetrius shouted back.

"It's going right back to the condos!" Cody looked over to the trail. "Hey, Hubert! That gator doesn't like your swampish national park any more than we do. I guess he's taken a liking to the taste of chlorine."

Demetrius was focused on pulling his foot free without losing his shoe, so he didn't think anything of it when he heard Cody calling Hubert's name over and over again. He finally managed to work both feet free of the muck with his shoes still on, and he made his way carefully back to the trail, dragging the stretcher behind him. He stood beside Cody at the back of the cart and they looked up and down the trail.

"Where's Hubert?" Demetrius said.

"That's what I'd like to know," Cody said.

CHAPTER TWELVE

Cody prided himself on maintaining his temper. He'd always been the calm inside the storm of his family. Even though he was disorganized and terminally late and more than a bit lazy about housekeeping chores, Cody was, he liked to think, a calm and rational person. He'd been that way all through school and even on the Parson's Hollow High School football team where he was known as Cool-Headed Cody.

The state trooper who was questioning him and Demetrius, however, was about to push Cody over the edge. Not only was the trooper a walking stereotype, but based on his comments, he was also a misogynistic racist bigot, and he had pushed all of Cody's trigger buttons in the hour he'd been questioning them about Hubert's disappearance.

"How did you come to have the key to this National Park gate?" Trooper Bentworth asked for the fifth time.

Demmy jumped in to respond before Cody could refer the trooper back to his little notebook he'd been scribbling in non-stop.

"Hubert had the key and opened the gate. He didn't tell us how he came by its ownership."

Trooper Bentworth turned his Ray Bans on Demmy. "You two licensed to work as animal control here in Florida?"

"No, sir," Demmy said. "Like we said, we were doing Mr. Potts a favor and helping out the Underwoods who had hired him to watch their dogs while they were off visiting their grandchildren in Utah."

"I see." Bentworth studied his notes, then looked up at Cody. "Where you boys from again?"

"Parson's Hollow, Pennsylvania," Cody said. "Look, it's really hot out here, and we're covered in insect bites. Can you take down our address and phone numbers and let us get back to the Singleton condo and clean up?"

Trooper Bentworth took a step closer and gestured toward the open gate that led to the trail into the Everglades. "A man is missing, Mr. Bower. I would think you'd have some respect for that fact."

"I have the utmost respect for that fact," Cody said. "But us standing here repeating answers to questions you already asked isn't helping to find him, is it?"

"You've got a bad attitude," Bentworth said. "Maybe a trip to the station will help set you to rights."

"I don't think that's necessary, Trooper Bentworth," Demmy said, pulling the trooper's glare to himself. "We're not used to this heat, so forgive us for any attitude. But we have told you everything we know, and we've provided our contact information. We're very concerned about Mr. Potts as well, but my mother is scheduled to have open heart surgery tomorrow, and I do need to get to the hospital and make sure everything is all set."

Trooper Bentworth took a couple of steps back and looked between them. "All right, I can appreciate that fact. I'm very close with my mother as well."

Cody just bet he was, and added 'mama's boy' to the end of his description of stereotypical misogynistic racist bigot.

"I'll call in a search team," Bentworth said with a look down the trail. "But we're stretched pretty thin what with all the other missing persons in this area." He gave Cody a long, steady look. "I just hope you didn't think to take advantage of that situation and do away with Mr. Potts out there in the 'glades."

"I can assure you, we had nothing to do with it," Cody said. "And I sincerely hope you find him safe and sound out there. But we do have to be going, as Demmy stated."

"Demmy?" Bentworth repeated, looking at Demetrius. "That's what he calls you?"

"It is."

"Sounds kinda gay to me," Bentworth offered. "Don't know if I'd like it if I was you."

"Well, I don't mind it." Demmy said, keeping any malice out of his tone. He always managed to hold his temper when dealing with douchebags like Bentworth. It was true Demmy through and through.

They nodded to Trooper Bentworth and got into the motorized cart. Cody got the cart started and drove back down the street, trying not to scratch the multiple insect bites or mourn his mud-caked shoes and socks.

"What a fucking tool," Demmy muttered from the seat beside him.

Cody let out a long, loud laugh, and they shared a smile. He squeezed Demmy's shoulder. "You doing okay?"

"I'm trying," Demmy said. "I just have no idea what happened to Hubert, and I feel awful about it. I mean, we were right there with him. How could he just vanish like that?"

"An excellent question," Cody said. He dropped his hand to the space between the seats and touched something metal, pulling up Hubert's large, heavy key ring. "Well, he's not planning to go breaking into people's places, that's for sure."

"That's even more worrisome," Demmy said. "What the ever-loving fuck have we gotten involved with now?"

"Your guess is as good as mine." Cody sighed. "And not to minimize Hubert's disappearance, but he stiffed us eight hundred bucks."

Demmy's phone buzzed in his pocket, and he pulled it out and checked the display. "It's my dad." He took a breath then accepted the call. "Hi Dad, sorry, we got into a bit of a mess helping Hubert with his favor. No, nothing like that. We got an alligator out of a swimming pool. No, we don't usually deal with alligators, so it was a bit of a learning process. It was at the Underwo...yes, the vegetarians."

He gave Cody an "Oh my God, really?" look and shook his head before returning to the conversation with his father. "There was a bit of a problem, though. No, we're fine, but Hubert's missing. Yes, I said missing. We don't know what happened, Dad. He took us to a trail into the Everglades with the Underwoods' cart...what? Yes, it's a very nice cart." Demetrius rolled his eyes at Cody. "Anyway, we let the alligator loose near the swamp. Sorry, right, I know it's not technically a swamp."

Demmy huffed out an exasperated breath. "Fine, we let it loose by the *water*, but it ran back down the trail toward the street, and when we looked around Hubert was gone. Yes, we called the state police and they sent someone to talk to us, but there's no sign of Hubert yet. I don't know, Dad, I guess we'll return the cart to the Underwoods' place and take the key ring to Eunice and let her know he's missing. Yes, he left his key ring in the cart. We figured he'd take that with him if he had the choice. I agree. Hey, how's Mom? Any word from the surgeon? Oh, they moved it out a day?"

"Everything okay?" Cody said as he pulled the cart into the Underwoods' garage and switched the power off.

Demmy held up a finger for Cody to wait a moment as he continued to talk with his father. "Why did they move out the date? Oh, okay. But they're not worried about it? Okay, that's good then. Hey, look, we just got back, and we're both a mess. Can you and Amelia visit with Mom tonight and tell her I'll see her tomorrow? Yeah, Cody and I will find something to eat, no problem. We'll just hang out at the condo."

Apprehension filled Cody as he realized he and Demmy would be alone for hours with nothing to do but watch TV or talk. This was his chance to let Demmy know how he had been feeling lately. The thought of it tightened Cody's stomach and sent a low wave of nausea through him. This could very well change everything between him and Demmy, and while Cody had been experiencing some very strong feelings for Demmy these days, he wasn't sure he was ready to risk their friendship.

But keeping quiet about this was really eating at him. He needed to figure out if he was just feeling too attached to Demmy because they spent so much time together these days, or if it was something more than that. Maybe he needed to see if gay sex was really for him, but how? He wasn't about to go cruise the gay bars, either here in Florida or back home, so what else could he do?

"Earth to Cody," Demmy said, shaking his shoulder. "You in there?"

"Huh? What?" Cody looked over at Demmy who had gotten out of the cart and was leaning in over the seat with a hand on his shoulder. "Oh, sorry. I drifted."

"Thinking about porn again?" Demmy said with a grin.

A lightbulb went off inside Cody's brain, and he smiled as he knew what he might be able to do to figure out if this crazy attraction was really for him or not.

"Who?" he said with a grin. "Me?"

"Yeah, you?" Demmy shook his head and held up Hubert's ring of keys. "I'm going to give these back to Hubert's wife and reminder her to look after the Underwoods' dogs until Hubert..." Demmy trailed off, took a breath, and then gave a single nod. "I'll be right back."

Cody watched Demmy walk toward Hubert's condo a moment before he hit the button to close the Underwoods' garage door.

CHAPTER THIRTEEN

Voices and thoughts filled Cody's head, distracting him from all external stimuli. He was so deep inside his own head, he nearly walked into Marshall and Olivia's condo wearing mud-caked shoes without a second thought. Demmy grabbed his arm and held him back, prompting Cody to give him a wide-eyed look as a crazy thought — it was crazy, wasn't it? — bubbled to the surface of his mind: *Demmy wants to kiss me.*

"Hey, we can't go in my parents' house like this," Demmy said.

Reality and disappointment surged to the forefront of Cody's brain. Demmy was not aware Cody was wrestling through feelings of attraction for him. They were simply covered with mud from the swamp and needed to remove some clothes clothing before they could go inside and clean up properly.

The thought that Cody would see Demmy in his underwear registered as a combination benefit and complication, but then Demmy pulled the front door shut and gestured for Cody to follow him.

"I forgot myself," Demmy said over his shoulder as he led the way to the attached garage. "Guess we'll have to strip to our skivvies in the garage and go in through the garage door."

"Yeah, sure," Cody said as Demmy entered the access code on the garage door. "I wasn't even thinking."

"Distracted, huh?" Demmy said, turning to look at him as the door rumbled open.

Cody met his gaze and tried to act casual. "Yeah, I guess I am."

"I am, too," Demmy said, shifting his gaze away from Cody.

"Oh?" Cody said, a glimmer of nervous hope sparking to life within him. Was Demmy going to make the first move perhaps?

Demmy turned away to enter the garage. Cody followed, perhaps a little too closely because when Demmy hit the close button near the entrance to the house, he jumped a bit and took a step back.

"Yikes, I didn't know you were so close behind me," Demmy said. The garage door shut with a quiet thump, sealing them inside the humid single car garage Demmy's parents used to store stacks of plastic storage bins.

Cody met Demmy's gaze and held it for a moment, waiting, *hoping* to hear Demmy say he'd been thinking about them, about their friendship, and how much more Cody had come to mean to him than just a friend.

"So, I guess we should take off these dirty clothes?" Demmy said in a questioning tone. "If you're okay with that?"

"What? Oh, yeah. Yeah, sure." Cody stepped back and, not taking his eyes off Demmy, kicked off his shoes.

Demmy half turned away and held onto a nearby bin for balance as he did the same. Cody realized he was staring and most likely making Demmy uncomfortable, so he half turned in the other direction as he peeled off his dirty socks.

"You said you were distracted, too?" Cody said.

"Oh, yeah. I mean, with my mom's surgery and now Hubert just... gone, I'm having a tough time focusing."

Cody nodded and tried not to feel disappointed. Demmy had a lot going on down here with his mom's condition, and now they were involved in a missing persons case, which didn't help. And Hubert simply vanishing while standing not fifty feet away from them was more important than whether or not Demmy wanted to kiss him. Wasn't it?

"I get it," Cody said. "It's so weird that Hubert just left without saying a word."

"Or was taken."

"But by who?" Cody said, shucking his shorts and forcing himself to keep looking at the bins in front of him that had CHRISTMAS written on them in black marker and not looking at Demmy.

"Or what," Demmy offered.

Cody had to look over at that. He managed to keep his eyes on Demmy's face even though he stood there in just his white briefs. "What are you suggesting?"

Demmy shrugged then made his way to a small laundry sink situated beside a stacked washer and dryer. Florida living meant having the washer and dryer in the garage, apparently. Demmy filled a nearby bucket with water, added a touch of laundry soap, then proceeded to wash his feet with a handful of paper towels. Demmy continued to talk as he cleaned off his feet and shins, and Cody was mostly able to focus on what he was saying, even as he grabbed quick glances at the rounded swell of his ass covered by the thin white cotton of his briefs.

"Anyway, what if an alligator got Hubert?" Demmy wondered. "I mean, I know we lugged one out there to release it, but what if another one was lying in wait on the other side of the trail?"

Demmy stepped back from the bucket and pulled off a couple handfuls of paper towels. He handed one handful to Cody and used the other to dry off his feet. Cody stepped up to the bucket and bent over, talking as he cleaned himself.

"I think we would have heard an alligator attack," Cody said. "Besides, our gator took off running back the way we had come, so I think he was scared of something."

Cody looked up as he finished cleaning his feet and was just in time to catch Demmy trying not to look as if he was checking out his ass. Demmy quickly turned away and walked through an aisle of stacked bins to open the door to the condo, saying over his shoulder, "What are *you* suggesting?"

Cody dried off his feet and found a path through the bins to stand before him, keeping his gaze on Demmy's face and not allowing himself to look any lower. "I'm just saying our gator should have been excited to get back to the swampy waters of home — "

"Swamp*ish*," Demmy said, and they shared a sad smile at the use of Hubert's word. Demmy opened the door to the condo and Cody followed him inside. As he trailed behind, Cody kept his eyes up and gaze locked on Demmy's back where the scrape from just two days ago was healing nicely. He kept his thoughts focused on the conversation and definitely not on Demmy's pale smooth skin, or the tuft of soft brown hair that grew at the small of his back. The touch of the cool air on his sweaty skin made Cody shiver.

"Anyway," Cody said. "That gator was not interested in sliding into the muckity muck it's used to, so something spooked it. And whatever could spook a ten foot long alligator must be pretty damn big itself."

Demmy stopped outside the guest bedroom and turned to

look at him again. Cody stood a couple of feet away and managed to affect a casual air as he shrugged at Demmy and looked him in the eye.

"Well whatever it was and however big it was, why didn't it spook us?" Demmy said.

"Maybe it was just stalking Hubert."

"Well, shit," Demmy said, shivering. "That creeps me right the fuck out."

Cody nodded. "And now we're back to the original question."

"Why does crazy shit like this keep happening to us?" Demmy let out a quiet, humorless chuckle.

"Well, yes, that. But also, what the hell can scare an alligator?"

Demmy sighed and turned his back, and Cody couldn't help checking out his ass again. Dammit, when had Demmy developed such a nice ass? Had he always had one and Cody had just never noticed?

"Are you checking out my ass?"

Cody jerked his gaze up to find Demmy looking at him over his shoulder. "What? No! No, I wasn't."

Demmy tried to look down over his shoulder at his backside. "Do I have a leech or something down there? Shit, is there a leech on me?"

"No, there's no leech," Cody assured him. "You've just got some mud there."

Demmy glared at him. "Is that a joke? We've got mud everywhere."

"Good point. Sorry."

Demmy studied him a moment longer. "I can shower in my parents' bathroom if you want to use the guest bathroom to clean up."

"Yeah, sure."

"Okay, let me grab my shaving kit," Demmy said and turned away to open the guest room door.

Cody followed him into the room and pointedly looked away from the two single beds positioned so close together. Demmy pulled his laptop out of the duffel bag and set it aside, then withdrew his bathroom kit and a clean pair of underwear and cargo shorts.

"Okay, I'll see you in a few," Demmy said and left the room.

Cody listened to him walk down the hall, and he eased the door shut. He pulled a T-shirt out of his own bag and spread it on the bed. Sitting on the T-shirt, he opened Demmy's laptop and tapped the trackpad, glad to find it was just in sleep mode and the screen lit up right away. The wireless connection symbol lit up as it automatically connected, and Cody clicked on a browser. He opened a search engine and, with his stomach in nervous knots and his thoughts spinning in a cyclone of acceptance and denial, he typed in *free gay porn videos*.

"So, it's come to this," he whispered to himself, then clicked Search.

About five million results were returned and Cody sighed. He glanced nervously at the door and then clicked the top link. His adrenaline was up, and his heart pounded, just like when he had been a kid and snuck a peek at his brother's *Playboy* and *Penthouse* magazines. His cock was like a steel rod beneath the laptop, stretching the confines of his briefs. It wasn't the images that had him hard and ready, but the thought of him and Demmy together, which was even more confusing.

The first couple of scenes he looked at did nothing for him, and he actually lost some rigidity. Maybe this gay sex idea wasn't for him after all? He looked at the time on the laptop, and then glanced at the closed bedroom door. It had been four minutes since Demmy had walked away. He'd give it a few more minutes and then try to put all of his crazy sex-with-Demmy thoughts out of his mind.

An image from another video caught his eye, and he sucked in his breath. A model in that scene looked enough like Demmy that Cody wondered if Demmy had actually done porn to help pay the bills some time in the recent past. He clicked on the image and the video started to play, the intro music loud enough to cause him to fumble with buttons until he managed to mute the sound altogether. When the models appeared on camera, Cody let out a relieved breath to find it wasn't Demmy, but a man who had similar looks: strong nose, rounded chin with a dimple and short brown hair. Where Demmy was slighter with toned muscle, this model was more beefed up, but still had that familiar look about him. This Demmy stand-in was paired up with a tall, blond stud, and they wasted no time with words.

Cody was entranced. The Demmy look-alike was flexible as all hell, twisting and contorting himself as he worked the blond stud's nipples and even, Cody was shocked to see, armpits. He'd never had anyone lick or suck his armpit. Frankly, it grossed him out right now what with all the sweat he'd worked up. But it looked like the blond stud was thoroughly enjoying it. Cody thought it might feel good to have someone give a little oral attention to his armpit. He wondered if Demmy had ever gotten into armpit licking with Oliver.

But that was all beside the point, because now the Demmy look alike was sliding down the blond stud's muscular torso, licking and kissing the entire way, and Cody's cock was a solid column of needy impatience. He hadn't been with a woman for months, and he hadn't jerked off in weeks, which was a pretty long dry spell for him.

Lately though, whenever he had tried to masturbate,

fantasies of being with Demmy barged their way into the front of his mind and confused and frustrated him. They'd been friends for so long, Cody didn't know how to feel about these new ideas and thoughts he was having. Should sex with Demmy be a natural extension of their friendship? If they did take that step, could Cody keep from fucking it all up? Even if Demmy was the one for him, the one Cody was destined to spend his life with, Cody wasn't sure about a number of things. Was Demmy a top, bottom, or versatile? Would Cody be open to being on the receiving end of anal sex with Demmy? He had read blog posts about men who enjoyed having their girlfriend or wife use a strap on to penetrate them, but Cody had never experimented with something like that. Would his being a bottom make him feel emasculated, or shouldn't it matter?

Too many questions always erupted around his fantasy scenarios with Demmy, and even his tried and true fantasy women like Sofia Vergara, Jessica Alba, or even Zooey Deschanel and her gorgeous blue eyes hadn't been enough lately to keep him focused long enough to finish. Now however, this blond stud and Demmy-lite model had little Cody all sparked up and rarin' to go.

Cody looked toward the door, then paused the clip just as the Demmy wannabe grabbed the elastic waistband of the blond stud's amazingly clean and tight fitting white briefs. He set the laptop aside and, with his dick pointing the way, hurried to the bedroom door and opened it a crack. He could hear the shower running in the master bathroom and the sound of Demmy whistling something.

He closed the door and was dismayed to find no lock. Really? No one in a senior living complex needed any privacy? Deciding he would be finished pretty quick anyway with the length of his dry spell, Cody peeled off his briefs and took himself in hand as he strode back to the bed and sat on the T-shirt he had spread out. He positioned the laptop on the foot of the bed and started the clip, keeping the sound muted in case Demmy finished before he did.

Pre-cum was already drooling down his shaft, and it provided enough slick for his fist without losing the best part of the friction. In the video, the Demmy wannabe ran his tongue up and down the blond stud's now exposed shaft and Cody closed his eyes, imagining Demmy doing that same thing to him. He wanted to feel Demmy's tongue and mouth on his cock, and he wanted to find out how Demmy's cock and balls tasted.

Cody opened one eye to check out the video and quietly groaned. The models had gotten into a sixty-nine position, each sucking for all he was worth, their shaved balls slowly pulling up. Cody closed his eyes again and thought about being in a sixty-nine position with Demmy. He wanted to nuzzle his nose under Demmy's balls and breathe in that special scent of him, know him that intimately, make Demmy feel good and have Demmy make him feel good in return. He wondered if Demmy shaved his balls, and if he would be surprised to find out that Cody shaved his own, since a girl he had been seeing a few years ago had convinced him to try it. Now he continued to shave them because he liked how it felt.

His hand pumped fast along his shaft, his orgasm so close now. It wouldn't be long.

He opened one eye again to check out the video and had to bite his lip to keep from moaning aloud. The blond had topped the Demmy wannabe in the missionary position and was driving into him hard. The Demmy wannabe's calves were braced over the blond stud's broad shoulders, and his feet bounced with every thrust. Cody thought about how it would feel to be in the blond stud's position and slide deep into the heat of Demmy's body, burying himself inside him, connecting with Demmy in the most intimate way.

So close now, it wasn't going to be long. He closed his eyes and leaned back on the bed, sweat standing out on his body, the stink of his efforts filling his nose as he curled his toes into the carpet. He heard a soft sound and opened his eyes to find the laptop screen filling his vision. The blond stud was now fucking the Demmy wannabe doggy style and had braced himself with his fists resting on the pale, firm globes of his partner's ass.

Cody lifted his head to check the door — so close, just a few more strokes — and saw it was still closed. He should check the hallway, but he couldn't stop now. His train was about to arrive in the station and it was a long one, loaded down with a lot of freight.

His balls pulled up and muscles throughout his body tightened as the rush came over him. Cum exploded out of his cock with a loud, wet *pop*. It splashed his cheek and chin, startling him as even more splattered across his torso. It was hot, and the sharp scent of it joined the odor of his sweat in the room. He slowed his strokes and milked out the last of his cum, then released himself and caught his breath. As his heart rate slowed back to normal, Cody opened his eyes and looked at the laptop. The blond stud stood on the mattress now, bouncing fast and pile driving his cock into the Demmy wannabe who supported himself on his shoulders, legs curled up over his head.

The sight of them caused Cody's cock to stir even as it lay in puddles of cum, and when the Demmy wannabe reached a gushing climax that splashed all over his own face, Cody's cock was hard once again. Jesus, what the hell was it about thoughts of sex with Demmy that got him so worked up?

A sound from the hall outside the door brought him around and he quickly closed the browser, then the laptop.

He tossed it onto Demmy's bed and grabbed some tissues from the box on the nightstand, trying to mop up as best he could. His heart pounded and his hard-on faded at the threat of being caught.

With the clump of sticky tissues clutched tight in his fist, Cody grabbed his shaving kit and eased the guest room door open. Demmy was in the kitchen, making noise with some dishes. Moving quickly and quietly, Cody hurried down the hall in the nude and ducked into the guest bathroom, closing the door behind him and leaning back against it as he let out his breath. That had been close.

He tossed the tissues in the trash and stood over the toilet, trying to pee. A soft knock on the door startled him, and he hurried back to the door, bracing his foot against it as he said, "Yeah?"

"Need body wash or anything?" Demmy said through the door.

Cody looked around and cursed quietly. He had forgotten to bring body wash. Son of a bitch. He opened the door a crack and peered out. Demmy stood in the hall with a towel around his waist, hair still damp from his shower and a bottle of body wash in his hand.

"Yeah, I forgot to bring any in with me," Cody said. He tried a relaxed grin that felt like it didn't fit right on his face.

Demmy looked him in the eye for a moment, then held out the body wash. "I just thought I would check."

"Okay, thanks."

"Yeah," Demmy said with another quick glance. "Of course." Then he turned and walked to the guest bedroom and stepped inside.

Cody wondered just how funky that room smelled, then decided he couldn't do anything about it, and he needed to clean up. He closed the bathroom door and headed back to the toilet to pee with a relieved sigh. Afterwards, he looked at himself in the mirror and wondered for a moment how Demmy really saw him. On the heels of that, he wondered if Demmy could ever think of him as anything more than a friend. Would he ever really have the guts to tell Demmy how he truly felt and hear how Demmy felt about him?

Dammit, when did shit get so complicated?

Cody started the shower and stepped under the water, sighing as the spray washed away the stink of the Everglades, the evidence of his attraction to Demmy, and, he hoped, his nervousness around his best friend.

CHAPTER FOURTEEN

Demetrius looked around his parents' bathroom as he dried off, noting the bottle of his mother's perfume sitting alongside his father's aftershave. It all seemed so familiar, he couldn't help feeling like a child again. It felt good to finally wash off the sweat and mud from the Everglades, but he was going to need some Afterbite or something by the looks of the number of insect bites on him. He would deal with that later. He wrapped the towel around his waist and walked through his parents' bedroom and down the hall. He paused outside the open door of the hall bathroom and frowned then flicked on the light. Cody hadn't showered yet. What was taking him so long?

Demetrius approached the door to the guest bedroom, hesitated a moment with his hand on the knob, then knocked lightly. He didn't hear a response, so he opened the door a crack and peered in.

Cody was stretched out across one of the beds, nude and masturbating. Sweat glistened on his skin, the dark hair on his torso damp with it, as was the hair that lay across his forehead. His eyes were shut tight and his brow furrowed as he stroked his cock hard and fast. Demetrius couldn't pull his eyes away from the sight, and his own cock roared to attention at seeing Cody in such a position.

He should have backed out of the room and closed the door as quietly as he'd opened it, but Demetrius was transfixed. He looked at the long, strong lines of Cody's body, taking in all the minute details, most of which he'd seen before, but some of which he'd only been able to fantasize about.

Until now.

Cody's cock was bigger than Demetrius had even imagined, and the sight of it ignited a fluttering feeling deep inside his gut and made his mouth go dry. The muscles in his ass tightened in anticipation of taking Cody inside him, and he had to swallow hard past a sudden lump in his throat.

He only looked for a few seconds, but the scene was emblazoned on the front of his brain. Demetrius noticed his laptop open on the bed in front of Cody, and he figured Cody had gone on the web to check out some porn site like *Hot Girlz Doing Hot Thingz*, or *Lowdown Dirty Slutz* or something. Whatever Cody had been looking at on the laptop had gotten him really turned on and initiated the jerk off session.

After letting his gaze run the length of Cody's body once more, drinking in all the details he could, Demetrius slowly, carefully closed the bedroom door. He stood in place for a moment, unable to think of what to do. His cock throbbed, but he couldn't take time at that moment to do anything about it. He needed to distract himself, and the best way to do that was with chores.

Because his clean clothes were in the room where Cody was... entertaining himself, Demetrius hurried into the kitchen, cinching the towel tighter around his waist. He busied himself unloading the dishwasher and replacing the clean dishes with those he and his Dad had left piled in the sink. Even as he worked on the dishes, his cock remained hard and insistent beneath the towel. If Cody decided to pay him a visit in the kitchen once he'd finished, he would most assuredly take note of Demetrius's condition and make some kind of comment about it.

A few minutes later, Demetrius heard the bedroom door open down the hall and paused in his wrangling of the dishes. Without a word, Cody scampered off to the hall bathroom, and Demetrius let out a relieved breath at not having to face him just yet. Once he knew the guest bedroom was clear, he hurried down the hall and ducked inside, then stopped, feeling a little dizzy as the powerful scent of Cody's sweat and semen hit him full force. His cock hardened even more and now throbbed with need as Demetrius cursed himself for not knocking louder, not looking away the minute he realized what was going on and just closing the door.

Goddamn, he could almost taste Cody's cock on his tongue.

He looked down and noticed he still had the body wash in his hand. He must have grabbed it off the counter where he had set it once he'd fled the kitchen. He didn't think Cody would have thought to bring his own, so he took a breath and, adjusting his towel to conceal his stubborn hard-on as best he could, walked down the hall to the guest bathroom.

He didn't have to do this. There was most likely bar soap or travel size body washes in the guest bathroom.

But he wanted to do this. Needed to look Cody in the eyes.

Taking a breath and letting it out, he knocked on the door.

"Yeah?" Cody said, his voice cautious.

Demetrius cleared his throat. "Need body wash or anything?"

He made a face and cursed himself for unintentionally offering up something he didn't think he could deliver. Obviously his body — and the speech area of his brain — felt differently, but Demetrius's heart was already boarding up windows and sealing the cracks in the stone wall around itself like some kind of hurricane was about to blow in. And maybe it was, now that he'd seen Cody in action.

Hurricane Cody was a category eleven that could pretty much level Demetrius's heart.

Cody opened the door a crack and peered out. His eyes widened at the sight of Demetrius standing there in his towel and his gaze bounced up and down his body before settling on Demetrius's face. "Yeah, I forgot it." Cody flashed a grin that didn't look very convincing.

Demetrius studied him a moment, trying to see what was making him so uncomfortable. But the longer he focused on Cody, the more his brain just revisited what he'd witnessed, so he held out the bottle. "I just thought I would check."

"Okay, thanks." Cody took it from him.

Cody's fingers — the fingers on the same hand he'd just used to jerk off — lightly touched Demetrius's as they passed the body wash between them. The center of Demetrius's chest heated up fast, like a supernova had gone off inside him, and he felt the heat traveling through him and up into his face. He had to get away from Cody and fast.

"Yeah," Demetrius said, helpless to avoid giving him another quick glance. "Of course." Then he turned and walked to the guest bedroom and stepped inside, closing the door and leaning back against it.

He drew in a deep breath, pulling in the heady scent of Cody's musk that hung heavy in the room, laced with just a trace of that familiar, intoxicating, bleach-like smell of cum.

"Fuck," Demetrius said with a quiet groan. He grabbed his hard, pulsing cock through the towel and squeezed it. Did he have enough time? He figured he did, but he cursed again when he saw there was no lock to engage.

Fine, it was worth the risk. Perhaps he could exorcise the scene of Cody masturbating. He undid the towel and stood between the beds. There he hesitated, one hand slowly stroking himself as he looked between the beds, contemplating his course of action.

Finally, he decided in for a penny, in for a pound, and stretched out on top of the comforter in the same spot Cody had been lying. The material beneath him was still damp with Cody's sweat, and Demetrius could not help letting out a moan. He dug his toes into the carpet in about the same place where Cody had planted his bigger feet and closed his eyes.

In his mind, on discovering Cody pleasuring himself, he imagined stepping fully into the room and walking right up to him, losing his towel along the way. He would walk around to the other side of the bed and lean down to kiss Cody hard on the mouth upside down like that hot scene in the first *Spider-man* movie with Tobey Maguire. Their tongues would tangle in a desperate, passionate dance. Cody would lift a hand and put his big palm on the back of Demetrius's head as they kissed, still stroking himself, but slower now as he focused more on the kiss than the fantasy.

Demetrius would move down Cody's body, kissing him, licking up the sweat, tasting him like he'd tried not to imagine all these years. All the while, Cody would lift his head to kiss and lick Demetrius's body as it passed by overhead until he would finally take Demetrius's balls into his mouth and stroke Demetrius's cock as Demetrius swallowed Cody's long, broad length. He would suck eagerly, ravenous to know him the way all of his girlfriends had known him. No other man had been offered the opportunity. Not until now. Not until Demetrius.

The fat head of Cody's cock would swell where it lay lodged deep in Demetrius's throat, and Demetrius would eagerly swallow his hot, tart semen.

"Oh...oh yeah," Demetrius said with a gasp, narrowing his strokes to the spot just beneath the ridge of his head. "Oh, fuck yeah."

He shuddered as he came, the hot, sticky cum splashing high up his torso. For a moment he lay still, clutching himself, his breath and heart rate slowing back to normal as the cum thinned and spread on his skin. He didn't have much time until Cody would be done with his shower, so he needed to get up and do a quick rinse down in his parents' bathroom.

He got off the bed and pushed back the tide of guilt that threatened to flood him over his fantasies of his best friend. He held his towel in front of himself and hurried out of the bedroom and down the hall.

As he stepped beneath the shower, Demetrius mentally chastised himself for fantasizing about Cody, who was not only his business partner, but his best friend to boot. He knew it had just been the fact that he'd caught Cody masturbating coupled with his recent break-up with Oliver. Not to mention the tension about the whole situation with his mom's health, and now Hubert going missing. This had just been about satisfying a carnal need, a simple quick release, nothing more. Catching Cody masturbating had been the trigger for the fantasy.

As Demetrius turned his face into the spray of the shower, however, his mind produced an image of Cody straddling him as he stroked his big cock to a sloppy finish and came all over Demetrius's face. His traitorous cock hardened in an instant and Demetrius punished it by soaping it up and then simply rinsing it off and leaving it further untouched. That would teach it.

HOURS LATER, Demetrius sat in a softly padded chair on his parents' patio. He pressed a button on his phone to check the time and sighed. It was 2:45 in the morning. Memories of Cody masturbating churned within his mind, interspersed with concerns about his mother's upcoming surgery as well as the mystery surrounding Hubert Potts. All of these things had kept him from being able to sleep, so he had snuck out of the guest room where Cody lay snoring quietly so close yet so far away, and crept past Amelia sleeping on the sofa, and padded out onto the patio.

He tipped back his head and looked up at the stars. A quarter moon sailed high in the sky, illuminating a bank of clouds gathered with ominous intent on the horizon. The weather reports had been filled lately with the tropical storm now referred to as Patrick, which was aimed right at Miami. Demetrius figured those thick clouds were the feeder arms of the storm. He added riding out a hurricane to his long list of worries.

The patio door slid open, and Demetrius looked around. He wouldn't have been surprised to see Cody step outside, his dark hair tousled adorably from the pillow, eyes half open. Instead, he discovered Amelia sneaking outside and easing the door shut. She smiled at him in the moonlight and soft glow of the landscape lights as she sat in the chair to his left.

"I thought I heard you get up a little while ago," Amelia said.

"Sorry if I woke you. You should have taken one of the guest room beds like Cody and I both offered."

"Oh, mangrove trees, the way both of you boys snore?" Amelia laughed and shook her head. "No thank you. Besides, I helped your mother pick out that couch I'm sleeping on, so I know it's more comfortable than those inexpensive twin mattresses you and Cody are using."

They both chuckled at that and fell into a comfortable silence until Amelia said, "You're worried about your mother, I know, but she's in good hands."

Demetrius nodded and flashed a quick smile. "I know she is. But I'm a Singleton, so I was born to worry about things outside of my control."

"What about the things within your control?"

Demetrius frowned. "Do you mean Hubert?"

Amelia shook her head. "No, that's outside of your control, too. The police and park rangers are searching for him. I'm talking about whatever is going on between you and Cody."

Shock and fear zipped through Demetrius like twin electrical charges. He sat back in the chair and tried to act casual and confused, but his leg was bouncing in an agitated tempo.

"I don't know what you..." His power of speech seemed to simply dry up, and he let the sentence hang in the slightly humid night air.

"I've known you all your life, Demetrius Barnaby," Amelia said. "For the sake of cypress trees, I've practically raised you. And I've watched you and Cody over the years as your friendship has deepened, and I know when something is going on between the two of you. He was desperate to get down here to be with you, you know."

Demetrius looked down at his hands clutched together in his lap. He didn't know what to feel about it all, and so his emotions seemed to have shut down completely. "He's my best friend, and he was worried about me."

Amelia leaned in over the patio table. "A worried friend will send you text messages more often than usual to check on your mother's condition. But someone who loves you, who really, truly loves you and feels protective of you and wants to try and make things all better for you? That someone drives across the country to be with you, see you with his own eyes, and make sure you're coping all right." She sat back and smiled. "That is the sign of someone who's in love."

Demetrius's heart seemed to stutter in his chest. "Love? What are you saying? That's ridiculous, it's Cody."

"Oh, just open your eyes, Demetrius," Amelia said with an exasperated sigh. "For the love of magnolias, it's all right there in front of you, and you keep backing away from it."

"But, Amelia," Demetrius said, lowering his voice even though it was too late for anyone else to be up, "Cody is straight. I don't have the right equipment."

"Oh, my dear, sweet boy." Amelia smiled and shook her head. "You're part of the younger generation, but you still don't seem to get it. Love doesn't care who you love. Haven't you ever heard about bi-sexuality? People are very gender fluid these days."

Demetrius sat and blinked at his retired schoolteacher aunt. Amelia, it seemed, could surprise him just as much as Cody. He looked out across the small yard toward the chain link back fence. Could Amelia be right about it all? Could Cody have developed stronger feelings for him than either of them had ever expected? If that was the case, could Demetrius himself love Cody back? He'd occasionally fantasized about sex with Cody, but never really considered the realities of it. Would they be compatible? Would Cody only be a top? Would he not want to kiss, or suck Demetrius's cock? How would it look to all of the people they knew back home?

"That's a lot to think about," Demetrius said in a quiet voice.

"I know it is, dear." Amelia reached out to touch his hand momentarily. "And I didn't mean to burden you any more than you already are, but I thought someone needed to make you aware of what was going on. I think you're a bit too close to the situation to be able to see it with much clarity."

As Demetrius stared out into the yard, he noticed movement in the trees beyond the fence. Someone stood in the shadows of the woods, watching the two of them on the patio. Whoever lurked in the humid darkness was tall, taller it seemed than Cody's six feet five inches, and kept in the shadows cast by the moonlight. A sliver of fear worked its way in between the confusion and emotional shock of Amelia's revelations. Who would be out at this time of night, and for what purpose?

"Demetrius? Are you all right?"

"Someone's out there," Demetrius whispered, "just past the fence."

"What?" Amelia looked out into the yard. "Where?"

A few things happened at once. The bank of storm clouds finally overtook the moon, and the night darkened even more. At that moment, the figure beyond the fence moved closer, looming over the chain link that suddenly appeared much more delicate. Amelia must have noticed the figure when it moved, because she let out a gasp. Demetrius pushed up from his chair and stepped forward to stand at the edge of the patio, squinting into the darkness in an effort to see better. The figure behind the fence stared right back, sending a chill up Demetrius's spine.

"Who is that?" Amelia's voice was barely above a whisper.

"Not sure."

"You there!"

Demetrius jumped and turned to find Amelia on her feet, waving her arms and speaking in a loud tone of voice that made his heart thump hard.

Amelia clapped her hands loudly. "We see you! Go on now, get out of here. Shoo! We're going to call the police if you don't move along."

"Amelia!" Demetrius said in a fierce whisper. "Lower your voice."

"Well, it's not right for someone to just skulk around outside peoples' yards at such an hour," Amelia said. She looked across the yard again and even in the gloom Demetrius could see her eyes widen and her mouth drop open.

He turned and had just enough time to let out a shout before a massive dark shape filled his vision. A fetid, damp smell invaded his nostrils, and the shape before him swung a heavy fist from which hung slick strands of wet material, catching Demetrius on the side of the head and sending him tumbling as somewhere close by Amelia screamed.

CHAPTER FIFTEEN

The scream woke Cody, and he was up and out of bed in an instant, standing and swaying in his underwear in the middle of a dark and unfamiliar room, his mind still trying to recall where he had been sleeping. Had he met a woman at a bar and gone back to her apartment? Another scream cut through the night and he turned, cursing and letting out a shout as he stubbed his toe on the foot of a bed across from the one where he'd been sleeping.

It all came back in a rush. He was in Florida, at Demmy's parents' condo. Demmy had been sleeping across from him, but now the bed was empty. Was Demmy screaming?

"I'm coming!" Cody shouted and limped to the door. He stepped out into the hallway, looked left and right, then headed toward the living room and the scream.

He stopped just outside the hallway and stood squinting into the darkness, trying to see if Demmy had come out to sit in a recliner near where Amelia was sleeping. The scrape of a chair leg out on the patio caught his attention, and Cody made his way to the sliding glass door and peered outside. It was dark, really dark, and the landscape lights only threw a weak golden glow that barely managed to make it through the gloom.

Toward the back of the yard, a hulking shadow shifted, and Cody was just able to see a flash of white material carried over someone's shoulder. Before Cody could slide the door open to shout to the figure, the tall stranger and the burden it carried stepped into the trees beyond the fence and darkness closed around them.

He looked around the patio at the chairs tipped over and the table standing askew, and then he caught sight of a pair of legs just beyond a toppled chair. His heart pounded as he flung the door open and stepped outside. The air was damp and heavy with the promise of a hell of a storm. Cody weaved around toppled chairs and the table, stopping dead at the sight of Demmy lying on the patio, arms flung to the side. A cold chill went through him even as the humidity made him sweat. No, he couldn't lose Demmy. Not now, not when he was on the cusp of opening up to him.

"Demmy!" Cody knelt beside him and hesitated, hands hovering over his still form. He was anxious to check for a pulse, but terrified at the same time. What had happened out here?

"Demmy?" Cody picked up his wrist and held it, mimicking Zenona, who had done it for him on a few occasions. A steady pulse beat in Demmy's wrist and Cody let out the breath he'd been holding. He turned Demmy onto his back and gently tapped his cheeks.

"Come on, Demmy, wake up," Cody said in a soft voice. "Wake up and talk to me."

Demmy groaned and turned his head away, frowning as he lifted his hand to wave Cody off. "Stop it."

"Wake up. Come on, tell me what happened."

Demmy's eyes fluttered open and he squinted at him. "Cody?" He pushed onto his elbows, winced as he drew in a hissing breath, and then sat all the way up and looked at his scarped elbow. "Ow."

"What happened?"

Demmy looked at him a moment and dropped his gaze to Cody's briefs gleaming white in the glow of landscape lights. "Are you outside in just your underwear? We're at my parents' condo. They could see you."

"Hey, focus," Cody said and snapped his fingers in front of Demmy's face. "What happened to you out here?"

"I came out here to sit and think, and we saw something out by the fence."

"We?" Cody looked around. "Who else was with you?"

"Amelia," Demmy said, looking around as well. "Where is she?"

They looked at each other, and Cody felt his stomach do a free fall as cold chills ran through him. "I'll check inside."

He hurried into the condo, calling Amelia's name but knowing in his gut he wouldn't find her. Marshall shuffled out of the hallway and frowned at him. "You might want to put some clothes on, Cody."

"Amelia's missing."

Marshall stared. "Missing? How? When?"

"Just a few minutes ago," Demmy said as he entered through the patio door. "We were out on the patio and someone came up to us from the trees behind the yard. He knocked me down and I blacked out, and now we can't find Amelia."

"Knocked you down?" Marshall switched on a lamp and approached Demmy. "Are you hurt?"

"Head hurts, but it's mostly just scrapes and bruises," Demmy replied, showing him the scrape on his elbow and matching one on his knee.

Cody checked the rest of the condo for Amelia but found no sign of her. He stopped in the guest room to pull on a pair of basketball shorts and a T-shirt, then joined Marshall and Demmy in the living room. Marshall was just picking up the phone to call the police, and Demmy had turned toward the patio door.

"Where are you going?" Cody said.

"To see if I can track her." Demmy switched on a flashlight he had grabbed from the kitchen utility drawer.

"Dammit, wait for me, we need shoes," Cody shouted after him. He ran into the garage and made a face as he slid his bare feet into the cold, muddy shoes he'd been wearing during their alligator drop off earlier that day.

Once he had tied his shoes, he grabbed Demmy's out of the utility sink and left the garage through the side door that opened into the backyard behind the fence. Cody saw Demmy standing at the back of the yard shining the flashlight into the trees just beyond the fence trotted over to him.

"I brought your shoes," Cody said and dropped them on the ground near Demmy's feet.

"Thanks." Demmy kicked off his flip-flops and stuck his feet into the shoes, grimacing at the sensation.

"Yeah, it's pretty gross."

"I want to go a little ways into the trees," Demmy said, shining the light on a flattened section of the cyclone fence and the trees right behind it. "Maybe we can pick up the trail."

"You didn't happen to bring another flashlight, did you?"

"Sorry, I just knew where this one was. Ready?"

"No," Cody said, waving toward the trees. "But go ahead, lead the way. You're the one with the light."

Demmy walked over the felled section of fence and Cody followed him. They stopped at the edge of the trees, and Demmy shined the light along the ground, searching for some kind of trail. The flash light beam picked out large footprints, big enough for Cody to stand with both his feet inside.

They were almost perfectly round with ragged marks toward the front where toes should be. Cody looked up and met Demmy's gaze as his stomach did a slow roll.

"He's a big fucker, isn't he?"

"Really big," Demmy agreed in a quiet, scared voice.

They looked into the woods, and Demmy took a breath and let it out as if building up his courage. Shining the light ahead of him, Demmy stepped between two palm trees and Cody followed. Within a few minutes, Cody had lost sight of the Singleton's backyard.

"Fucking creepy in here," Cody muttered.

"Just think of it as being in the woods back home."

"Fucking creepy there as well. At least this time there's no monster dog or farmer suffering from 'roid rage chasing after us."

"No, just a swamp monster," Demmy said.

"Goddammit Demmy," Cody whispered. "Stop jumping to conclusions, that's usually my job. I'm the Mulder, you're the Scully, right? And if this turns out to be a swamp monster, I swear I'm going to find a way for us to apply for some kind of monster hunter license or something."

"Shh. Let's keep quiet so the swamp monster doesn't circle around and come up behind us."

Cody looked over his shoulder, completely spooked, but could only see a few feet behind him in the back glow of the flashlight. He turned forward again and followed Demmy, both of them stepping over roots and branches and around trees. Now and then they came across another footprint just as big as the one they'd seen outside the trees.

They walked for a few minutes in silence, and then Demmy stopped at a fallen tree to shine the light around the ground, looking for footprints. Cody tried to help, but with only one flashlight, all he could do was sit on the tree and try to look everywhere at once. Lightning flashed through the heavy canopy of leaves, startling them both. Several seconds later it was followed by the rumble of thunder.

"Perfect," Cody grumbled.

"We're going to lose whatever tracks it might have left," Demmy said, searching more frantically for footprints.

"You keep saying 'it,' and you're freaking me out."

Demmy shined the light in his face. "Fine, I'll call it 'him', okay? Will that help? Just help me look for tracks!"

Cody squinted against the light and brought up a hand to shield his eyes as he turned his head away. "Get that damn light out of my eyes!"

"Cody!" Demmy shouted. "Behind you!"

Cody turned his head, the movement seeming to take minutes instead of seconds. A putrid stench assaulted him, similar to that of the rotting vegetables he often encountered in his refrigerator crisper drawer, and it was combined with the musky damp odor of dirt. Fear made Cody's heart gallop, and his stomach and bladder shriveled up as his mouth went completely dry.

It was perfectly illuminated in the beam of Demmy's flashlight where it stood just a few feet away, peering between a trio of trees grown close together. The thing lifted a hand and let out a roar of irritation that sent a repulsive wave of air over him. At least seven feet tall, its body appeared to be made up of moss, leaves, algae, and large pieces of bark. Arms of thick branches ended in clawed twig hands. A leaf had sprouted from the twig thumb of the thing's left hand and as Cody stared at it, the leaf shivered in the breeze.

Cody sat transfixed by the creature, staring as it extended its twig claws toward him. The thing — swamp beast, swamp creature, swamp *monster*, whatever it was — let out another roar that finally snapped Cody out of his stupor. He pushed off from the fallen tree at the same time he heard Demmy shout, "Get back!"

His heart thundered hard now, way past the gallop stage, sending the blood rushing through his veins. The swamp monster's claws swiped through the space where Cody had been sitting just as he moved. His relief at evading the thing was short-lived, however, as Cody tripped over his own feet and fell to the ground, arms extended to break his fall. His hands sank to his elbows into the swampy ground, and even over the monster's roar he heard Hubert's voice in his head grumpily correct him. "*Swampish.*"

With his hands mired deep in the soggy ground, Cody was stuck in place. His breath came in short, panicked pants as he tried to pull his hands free, but the swampy muck held them fast. Demmy knelt in front of him and dropped the flashlight on the ground to grab hold of Cody's forearms with both of his hands. He tugged hard, grunting and cursing as he worked to get Cody free.

"I'm stuck!"

"I know!"

Rough, wet fingers grasped Cody's ankles and lifted his legs off the ground. Cody let out a shout as he hung, staring into Demmy's eyes with his hands still anchored deep in the muck and his feet held high as if he were part of the wheelbarrow position.

Everything slowed down.

Cody saw drops of rain splash against Demmy's cheeks that made him blink. He watched Demmy's long eyelashes sweep closed and then open again. He saw a couple of scratches on Demmy's face, probably caused by branches, and knew he had a few himself.

The fingers tightened around his ankles, the skin rough and scratchy like the bark of a tree. The cool, slick mud clutched at his hands, but he could feel the strength in the monster's grip on his ankles, and he knew how this was all going to turn out.

He stared into Demmy's eyes, the backwash of the flashlight beam making them glow like sapphires as everything around the two of them stood in timeless suspension. Cody's entire world had paused to take a deep breath. From a place deep inside him, the words came up without any forethought or fear.

"I love you."

Those words triggered the moment to pass.

The monster gave a tug, seeming to Cody that it had not even pulled as hard as it could have. His hands pulled free of the ground with a slick, wet sound. Demmy tried to hold onto him, eyes wide as he shouted "No!" But he was no match against the monster, and his fingers slid off Cody's mud-slick arms.

The thing hauled Cody up and slung him over its shoulder as if he weighed nothing at all. He felt the rough scratch of its bark skin scrape against his belly where his shirt had rucked up. He braced his hands against the monster's back and tried to raise the upper half of his body, but his hands were slick with mud, and he kept slipping back down. The creature's shoulder pressed up into his gut, limiting his ability to draw a deep breath, and it felt as if he were suffocating as the thing stomped off into the woods. Cody knew he had to get free and quick before he was carried too far away from Demmy and the way back to civilization, but when he pushed up once again, the back of his head struck something—a low tree branch maybe—and darkness took him.

CHAPTER SIXTEEN

Demetrius was beside himself. One side was terror: what had he just witnessed and where had it taken Cody and Amelia? The other side was pure panic: what was he going to do about it?

He held the flashlight in a trembling hand as he forced his way through the thick trees. Branches scratched his skin and clawed at his eyes. The beam of the flashlight bounced back and forth, sometimes picking out a massive footprint that let him know he was still going in the right direction. His thoughts were a jumble of images and feelings and memories, thinking of Cody and Amelia, wondering if they were still alive and hoping he could figure out a way to save them.

Memories of the swamp monster kept coming back. The dank, noxious smell of it, and the mossy skin that covered bark and branches. It had been tall, incredibly tall, taller than Cody by almost a foot, and Cody was the tallest person Demetrius had ever met.

Cody.

Demetrius's heart seemed to quiver as he thought about

him, remembered those words and, even in his panicked state, tried to decipher exactly what they meant.

I love you.

Well, of course Cody loved him. They were best friends, after all, and had been for over twenty years. But there had been power behind those words, a force Demetrius had never sensed from Cody before. It made Demetrius feel a whole host of emotions that seemed to live separately inside him, shunted off to a corner while the main emotions of the moment guided him: concern for Cody and Amelia, fear they were injured, terror at what he'd witnessed, and determination to get them back safe.

He tried to keep these other emotions locked away, but try as he might to keep them at bay and focus on tracking the swamp monster, they kept sliding in from the corners of his mind. One minute he was able to focus on what he was looking at, and the next he was concerned he might misunderstand the intention behind Cody's words.

Then right behind that came the fear Cody *had* meant it the way Demetrius quietly hoped. On the heels of that one followed terror over what the future might bring if they tried to get together as a couple. Finally, something steelier settled within him as he at last placed everything in its proper order. Top on his list was a grim determination to find Cody, Amelia, and hopefully even Hubert. Everything else was secondary.

As Demetrius picked his way between trees, scanning the wet ground for tracks, he pushed everything out of his mind but the need to find them. He forced himself to not dwell on the fact that Cody had been acting much differently the last few months, even before the wolf man case. Right now he was the only hope for Cody and Amelia, and that was his priority, not whether or not something more than friendship was possible between him and Cody.

Demetrius cursed at himself as he followed the monster's footprints.

"Stop being an asshole," Demetrius grumbled. "You're anticipating the end of things before you've even found out if there's a chance to start those things up."

The rain was falling harder now and the wind had picked up. He'd tried to call his dad, but his cell phone had no signal out here. He wished now they'd waited for the police, for a proper search party. But, no. Although he usually over-thought every decision, Demetrius had this time reacted before he'd thought the situation through. He had stormed off into the trees armed with only a flashlight, and Cody had followed him as usual, trusting in him, wanting to please him. Well, Demetrius had gone too far this time. All he could do was try his best to save Amelia and Cody from the swamp monster.

Swamp monster. Even with everything they'd seen over the last year — the wolf man, Agatha's dog that had turned into a blood-craving beast, and Reed Wilkes who had turned into a steroid-fueled rage monster — Demetrius still found it difficult to grasp the concept. How had this creature come to life? Was it something that had adapted to the specifics of its environment, or had it been created out here from some weird mix of chemicals and happenstance? And why all of a sudden was it grabbing people, and what did it do with them?

He thought about all the missing persons posters at the hospital, and then Hubert, and now Amelia and Cody and his stomach tightened with fear. He hoped they weren't intended to be food, but that terrifying certainty seeped into his system. The way the alligator they'd tried to return to the swamp had literally turned tail and run the other direction had been a sure sign something was off. The swamp monster was big enough and, from what Demetrius had witnessed, strong enough to be the alpha predator in this part of the Everglades. And Hubert's comment about there being a lot more alligators showing up in swimming pools recently now seemed to make sense. Maybe the swamp monster had just migrated to this area for a new food supply.

Demetrius leaned against a tree to catch his breath. He shone the flashlight around the ground, noticing how swampy this area was compared to where they had encountered the creature. Murky water stood in spots, the depth impossible to gauge. The raindrops that made it through the leaf coverage sent ripples across the dark surfaces. Demetrius shivered, wondering what those disturbances might be awakening.

A scream from off in the distance made his breath catch in his chest. He jerked his head up and directed the flashlight beam into the dark tangle of trees before him, trying in vain to see how far he had yet to go. The silence stretched out, frightening in its implication. Had that been Amelia's death scream?

Demetrius refused to consider that possibility. He pushed off from the tree and made his way along the softening ground between the ever increasing and widening puddles of swamp water. He didn't dare shout encouragement to Amelia or Cody for fear of alerting the creature. Demetrius hoped he had it in him to be stealthy.

CHAPTER SEVENTEEN

Cody drifted in and out of awareness. He was on his feet but hanging slack with his head down and arms stretched out and supported. How he'd gotten into this position he couldn't recall. Rain fell on his head and the back of his neck, and the smell of it, mixed in with the ripe smell of mud and plants, took him back to a day not too long ago. He and Demmy had been caught in a surprise thunderstorm during a job. They'd run through the downpour and taken shelter inside a small garden shed at the back of the property. It had been a tight squeeze for them both to get inside and they'd stood looking at each other in silence a moment before busting into laughter.

Cody could have leaned in and kissed Demmy. Just a space of a few inches was all it would have taken, but he held back. That simple movement would have had a tremendous impact on their relationship, and he wasn't sure either of them were ready for it. He had, however, hardened at the thought of it, so he had leaned away from Demmy until his back pressed against the handles of shovels stacked in the corner behind him. He didn't want Demmy to accidentally brush against him and... what? Be shocked? Be aroused? That was the trouble with this entire possibility of a relationship. Besides neither of them being ready to discuss or deal with it, Cody had no idea how Demmy would react to the news. Even after all these years of friendship, he couldn't quite predict it.

There in the garden shed, the laughter had faded away, and they had stared at each other. The light was dim. Rain pounded hard on the shed's sloped roof. The smell of damp earth had been thick inside the shed.

As he stood inches away from the person who might be the one true love of his life, Cody had to resist the strong urge to act on his impulses.

The memory of being in the shed with Demmy vanished when something big splashed in water close by. Thunder rumbled as well, bringing Cody back to his present situation with no idea how he had gotten there. An ache in the back of his head made him wince and groan quietly. He felt cold and wet and confused, unsure where he was and what had happened. Then a memory surfaced of following Demmy through the woods behind the Singleton condo. They had been tracking someone or something. Were they on a job in Florida?

A growl from close by sent a chill through Cody. His adrenaline spiked, sharpening his senses and making him more alert. He very slowly opened his eyes until he squinted through his lashes. He appeared to be on a small island of mud and stone. Dark swamp water surrounded him, the surface pebbled from the heavy rain. With slow, cautious movements, Cody looked up at his hands and found his wrists bound with vines to two trees, leaving him sagging between them.

He tried to look around, but movement in either direction made him wince. Something had smacked the back of his head pretty good, and pain radiated down his neck into his shoulders. He let his head drop again as he remembered the sensation of being carried over someone's shoulder, the scratch of tree bark against his skin, and the stink of rotting vegetation.

Swamp monster.

It came back in a terrifying rush, all of it. The drive down to Florida; Demmy's surprise and anger at seeing him in the hospital; the alligator in the pool and Hubert going missing; Amelia going missing as well.

A high, terrified scream from very close by brought his head up quick. He ignored the throbbing inside his skull and peered through the gloom around him. The rain was falling hard, thick as a curtain. It smashed against the surface of the swamp, creating a spray that hung like mist above the water. Thunder boomed and the wind picked up as if someone had flicked a switch, blowing the rain sideways and shaking the trees.

Cody shook hair out of his eyes and regretted it as the resulting blast of pain made lights flash across his vision. He peered through the heavy rain and punishing wind, twisting each hand back and forth within the vines holding them up. The plants scratched and scraped his skin with each movement, but he thought they might be loosening up a bit. At least he hoped they were.

Another scream helped him zero in on the location, and he turned his head more, wincing at the pain it caused. Just over his left shoulder, he could see around the tree he was tethered to. The island of mud and rock on which he was imprisoned extended as a slender finger of land with trees and bushes scattered along its length. Branches and palm leaves and other flotsam littered the surface of the island. Beyond a large pile of bleached white branches, Cody could just make out a struggling figure.

The figure's feet kicked out at a dark shape standing nearby. "Leave me alone! Go away!"

"Amelia? Amelia! No! Leave her alone, you bastard!"

"Cody?" Amelia said. "Oh my God. Cody! Oh oh, look out, it's coming to you."

Cody pulled harder against the vines that held him in place. A splashing sound approached, just audible over the driving rain and the moan of the wind. He closed his eyes and twisted his hands faster, the vines biting into his skin. The smell of decay washed over him, pungent despite the strengthening wind of the storm. He felt as if his internal organs were all one big trembling mass inside him as he slowly opened his eyes.

It stood eye to eye with him, even though its feet were below the water line. In the dim light, the depthless eyes glowed green within a face shaped by moss and wood. Its nose was a lump that could have been a cut off branch, and the mouth a gaping dark maw ringed by sharp wooden teeth. Moss and tree bark made up the rest of its body, giving way to long ropes of vine wound together to form strong, trunk-like legs.

The thing was like some kind of special effect and Cody couldn't help feeling like he was watching some all too realistic movie on one of those science fiction channels.

"Cody, be careful," Amelia said. "It's killed people."

"Great." Cody could feel the vines around his wrists weakening, but not fast enough for him to get free and get away. "Can you get loose?"

"Just my feet. My hands are too tight."

"Feet?" Cody tried to lift one of his feet and whispered a curse when he found a vine wrapped right around his ankles.

The swamp monster stomped one foot on the mud of the island and leaned in closer. Cody watched as the moss, leaves, and bits of bark that made up the thing's face changed into a hostile expression. Fear shifted to terror within him, amping up his adrenaline, and Cody yanked his right arm down hard enough to snap the vine. He spun in place a few times with his left arm extended over his head, putting all his weight on the remaining vine until it snapped as well. He fell flat on his back with his ankles still bound as the monster swiped at him, the twig fingers whooshing over his head. The monster took another step closer and put its hands on the trees and leaned between them, looming over him.

Cody rolled over and dug the fingers of his free hand into the mud above his head, pulling himself away as far as possible, left arm still stuck over his head. He looked over his shoulder and found himself staring into glowing green eyes as the monster leaned in closer. He thought he was a goner, but a bright flash of lightning startled the monster. It slipped in the mud and fell back heavily onto the bank of the island. On its way down, however, the monster's twig-claw snagged on the vine tied around Cody's ankles and dragged him back between the trees.

"Shit!" Cody shouted, scrabbling for purchase. He dragged his fingers through the mud, unable to find anything to grab on to as he pulled his legs up as hard as he could.

The vine around his ankles snapped, and his legs fell into the mud with a wet slap. The monster grabbed for him, but Cody yanked his knees up to his chest, pulling his feet out of reach. He noticed the trailing end of the vine was still wrapped around his ankles, keeping his feet tied together. Rolling onto his side, he reached down to tug at the vine with his free right hand. The monster was having trouble regaining its footing on the muddy slope of the island and Cody rolled on to his back with his knees pulled up to his chest. He pulled at the vine around his ankles as he kept an eye on the swamp monster.

The wind picked up even more, whipping rain into his

face as he plucked and tugged at the vine, and he had to turn his face to the side in order to gasp for breath.

"Cody!" Amelia shouted, her voice barely carrying to him over the now roaring wind.

"I'm okay!" Cody shouted back, gulping in rain and coughing it back out again.

The vine around his ankles came loose just as the monster managed to grab hold of the trees where Cody had been tied up. It pulled itself to its feet and towered over him. Lightning seared the dark clouds, backlighting the thing as if on cue in a horror movie. Vines and leaves that hung off the monster snapped and twisted in the wild wind, and its eyes shone green in the night like swamp fire.

Cody rolled onto his belly and pushed to his hands and knees. He crawled away from the thing as fast as he could, his hands sliding out from under him every few feet and planting his face in the mud. Rain pelted his back as he made his way along the island. Behind him, either the monster roared in aggravation or the wind had gusted stronger than ever. Whichever one it was, Cody continued crawling away, refusing to look back. The wind splashed swamp water on him and the rain pounded his skull and back as he made his way toward Amelia.

A heavy thud vibrated through the mud in which his fingers were encased, and he risked a glance over his shoulder. The swamp monster had fallen, maybe blown off his feet. However it had happened, Cody was grateful, and he doubled his efforts to reach Amelia.

When at last he reached her, Cody grabbed hold of one of the trees to which she had been lashed. He pulled himself to his feet and wrapped an arm around the trunk to keep himself in place as he leaned in against the wind to squint at her. She was struggling to get loose from the vines around her wrists. The rain lashed them, stinging as it blew into Cody's face, making it difficult to catch his breath.

"Amelia!" he shouted, barely able to hear himself over the wind.

She turned her head toward the sound of his voice. Her eyes were closed against the force of the rain and wind. He grabbed the vine closest to him and pulled hard until it snapped. Her arm fell to her side and with a scream, she swung away from him to bump into the opposite tree. Cody swore and pushed off from the tree, reaching for the next one. The wind got hold of him, however, and pushed him to the edge of the island. Unable to find purchase, he slid through the mud.

Lightning forked across the sky and temporarily blinded him. He dropped to his hands and knees to make a smaller target of himself against the wind, and rubbed at his eyes while spots swarmed across his vision. When he could see again, he clawed his way back to Amelia, glad to see she was okay and pulling against the remaining vine holding her in place. Across the swamp, branches slammed to the ground and trees bent to their breaking point.

Just before he could reach Amelia, the swamp monster rose up behind her. Its glowing green eyes glared down at Cody from above her, and it raised a massive fist high overhead, ready to bring it down on Amelia's neck.

"No!" Cody shouted, and he launched himself forward in a slipping, stumbling run.

CHAPTER EIGHTEEN

The storm was getting worse, and Demetrius feared it was amping up to a hurricane. He had never been through a hurricane before, but he knew his parents had weathered several since they'd moved to Florida. Of course, they hadn't had to ride out a hurricane in the middle of the swamp. He'd just have to do it while lost in the Everglades with his aunt and his best friend having been taken away by a terrifying swamp monster.

"No problem," Demetrius muttered to himself.

He slipped in ankle deep mud and went down hard on one knee. Cursing, he struggled back to his feet, but a heavy gust knocked him to his knees. The crack of a breaking branch made him turn his head, and the wind stole his breath. He scrambled through deep mud, trying to get out from the full force of the wind. Rain pummeled his back and the top of his head. A heavy branch crashed to the ground directly behind him, so close he felt the leaves brush his ankles.

Demetrius crawled a little farther before using a tree to pull himself to his feet. He used his shirt to wipe mud off the lens of the flashlight, and he shined the beam over the fallen tree branch, watching the leaves whip back and forth. Turning his face out of the wind, he drew in a deep breath and wiped away rain and mud. Lightning flashed, momentarily blinding him. Demetrius rested his head against the tree and closed his eyes as the rain lashed him. He had to keep moving, Cody and Amelia's lives depended on him.

"Come on, Demmy," he said. "Time to show what you've got."

He pushed off from the tree and walked on through the rain. The storm had obliterated any sign of the swamp monster's tracks, so now he moved on pure instinct. He hadn't heard Amelia scream in a long time, and that worried him more than if she'd continued. As long as she was screaming, she was alive.

Several minutes later, Demetrius stepped out of the trees onto a moss-covered bluff. He was looking out over a small cove of water covered with algae. A narrow island of rock and mud lay in the middle of the cove. Movement out on the island caught his attention, and Demetrius put his arm across his forehead to shield his eyes. As he squinted through the rain and gloom, his mouth dropped open in shock. Was he really seeing what he thought he was seeing?

A number of trees stood in staggered pairs along the muddy island, bent by the force of the wind. Between two of the trees stood a man with his arms extended out and up. He appeared to be tall, very tall, and Demetrius knew it had to be Cody.

"Cody!" Demetrius shouted, but the wind took his words even as they left his lips.

A woman screamed, and he looked down along the island. She was bound between two more trees in a similar fashion to Cody.

"Amelia," Demetrius said to himself. "Jesus, what the hell?"

Movement in the water near Amelia caught his attention, and he gasped. Through the heavy downpour, he saw what he had first thought to be a tree growing out of the swamp was in actuality the monster.

"No," Demetrius whispered as he tried to see through the rain. "No, no, no, no, no."

He lost sight of the island within the rain and knew he had to act. Moving carefully, Demetrius picked his way through the ferns and fallen branches around the bank of the cove. He intended to circle around closer to the island and somehow attract Cody or Amelia's attention.

After stepping into a small clearing, he paused to check on Cody and Amelia. A break in the storm and his new position allowed him to see better. Cody had gotten loose and was trying to get Amelia free, but the swamp monster was approaching from behind Amelia.

"No!" Demetrius waved his arms overhead and took a few steps to the side, more toward the center of the clearing.

The storm picked up again, sudden and ferocious. Trees all around Demetrius bent almost in half. Branches crashed to the ground nearby and the force of the wind drove Demetrius to his hands and knees. The flashlight tumbled out of his grip, the beam spiraling crazily in the heavy rain. He reached out for the flashlight, feeling along the muddy ground.

The heavy rain blinded him, but he gave a shout of triumph when he grabbed the shaft of the flashlight. He noticed it felt different, and tried to look at it in the dark. A streak of lightning lit up the area briefly, and Demetrius realized he was holding a large bone and not the flashlight.

He screamed and dropped the bone. Looking around, he noticed what he had thought had been branches were really bones. He started to hyperventilate as he pushed up to his knees and looked all around him.

Another flash of lightning revealed a mound of bones a bit farther back. A human skull rested on its side near the top, the dark sockets staring right at him. Mixed in with the human bones were what looked to be animal bones, including alligator jaws and long strings of tiny bones that were most likely tails.

Nausea rushed through him, but Demetrius fought the feeling back. He had to stay focused and save Cody and Amelia. Getting to his feet, Demetrius struggled to stay upright in the wind. He staggered across the clearing, slipping and stumbling over bones and through mud until he reached a tree. Wrapping his arms around it, he looked out over the swamp but everything was in turmoil. He couldn't see more than five feet in front of him.

Demetrius swore and pushed off from the tree with the intention of continuing around to the opposite bank. The wind, however, had other ideas for him. A sudden gust sent him lurching toward the swamp. He couldn't stop himself. Once he reached the muddy bank, his feet went out from under him and he sat down hard. The rain felt like tiny rocks against his skin as he floundered for purchase in the muddy bank. His hand landed on something sharp and he jerked it away then leaned down to inspect what he'd touched. An alligator's lower jawbone lay in the mud, and Demetrius picked it up. He grabbed a long, heavy bone — most likely a human femur, but he refused to think about that at the moment — and struggled to his feet. With a weapon in each hand, he stumbled blindly into the trees.

CHAPTER NINETEEN

Cody knew he would never forget how the swamp monster felt under his hands. He'd launched himself at the thing like it was a Friday night back on Parson's Hollow High's football field, and the monster was a quarterback with the ball. He grabbed it around the middle and threw his shoulder against it. At first it felt like he'd just hugged a tree. The bark was rough, and the moss soft beneath his touch. But then it moved, and Cody felt the muscles shift just beneath the bark. It made him shudder even as he dug his toes into the mud and pushed with all he had, driving it back and away from Amelia.

His feet slid in the mud, but Cody put all his strength into the move. When he felt the monster's weight shift, he shouted and drove his shoulder even harder into it. The twig branches of its fingers scratched down the length of his back, turning his shout of effort into a cry of pain. But he didn't let up. He continued to push against the thing, tightening his grip on the bark that made up its rib cage. The crack of bark breaking beneath his fingers gave him extra energy and finally he and the monster both toppled off the island and into the swamp.

Cold water closed over his head, shocking him into exhaling. He was under before he could take a breath, and the monster continued to scratch at him. One of its legs came up between Cody's thighs, but the water slowed its movements down enough for him to be able to shift his hips and save his balls. His lungs burned, and he would need to take a breath soon, but the monster had tightened its stick arms around him. Fear exploded inside his chest and the resulting adrenaline sent a surge of strength into his limbs. He bucked hard, breaking the monster's grip, and then pushed up and away from its desperate, grasping arms and kicking legs. His face broke the surface, and he drew in a deep breath, sucking in swamp water along with the air. Heavy coughs left him bleary-eyed as he struggled to find his footing. The water hadn't looked that deep when the monster had been wading toward him.

Some kind of movement on the bank of the swamp caught his attention. He thought for a moment it was Amelia, but she had still been tied up when he'd run at the monster. It hadn't been a tree blowing over as the movement was continuing. It could be a person.

"Hey!" Cody shouted. "Here!"

"Cody!"

Relief and joy spun together inside his chest. It was Demmy, here to save them. He knew Demmy wouldn't have given up on him.

"Demmy!"

"Keep shouting so I can find you."

"Right here. Keep coming toward the sound of my voice."

Cody finally found the soggy bottom of the swamp, and he tried to stand up against the wind and blowing water. But thin, hard fingers wrapped around his ankle and yanked him off balance.

"Look out — !" Cody managed before the monster pulled him under.

He flailed his arms and kicked with his free foot. The monster tugged harder and tried to grab his other foot, but Cody pulled it out of reach. Something touched his hand, and he jerked it away. Then someone caught his hand and held it tight and he grabbed back. It had to be Demmy. His grip helped Cody steady himself so he was able to plant his free foot on the monster's chest and push up hard enough to break free. He popped above the surface and gasped in a deep breath.

"I've got you," Demmy said. He stood behind him and put an arm around his chest, still holding tight to his hand.

"Go," Cody managed between coughs. "Go! Get us away from it. Get to the island. Amelia."

Demmy was standing in water up to his neck, and Cody kicked to put distance between himself and the monster before putting his feet down. He touched bottom and stood up, the water coming up to his chest. He put his arm around Demmy and together they slogged to the island. Demmy held something in his free hand, but Cody couldn't see what it was.

"Are you hurt?" Demmy asked.

"Scratches and stuff. Nothing serious. Let's free Amelia and get out of here."

"We're in the middle of a hurricane," Demmy said.

"Oh really? I hadn't noticed."

That earned him a pinch in the side, which Cody gratefully accepted. He was just glad to have his arm around Demmy. For a time, he'd thought he would never see him again.

They reached the island and struggled to get up the muddy bank. Cody caught himself looking over his shoulder every couple of minutes, expecting the monster to lunge up out of the water at them like at the end of pretty much every horror movie ever made.

"Where is it?" Demmy said, apparently envisioning the same thing. "Did it drown?"

"It's a swamp monster. I don't think it *can* drown."

They finally managed to get to the island, crawling to the trees where Amelia had been tied up. There was no sign of her, just the vines that had bound her snapping in the wind.

"She's gone!" Demmy said, turning to look at him with wide eyes. "Did she escape?"

"I don't know." Cody looked all around the island, but there was no sign of her. "One of her arms was still tied up when I left her. Maybe she got free and ran off?"

Demmy shook his head. "She wouldn't have left you."

"Dude, *I* would have left me," Cody said. "I would never hold it against her if she got away and took off through the woods."

"It's just not like her." Demmy looked at the sky. "Hey, the storm's letting up."

Cody inspected the clouds. "Looks like it."

"Oh shit." Demmy pointed to a massive wall of clouds just visible over the tops of trees. "I think we're in for another round of it soon."

"Great. Let's get a move on before it hits again."

They got to their feet, and Cody noticed what Demmy was holding. "Are those bones?"

Demmy held them up. "I found a pile of them on land."

A scream made them both turn quick and look across the water. On the far bank, Amelia struggled to escape from the swamp monster who was dragging her out of the water and through the mud.

"Amelia!" Demmy shouted. "He's taking her toward the bones."

"Help!"

Cody did not hesitate. Most times he acted without thinking something through, and today proved no different. He ran to the end of the island and dove into the water. With strong, sure strokes, he made it to shore and climbed through the mud. The monster had released Amelia and turned, ready to defend itself.

"Amelia, get out of here," Cody said, not taking his eyes off the monster. "Run!"

Behind him, he heard Demmy swimming in from the island. From the corner of his eye, Cody could see Amelia scrambling away in the mud. For the moment, it was just him and the swamp monster, and Cody was more than ready to bring it some pain.

Apparently, the swamp monster felt the same way. It let out a loud roar and leaned forward, charging at him. The twig fingers were extended, ready to deliver gouging scratches, and its glowing green eyes glared.

Cody took a step back, bracing himself for the thing's attack. His foot landed on something that rolled, and he fell on his back. As the monster neared, Cody had just enough time to raise his arms in an effort to protect himself.

At that moment, Demmy launched himself out of the water and stepped between Cody and the monster. Cody was about to shout a warning when Demmy brought his arms back as if getting ready to swing at a pitch. For a moment, Cody was annoyed and confused. Demmy didn't play sports, why the hell had he chosen this moment to start?

Then Cody saw Demmy held an alligator jawbone, its teeth pointed out. When the swamp monster was within range, Demmy swung. His aim was high and true. The heavy bone inside the alligator jaw gave the brittle cartilage extra weight. The teeth slashed across the monster's face and punctured its left eye.

The monster's terrifying roar became a shriek of pain. It

put its twig hands over the black socket that used to be its eye and turned away. Demmy's follow through spun him off balance, and his foot slipped out from under him in the mud, sending him crashing to the ground beside Cody. They sat side by side in the mud and watched the monster stomp around its feeding grounds, shattering bones beneath its big feet. It held its hands over the left side of its face and howled in pain.

"Did you ever think something like this lived down here?" Cody said.

"Not even after we killed the werewolf."

"Wolf man."

A sound from off in the woods reached them, and Cody exchanged a worried look with Demmy. "What is that?"

"It sounds like — " Demmy was cut off by a sudden gust of wind that brought sheets of driving rain along with it.

"The storm!" Demmy shouted, grabbing Cody's arm to help him to his feet.

They staggered against the wind toward the trees. At one point, they were holding on to each other, both leaning into the wind and almost parallel to the ground. Cody had lost track of the monster, but he didn't care. He wanted to be out of the wind and within the shelter of the trees. The crack of trees splitting and branches breaking sounded like gunshots, making Cody wonder if being near the woods was a smart idea after all.

Twig fingers gripped his shoulder and spun him around. Cody lost his hold on Demmy as he found himself staring up into the monster's face. Thick black fluid oozed from the scratches and empty eye socket left by Demmy's alligator jaw. Cody tried to pull free, but the monster had too strong of a grip on him. It roared into his face and raised its free hand to deliver a swipe with its long, sharp twig claws.

A loud, angry shout caught Cody's attention. He looked

over his shoulder and figured the dirt and rain being driven into his face by the wind was causing him to see things. Either that or Amelia thought she was some kind of track and field star. Lightning flashed, and he was able to see Amelia running toward them, holding a tree branch in both hands like a pole-vaulter. The branch had splintered, and she held the jagged end out and up.

Before Cody could truly process what he was seeing, Amelia drove the branch into the thing's gut. The impact spun the monster around, and it scratched long furrows across Cody's shoulder with its claws. He screamed up at the black clouds, lightning and thunder acting as punctuation. Amelia stumbled and fell flat on her face in the mud next to Cody. The monster staggered backward toward the swamp, the branch sticking out of its midsection.

A hand gripped Cody's injured shoulder and he cried out. Demmy put his mouth next to Cody's ear to be heard over the storm.

"We have to go!"

Cody nodded. He wanted nothing more than to be far away from this place. Demmy helped him to his feet, and they both helped Amelia stand.

"You saved my life," Cody said into her ear.

"Oh birch trees," Amelia said. "You saved me first."

Cody laughed, the sound of it surprising all three of them. He looked over his shoulder for the monster, but could see nothing except rain and trees being lashed by the wind. Lightning crackled across the sky, followed immediately by a clap of thunder that made them all crouch down.

"We really have to go!" Demmy shouted.

He got no argument from Amelia or Cody. Clinging to each other, the three of them headed off into the trees.

CHAPTER TWENTY

Demetrius struggled through the dense woods. Amelia staggered between him and Cody, both of her arms linked in one of theirs. The wind screamed around them, throwing dirt and other debris in their faces and stealing their breath. Trees snapped in half or were completely uprooted. Rain battered them as they waded through the flooded Everglades, hopefully headed in the right direction. All Demetrius knew for certain was that they were putting distance between the monster and themselves.

Amelia stumbled and went down to her knees. Demetrius and Cody stopped and helped her back up. As Amelia steadied herself, Demetrius glanced back the way they had come and felt a shiver of fear go through him. A tall figure lurched toward them, barely visible through the wind-driven rain. Lightning flashed, followed closely by booming thunder that made all three of them jump. In the flickering lightning, Demetrius saw the swamp monster plodding toward them.

He put his head close to Amelia and Cody and shouted, "We have to go faster!"

Cody looked back and Demetrius was pretty sure he

heard him let loose a string of curses at the sight of the monster. They got back to the business of walking against the wind as a team, holding on to each other and using trees to pull themselves forward. Slowly they made progress. Each time Demetrius looked over his shoulder, they seemed to be keeping distance between them and the monster. He just hoped they were moving in the right direction.

He lost track of time as he continued to focus on keeping ahead of the monster. One slip from any of them could mean death if the thing were to catch up. With his attention focused on keeping his footing, Demetrius didn't really notice the wind losing force until Cody mentioned it.

"Wind's dying down," Cody said, no longer having to shout to be heard.

"Oh thank God," Amelia said and drew in a deep breath. "I can finally breathe again."

Demetrius checked on the monster's progress. He could see it easier now that the wind and rain had let up, and the sight of it slowly gaining on them gave him a boost of energy.

"We need to keep moving," Demetrius said. "Faster now. Come on, we should be getting close to the village."

"How the hell can you know that?"

"I don't," Demetrius replied. "It just feels like this is the right direction, that's all."

Lightning still flashed, but the thunder took longer to rumble in response which Demetrius hoped meant the storm was moving on. They sloshed through the dirty floodwater, and Demetrius tried not to look behind them too often. The village had to be close. He looked back again and saw the monster had fallen farther behind. He let out a relieved breath and stopped to pull his cell phone from his pocket.

"What are you doing?"

"Checking for a signal."

"Your phone still works after being submerged in the swamp?"

Demetrius pressed buttons and tapped the screen to no avail. "Shit."

"I hope you're due for an upgrade," Cody muttered. He looked around as he ran a hand over his head, smoothing his hair back from his forehead. "Are you sure we're going in the right direction?"

"No," Demetrius said.

"I've completely lost track of where I am," Amelia said from where she leaned against a tree trying to catch her breath. "We could be back in Parson's Hollow for all I know."

"Don't I wish," Demetrius grumbled. He looked at the sky, but the cloud cover was still too heavy to be able to see the stars, moon, or sun. Hell, he didn't even know what time of day it was.

Another check of the monster's progress gave him a chill. It had closed the distance between them much too quickly for his comfort.

"Come on, we need to keep moving," he said.

"Why don't we stay and fight it?" Cody asked. "Finish it off once and for all."

"With what? We've got no weapons."

"Amelia made a tree branch into a hell of a weapon," Cody said.

"Be that as it may, I think Demetrius is right," Amelia said. "Let's put some more space between us and that thing. I don't want to spend another night lost in the Everglades. Especially after being drenched."

"Majority rules," Demetrius said. "Let's go."

Some time later, they came upon a tall power line tower and stopped to lean against it for a rest. When Cody had caught his breath, he climbed up the maintenance ladder just high enough to be able to see over the trees while Demetrius kept a nervous eye on the monster. It had fallen a bit farther behind but was still doggedly following them.

"I see buildings!" Cody shouted down to them. "Probably just over a mile that way."

"Oh thank God," Amelia said. "Let's hurry."

"Uh oh," Cody said.

Demetrius checked on the monster's progress even though he'd just seen it was still at least one hundred yards away. "What uh oh?"

"Cody Bower, come down here this instant," Amelia shouted to him.

"You two might want to consider climbing up."

Demetrius exchanged a worried look with Amelia. "Why?"

"We've got incoming alligators swimming toward us through the flood waters."

"Alligators?" Amelia whispered. She looked back at the monster and then up to where Cody stood on the ladder, dozens of feet in the air. "We'll be trapped up there."

"Trapped but far away from the alligators," Demetrius said. "I'll be right beneath you."

"Oh, Demetrius, I don't know." Amelia stood looking up the steel rungs.

"Stop looking up my shorts, Amelia, and get to climbing," Cody called. "You've got about two minutes to get out of reach of those alligators."

"Son of an aspen," she muttered before gripping the rung before her and starting to climb.

"There you go," Demetrius said. "Nice and careful."

He let her get a few rungs up before he followed. A gentle rain was falling, nothing like the downpour from before, but it made the rungs slick beneath his mud-coated shoes.

"How close are they?" Demetrius asked.

"Which party? Alligators or swamp monster?"

"Either. Both."

"Swamp monster is about twenty yards out," Cody said. "And alligators are swimming in from about forty yards. Odds are swamp monster will reach us just before the gators."

"Let's hope he hasn't figured out how to climb a ladder," Amelia said.

Demetrius climbed slowly, minding his footing as he let Amelia ascend ahead of him. When she reached the spot just below Cody, she stopped and hooked an arm through one of the rungs and Demetrius moved up to the spot a few rungs beneath. He could hear the hum of power through the wires overhead and marveled at the fact that the storm hadn't brought the lines down. It was lucky for them the lines were still up, otherwise they would have probably been electrocuted while standing in the calf-deep water.

"Here's the monster of the hour," Cody said, "hold on tight now."

Demetrius's heart pounded as he watched the monster wade out of the cover of trees. It moved slower than it had before and held a hand over the wound in its midsection. The monster stood in place and scanned the open ground around the electrical tower. Demetrius looked up at Amelia and Cody and held a finger to his lips, and they nodded. He looked back at the monster and held his breath. His heart pounded so hard he could hear the blood rushing in his ears.

The monster wiped at the eye Demetrius had gouged out with the alligator jaw. It made a kind of whimpering sound that almost made Demetrius feel sorry for it. Almost. He wished it would turn around and walk away, disappear back into the Everglades and never be seen again.

Just when Demetrius thought it might actually return to the heavy woods, the monster happened to look up. The glowing green eye looked right at Demetrius and the thing roared, instantly enraged.

So much for feeling sorry for it.

With long strides, the monster approached the tower. It gripped either side of the leg they were currently perched on and glared up at them.

"We're about to find out if it can climb," Cody said.

Demetrius swallowed hard as he stared into the monster's eye. It tried to shake the leg of the tower and when that proved impossible, it roared angrily at them. Demetrius reflexively climbed up another step and felt his head bump against Amelia's calves.

"Sorry," he said without taking his eyes off the monster.

"No worries, dear," Amelia replied. "This is a fine mess we're in. Now what?"

"I left my phone back at the condo," Cody said.

"So did I," Amelia said.

Demetrius sighed. "I had mine with me, but it's water-logged now. Won't even turn on."

"Well, shit," Amelia said.

Demetrius looked up and found Cody grinning at him past Amelia.

"What happened to using trees instead of curse words?" Demetrius said.

"A swamp monster is more than cause enough for cursing."

The monster lifted its left foot and tried to fit it on the rung. Luckily the thing's foot was too wide and it slipped off to splash back in the water. It roared at them again and stretched up as far as it could, twig fingers extended toward them. Demetrius climbed up yet another step even though he was at least ten feet out of reach.

Movement behind the monster attracted Demetrius's attention. As he watched, an alligator swam past the thing, slow moving tail propelling it through the water. Another alligator followed that one, and behind that came a third, bigger than both of the preceding ones.

"I don't know about this," Cody said.

"Me neither," Demetrius said, switching his gaze between the alligators circling the tower and the monster still trying to reach them.

One of the alligators swam in closer to the monster, and its tail broke the surface. The monster turned and dropped into a low crouch, arms extended while it let out a growl. Another alligator swam in front of it, and the monster snatched its tail out of the water. The alligator thrashed, but the monster held the tail tight. Without a second look up the ladder, the monster headed back the way it had come, dragging the struggling gator behind it.

"Let's hope it's satisfied with the meal it found," Amelia said.

"It doesn't look like the other gators are going to let it just up and leave with one of their own," Cody said.

Demetrius had to agree with Cody as he watched the other two gators swim past and under the tower toward the monster. Behind them swam three others, all five quickly closing on the swamp monster. These five ignored the flailing alligator and focused instead on its captor. Two attacked from the front, one on each leg. The monster staggered, and the alligator it had been dragging broke free from its grip.

"Alligators aren't pack hunters, are they?" Demetrius said.

"Maybe they are if the threat is big enough," Amelia said in a quiet voice.

"This, my friends, is karma in action," Cody said. "That thing has been feeding on alligators for weeks, at least."

"And the gators are mad as hell and aren't going to take it anymore," Demetrius said.

Amelia looked down at Demetrius. "Do you think this

would be a good time for us to climb down and head for those buildings?"

Demetrius watched the alligators circle the monster as it turned in place, trying to grab them. The gators bit and tore at the monster's legs, tearing off pieces of moss and bark that floated away.

"Probably a good idea," Demetrius said.

He descended the ladder, but before he set foot into the water, he looked around the area for any straggler alligators. The coast was clear, and he stepped off the last rung. Across the clearing, the monster stumbled and went down to one knee in the middle of the alligators.

"Come on, we have to go," Demetrius said in a low voice as he helped Amelia off the ladder. "Go that way."

She started wading toward the trees, and he remained by the ladder as Cody descended, his attention on the battle a dozen yards away. An alligator came up out of the water and grabbed the monster's left arm in its powerful jaws, tearing it off at the shoulder. The monster roared in pain as it struck at them with its remaining arm.

Cody stood beside Demetrius to watch for a moment. "Not much longer now."

"No, probably not," Demetrius said.

"Won't be much left in the way of proof for our story."

Demetrius shared a sad smile with him. "Just like our other paranormal cases."

"No proof, and yet we keep getting pulled into them."

The monster lost its other arm and fell to both knees. It screamed at the sky until a large gator grabbed the upper portion of its chest and dragged it under. The water splashed and churned with the struggle, and they lost sight of the swamp monster for good.

"Hey, lollygaggers," Amelia called from the tree line. "Let's go!"

"Yeah, we'd better get out of here before those gators realize he's just tree and moss," Cody said, tugging on the sleeve of Demetrius's T-shirt.

Cody headed toward Amelia and Demetrius followed. He looked over his shoulder in time to see the swamp monster's head bob up and down in the water, both eyes now dark. With a shudder, he focused his attention on where he was stepping and followed Amelia and Cody into the trees, headed toward civilization.

CHAPTER TWENTY-ONE

Over an hour later, Demetrius finally saw buildings through the trees. His relief was followed quickly by exhaustion and a deep desire to check on his parents and explain what they had experienced. After that, he was going to take the longest shower of his life and try to get some sleep.

"I see buildings," Amelia said. She was following Demetrius, being careful to step where he stepped in the calf-deep water left by the storm. "Thank God."

"You didn't enjoy our little nature walk?" Cody said from where he brought up the rear.

"Not a bit. I prefer to ride out tropical storms indoors."

Demetrius stopped and turned to face them. "I think we need to discuss what we're going to tell the police."

Amelia and Cody looked at each other, then back at him. Cody said, "Were you thinking of telling the nice, level-headed members of the local police force that Amelia was carried off by a swamp monster and we tracked it down, rescued her, and then we watched it get torn apart by alligators?"

Demetrius grinned. "Well, when you say it like that..."

"We have to tell them about the skeletons we found," Amelia said. "Those people have families who are missing them and need closure. And the victims deserve to be laid to rest."

Cody put his arm around Amelia and pulled her up against his side in a hug. "I know I stink, but I have to hug you right now."

"You don't smell any worse than I do," Amelia said, putting her arm around his waist and hugging him back. She looked at Demetrius with tears in her eyes. "If it weren't for you boys, I would have ended up on that pile of bones as well."

Demetrius put his hands on his hips and dropped his gaze as he fought back tears. But then Amelia and Cody both pulled him in close for a three-way hug, and Demetrius couldn't hold back. A quiet sob slipped out, and tears ran down his face as he rested his head against Amelia's.

"I thought we'd lost you," Demetrius said. "That would have killed me."

"Would have killed both of us," Cody added.

"Oh sycamore trees, now you've got me crying," Amelia said, and all three of them laughed.

Demetrius pulled her in for a tight hug. "I love you." Saying those three words brought back the memory of Cody looking at him and saying the same thing before the swamp monster pulled him away. Demetrius still had no idea what to do about that, so he pushed the memory down along with the very carnal and complicated feelings that came along with it.

"So what's our story then?" Cody said.

Demetrius released Amelia and wiped away tears as he considered their options. "Alligators?"

"Alligators kidnapped Amelia from out of your parents' back yard?"

"Oh yeah, I forgot that part." Demetrius sighed. "Escaped convict?"

"I would think they could check on something like that," Amelia said. "How about a strange man came into the yard, hit Demetrius and carried me into the Everglades. He tied me up on that island, but then was eaten by an alligator just before you two tracked us down."

Demetrius looked at Cody who shrugged and nodded. "Works for me."

"We always seem to lose credit for the really big jobs," Demetrius said.

"And you keep finding these weird and dangerous cases," Amelia said. "How about just a raccoon removal or a squirrel situation?"

"From your lips to God's ear," Cody said. "Okay, so a stranger we can't describe took Amelia off into the swamp. He tied her up and then became an alligator's brunch. We found Amelia along with the alligator feeding ground where, hopefully, they'll be able to identify all of the bodies."

"There were so many bones," Demetrius said as he thought back on the remains that littered the ground near the monster's island hideaway. "I wonder why it tied you both up on the island first."

"Maybe it wasn't hungry yet?" Cody offered. "Or it was going to use us to lure alligators to it?"

"I'm not asking questions," Amelia said and clutched her hands together. "I'm just glad that's how it happened."

Demetrius nodded. "Me too. Let's get moving. The sooner we get there, the sooner we can check on my parents and get cleaned up."

They set off in a single file once again with Demetrius in the lead. It wasn't long until they finally stepped up onto a grassy berm that ran the length of a fence. Tree limbs, palm leaves, patio furniture, garbage cans, and other items lay scattered about the yards. In one yard, a tree had blown down and crushed the wire fence beneath it.

"Let's see if we can get to the street through that yard," Demetrius said. "It'll probably be easier to figure out where we're at from out on the street."

They carefully crossed the ruined fence and stepped around the uprooted tree. The condo and yard had been neatly maintained before the storm, but Demetrius saw the owner would have a lot of repair work ahead. Shingles had been peeled off the roof, and a tree branch had been blown through a window.

"Oh, my," Amelia said. "I hope your father's okay."

"Think they would have evacuated your Mom?" Cody said.

A cold pit opened up in Demetrius's stomach. "No idea. Come on, let's go."

It took both Cody and Demetrius to force the wooden privacy gate open so they could access the street. Cars moved slowly along the road, weaving in and out of debris that lay scattered around. A police car pulled up, and the officer behind the wheel looked at them.

"You folks okay?"

"Not really," Amelia said. "We need to make a police report."

The driver exchanged a look with his partner, then pulled the patrol car as far as he could to the side of the road. The light bar on top of his car flashed into life before both men stepped out.

"What happened?" the driver asked.

IT TOOK over an hour for them to explain it all. By the time they had finished, Demetrius felt as if he might fall asleep on his feet. The officer looked up his parents' address and had them all squeeze into the backseat with Amelia in the middle. The radio squelched continuously as units reported in, each sound sending a needle of pain deeper into Demetrius's brain.

"I love that song," Cody whispered over the top of Amelia's head.

Demetrius couldn't help a smile. Cody had always been beside him, ready to help distract Demetrius from life's challenges. What would he ever do without him? Hopefully, he'd never have to find that out.

He was glad to see that his parents' condo had only minor damage. One of the windows was broken, a few shingles were missing, but the roof was intact and the walls were still standing. Demetrius climbed out of the back of the police car and then turned to help Amelia out.

"You need to stay in town for a few days," the policeman said. "All three of you. We'll need your help finding that place in the 'glades to recover the bodies."

"We'll help if we can," Demetrius said. "The storm got us pretty much turned around out there."

"That's fine," the cop said. "We're pretty busy now with the storm clean-up, but we'll need a formal statement later. Don't leave town."

They watched him drive off, and then they turned as a group toward the condo. To Demetrius, the last few yards they needed to walk up the driveway to get to the garage seemed like miles.

"Carry me," Cody said in a low, quiet voice.

"Come on, you two." Amelia linked arms with each of them and, with a little effort, got them to move.

As they approached the garage, Marshall Singleton opened the front door of the condo and stepped out on the porch.

"Demetrius!"

"Dad!"

Demetrius shifted their trajectory and met his father halfway between the driveway and the door. Marshall grabbed him in a strong hug, and Demetrius closed his eyes, savoring the moment. His father held him longer than he ever had before, and when Demetrius finally pulled away, he saw tears in his father's eyes. The sight made his own eyes burn with tears, and he put his hands on his father's shoulders.

"We're okay," Demetrius said. "We're all okay."

"I was so worried," Marshall said. He gathered Amelia close, then shifted his attention to Cody, reaching up to give him a tight hug. "You all went missing, and then the storm came in, and the hospital called — "

"Hospital? Is Mom okay?"

"She's fine. They just wanted to let me know they were taking her to a lower floor and pushing her surgery off another day."

"So she hasn't had surgery yet?"

"Tomorrow."

"Oh, good, we didn't miss it," Amelia said. She took Marshall's hand and gave him a gentle smile. "Marshall dear, it's so good to see you again. But we are dead on our feet and need to get cleaned up. May we go inside?"

"Of course! I'm sorry, I was just so excited to see you all. Come in, come in."

"We're pretty dirty," Cody said. "We can go in through the garage."

"No worries, Cody. I had police and neighbors traipsing in and out while you three were gone. The house will need to be cleaned top to bottom anyway. Come on in. All of the units here in East Glades Bayou came with whole house natural gas stand-by generators, so we've all got power." He grinned as he held the door open for them. "I bet those suckers in Palm

Oasis are wishing they'd decided to pay the extra one hundred dollars a month now. Cheap bastards. Anyway, you all clean up and get changed and then tell me everything over dinner."

Demetrius exchanged a look with Cody and gave him a small shrug. His father wanted to know the truth. Maybe they should tell him so he would know to keep an eye out in case another swamp monster started making the rounds.

But first he wanted to get a shower and put on some clean clothes. He would probably need to buy a new pair of shoes, too. He didn't think his shoes would ever dry out. When he stepped into the air conditioning of his parents' condo, Demetrius stopped to let out a grateful sigh.

"Amelia, you can use the shower in the master bedroom," Marshall said over his shoulder as he hurried past them into the kitchen and returned with three garbage bags. "Put your shoes in these, and then the rest of your clothes. I'll set them out in the garage and we'll wash them later. Demetrius, you and Cody can take turns in the hall bathroom."

"Flip you for first dibs," Cody said.

"Deal."

He squawked in alarm when Cody bent down to grab him around the waist and lift him off the ground. Cody tipped him sideways, forcing Demetrius to brace himself on Cody's strong thigh.

"Cody! Put me down! What are you doing?"

"I'm flipping you."

Demetrius pinched his thigh, and Cody let out a combination shout and laugh before setting Demetrius back on his feet. Cody stood grinning down at him, and Demetrius couldn't help smiling back. He saw Amelia exchange a look with his father, both of them shaking their heads, but he didn't care.

"Guess I win, huh?"

"You win," Demetrius said. "Like usual."

"Oh, that's up for debate," Cody said with a laugh, and then he leaned down to untie his mud-caked shoes.

Demetrius automatically checked out the curve of Cody's ass, and he forced himself to look away as he removed his own shoes. They had a lot to get through this week, but he and Cody were going to have to have a long conversation, and soon. He just had no idea where to even begin with something that important. Would it be something along the lines of, "So, Cody, back when the swamp monster and I were playing tug of war with you, and it was about to win, you said you loved me. Can you expand on that, please?"

A quiet laugh snuck up on him, which sounded more like a snort once it came out. Cody grinned at him.

"Did you just snort?"

"No," Demetrius said and looked away from him.

"Okay, Snorter McSnortington." Cody grimaced as he pulled off his T-shirt. Scratches left by the monster's twig claws looked red against his skin, but Demetrius was glad to see they had scabbed over.

"Good Lord, Cody," Marshall said. "What happened to you?"

"That is part of our long and involved story. Demmy, think you can play nurse this time?"

"Yeah, of course." Demetrius thought about Cody tending to the scrape on his own back. Had that just been a few days ago? He could almost feel Cody's gentle touch, still hear the concern in his voice.

"I'll try not to use up all the hot water." Cody winked before he walked down the hall, the garbage bag he carried crinkling with each step.

"Well, I'm not making any promises like that," Amelia said with a firm nod. "I just might use up all the hot water."

Demetrius and Marshall both laughed.

"You go ahead and do that if you want, aunt Amelia," Demetrius said. "You've earned it."

She walked away along the hall, carrying her own garbage bag.

"How about a drink?" his father said.

"I don't even know what time it is."

"It's almost noon."

"We were out there that long?" Demetrius said.

"You can see why I was so worried."

"Yeah, you and me both." Demetrius dropped his shoes into the garbage bag and nodded to his father. "I think a drink would be just the right medicine."

Marshall put an arm around Demetrius's shoulder and directed him toward the kitchen. "Come on, let your old man buy you a nice, smooth scotch." He looked down at his muddy and torn clothing. "And I'll get another garbage bag for you to sit on."

"Do you have a bag of rice?"

"You hungry?"

"Well, yes, but not for rice." He pulled his unresponsive phone from his pocket. "I need to try to dry this thing out."

"You just sit down and relax," Marshall said. "I'll take care of everything."

Demetrius sighed as he sat on the garbage bag his father spread over a kitchen chair. It felt good to hand everything off to someone else for a bit. Even if it might not last more than an hour, his brain needed the break.

CHAPTER TWENTY-TWO

Demetrius sipped his scotch and watched the news while he waited for his turn in the shower. News reports were, of course, filled with storm stories. The tropical storm had roared ashore with near hurricane force winds. Although it wasn't technically a hurricane, it did cause widespread power outages and travel delays.

Once they had all showered, the four of them sat in the living room. Demetrius, Cody, and Amelia explained everything that had happened, and Marshall's eyes kept growing wider and wider. Finally, he looked at Demetrius and said in a quiet voice, "This is all true?"

Demetrius nodded. "All of it. And that's just what's happened to us down here."

"What do you mean? What else have you boys gotten involved in?"

Between the two of them, Demetrius and Cody told Marshall about Arnold Klemper, the wolf man of Parson's Pines nursing home. Then they explained about the possible chupacabra they'd tracked down, only to discover it was actually a dog that had been used for medical drug testing.

But those same drugs had turned a steroid shooting local farmer into a raging monster.

"My God," Marshall said once they had finished. "And now a swamp monster?"

"Only we're not telling the police it was a swamp monster," Cody said.

"You're going to lie to the authorities?"

"That's right," Demetrius said. "Because we don't want to end up having to take psych tests."

"There's no evidence left anyway," Amelia added. "Those alligators tore the monster apart. We watched it happen."

"Just rewards," Cody said.

Amelia nodded, her lips pressed tight together. "You've got that right, Cody." She looked at Marshall. "That thing was planning to eat Cody and me. We would have ended up just another bunch of bones scattered on its refuse pile."

"And it's been living out there this whole time?" Marshall said.

Demetrius shrugged. "We're not sure."

"It might have been living deeper in the Everglades," Cody said. "Since Hubert said the alligators just recently started showing up in the pools around here, the swamp monster may have migrated to this area due to lack of food where it used to live."

"And you're sure Hubert is...?" Marshall's voice trailed off and he made a face.

"Most likely," Demetrius said. "We didn't see him out there, but there are a lot of bodies. A lot."

"All of those missing persons? Did they become food for it, too?"

"Probably," Demetrius said.

Marshall shook his head. "How awful."

Marshall decided to give them all some time to rest and visit Olivia in the hospital.

"I didn't tell her you all went missing," Marshall explained as he packed a bag with magazines, bottles of water, and granola bars.

"We understand," Demetrius said. "Give her my love and tell her I'll be there tomorrow."

"We'll all be there tomorrow," Cody added.

Marshall hugged them each in turn. He said to Amelia as he gathered up the handles of the reusable shopping bag, "Why don't you sleep in our bed, Amelia? It's much more comfortable than that couch. I just put fresh sheets on this morning, so it's perfectly clean."

"Thank you, Marshall. I think I'll take you up on that offer."

He grabbed his wallet and keys and headed toward the door. With one hand on the knob, he looked back at Demetrius again and gave him a sad smile before he left. Amelia yawned, lifted her hand in a wave, and walked along the hall to the master bedroom where she closed the door.

"I don't know about you, but if I don't lie down soon, I'm going to fall down," Cody said.

Demetrius nodded. "Right behind you."

He followed Cody into the guest room. Sleepiness had shifted quickly into exhaustion toward the end of their discussion with his father. The skin around his eyes felt tight, and his thoughts were bouncing between subjects. For now he pushed aside all thoughts and concerns about his and Cody's relationship. That could wait until later. He stripped down to his underwear, eased his aching body under the covers, and closed his eyes.

IT WAS dark when Demetrius awoke. He was confused about where he was and what had happened. Someone was breathing slow and deep nearby, but he couldn't come up with a name. Something buzzed from across the room. It had to be a cell phone, and Demetrius rolled over to check the nightstand. No phone on his side of it, but one was near the other bed.

Clarity returned. He rolled onto his back and stared up at the ceiling as the memories slowly came back. His phone was water-logged, and he'd left it in a bowl of rice before getting in bed. He would most likely need a new one. Outside the bedroom door, he heard someone walk past and decided to get up. Now that he was more awake, he realized he really needed to pee.

He got dressed in the dark and slipped out of the bedroom, headed to the hall bathroom. After peeing for what felt like hours, he shuffled along the hall to the living room, yawning and stretching. His father sat at the table in the dining room between the kitchen and living room, looking down at a long receipt.

"Hi Dad," Demetrius said.

Marshall smiled. "You're up. I wondered if you would sleep through the night."

"Feel like I could. What time is it?"

"Midnight."

"We slept for almost eleven hours?"

"Amelia's still sound asleep," Marshall said and gestured to the sofa. "I was going to sleep out here tonight."

"Cody's still sleeping, too." Demetrius sat at the table. "What's that?"

"A receipt from the mobile phone store," Marshall said. He picked a bag up from the floor and placed it before Demetrius. "I replaced your phone. You like iPhones, right?"

Demetrius blinked in surprise. "Dad, you didn't have to do that."

"I know that, but I wanted to do it. You came down here to

help out your mother and me, all three of you. And look what you got mixed up in. I know Cody and Amelia both left their phones here, but I got them new ones as well."

"I don't know what to say." Demetrius reached into the bag and pulled out the phone still inside the box. "Thank you. I really appreciate it."

"There's no plastic because I had the girl at the store open it and get it ready to go," Marshall said. "What do they call that?"

"Activate it?"

"Right, that's it. She activated it for me. I have all of your numbers in my contact list so I just went ahead and activated them all." Marshall smiled. "I figured you all wouldn't mind since they're the latest models. Oh, yours is that silver color, Cody's is black, and Amelia's is something new. Rose gold, I think they call it."

Demetrius opened the box. The new phone gleamed up at him.

"I'm really kind of overwhelmed," Demetrius said. "You spent a lot of money."

"Well, it's nothing compared to what you and Cody have been through in less than a year." Marshall took Demetrius's hand across the table and looked him in the eye. "You have always been your mother's and my proudest accomplishment. But after everything you've told me, everything you lived through last night, I am amazed and overwhelmed myself at your courage and devotion. Not only to your mother and me, but to Amelia and Cody as well. You have grown into a brave and loving man with a generous heart, and I wanted to do something generous for you in return."

Tears ran freely down Demetrius's face. When his father had finished speaking, Demetrius got up, and Marshall hugged him tight.

"Thank you for saying all of that," Demetrius said against his father's shoulder. "That means so much to me."

"I love you, son."

"I love you, too."

"Everything okay out here?" Cody asked.

Demetrius stepped back from his father and wiped his eyes before he turned to see Cody standing at the hallway entrance.

"Everything's great, Cody," Marshall said. "Come over here. I have something for you."

"Yeah? I hope it's a new phone, because it seems like mine suddenly decided to up and die on me."

Demetrius laughed along with his father, and he thought a laugh had never felt so good.

———

DEMETRIUS SLUMPED LOWER in the waiting room chair and forced himself to keep his gaze on the shiny new phone. Amelia sat beside him, similarly held rapt by her own mobile phone, and Cody sat on her right. His father paced in front of them. When they had arrived early that morning, the surgical waiting room of Coastal Waters Memorial Hospital had already been full of family members and friends waiting for word on their own loved ones. The only open chairs were situated directly beneath the flat screen TV mounted in a corner. Now Demetrius felt like everyone in the room was staring at him while they watched TV, hence his fascination with his new phone.

"What the ever-loving fuck?" Cody said.

Demetrius could practically *feel* an inaudible gasp from the people around them.

"You need to learn the names of some trees," Amelia said.

Cody looked up and Demetrius saw his cheeks turn a

little pink. "Sorry everyone." He leaned across Amelia to whisper to Demetrius. "I just got a bunch of voice mails and text alerts, like just now."

Marshall paused his pacing in front of Cody. "Oh, the girl at the phone shop said that might happen. Something about the network taking a while to send the alerts to the new phone."

Cody smiled at him. "Great. Thanks, Marshall."

Marshall resumed his pacing and Cody looked at Demetrius then jerked his head toward the door. "Care to go down to the cafeteria and get some beverages?"

"I'm fine," Marshall said. "Oh, do you need money?"

"We're all set, Dad," Demetrius assured him. "Do you want anything, Amelia?"

"If you could bring me back a large coffee with two sugars, I'd be very appreciative."

Amelia grabbed Marshall's hand as he was passing her and pulled him down into a chair. "Sit down, Marshall. For the love of sassafras, you're making all of us a nervous wreck."

Chuckles from the other people in the waiting room made Demetrius feel a bit of relief. Amelia seemed to have smoothed over any agitation Cody may have caused with his outburst. He followed Cody into the hall, bumping into him when he stopped fast.

"These are all messages from Jugs," Cody said.

"Jugs?"

"Darnell Perramon, from Harriettville High," Cody said. "He's the one who's been handling Critter Catcher jobs while we've been down here."

"Right, okay, I remember now. What do they say?"

"The text messages are all about that animal under Abigail Barcelona's house."

"That older woman who has the hots for you?"

Cody glared.

"What?"

"Anyway... Apparently, that animal came back."

"And? Did he catch it?"

"He did. Guess what it is?"

"A big rat?"

"Nope. A Yorkie."

Demetrius lifted his eyebrows. "That thing was a Yorkie?"

Cody nodded. "It was. And Jugs took it to a groomer and is keeping it."

"Well, perfect," Demetrius said. "It's a happy ending."

"Yeah, for that case," Cody said. "But he's left nine voicemails."

"Listen to them while we walk to the cafeteria, come on."

The messages from Jugs covered a wide range of questions, from where they kept any extra coffee to how exactly he was supposed to remove bats from an old man's attic. They discussed how to answer Jugs's questions as they waited in line to buy coffees. Demetrius left Cody in the cafeteria with the phone to his ear and a large cup of coffee steaming before him. He returned to the waiting room and sat in Cody's seat before handing Amelia her coffee.

"Where's Cody?" Marshall said.

"Returning a call to the guy who's managing our business back home."

"Everything okay?"

"Better than it was down here," Demetrius said. "Cody will be up in a little while."

Demetrius noticed a number of people had left while he and Cody had been gone, and he hoped that meant his mother would be out of surgery soon. As if summoned by that thought, his mother's surgeon, Dr. Ralston, stepped into the waiting room and paused just inside the door to look around.

"Dad," Demetrius said.

They all stood up and Dr. Ralston smiled.

"She's doing great," Dr. Ralston said. "Let's go to a consultation room."

"She did well?" Marshall said as he followed the surgeon down the hall to a small room that held a round table and a number of chairs.

"She did better than well. Sit down, let's talk."

As Demetrius listened, his shoulders lowered and muscles relaxed. The surgeon was extremely pleased with how the surgery had gone and even suggested his mother could be released in less than a week.

"Wow," Demetrius said.

Dr. Ralston nodded to him. "Wow, indeed."

"When can we see her?" Amelia said.

"Maybe another hour or so. Stay in the waiting room and a nurse will come to take you to see her."

Relief mixed with exhaustion left Demetrius stunned. A buzzing had started inside his head, and he wanted to both go out to celebrate and lay down for a long nap. They met up with Cody in the hall and passed on the good news. His smile was broad and bright, and he pulled Demetrius into a strong hug.

"This news has made the trip worth it," Cody said.

"I know," Demetrius said. He had his eyes closed and couldn't help savoring the feel of Cody's strong arms around him.

CHAPTER TWENTY-THREE

"Are you really sure you won't need your car until we get home?" Demetrius said.

Amelia smiled and shook her head. "For the fifty-seventh time, Demetrius, I will be fine without a car until you and Cody drive it back to Parson's Hollow. It will only be a few days."

"She'll be fine, Demmy," Cody called from his spot behind the wheel of Amelia's late model Explorer. "Hug her again and let's go. This cop is giving me the stink eye."

Demetrius waved at Cody without looking at him and said to Amelia, "Text me when you land, okay?"

"You're starting to sound like your mother now." Amelia pulled him in for a strong, tight hug. "I love you, my dear boy. So very much."

He blinked back tears and whispered, "I love you, too. Safe flight."

Amelia pulled back and smiled at him. "You and Cody take your time driving home. Otis is excited to be picking me up at the airport and chauffeuring me around for the next few days."

"Sounds like you and Otis are getting serious," Demetrius said.

"Oh, do you want to discuss the potential seriousness of our current relationships?" Amelia said with a sassy twinkle in her eye. Her voice was too low for Cody to hear, but Demetrius's pulse raced anxiously. He wasn't ready to get into that conversation with Cody just yet, and he definitely was not ready to discuss anything about him and Cody with anyone else.

"It's not the same, and you know it," Demetrius whispered.

"Isn't it?" She kissed him on the cheek, bent down to give Cody a finger wave through the passenger window, then grabbed the handle of her suitcase and headed for the airport entrance.

"Come on, let's go before they think we're terrorists," Cody called.

Demetrius got into the passenger seat and buckled up. Cody was distracted watching for a break in traffic so he could pull out, and Demetrius took the opportunity to look him over. Same old Cody as before, with the same square jaw, dark stubble, and tousled dark hair. But something was different now. For some reason there was a tension between them. It was almost as if they'd had a disagreement of some kind even though neither of them had said a cross word. Demetrius had no idea how to go about lancing whatever the tension might be in order to clear out the gunk.

Well, he knew what the tension was, of course, but neither of them seemed in a particular hurry to broach the subject. Under extreme duress out in the Everglades, Cody had told Demetrius he loved him. Whether or not that was on a friend level, Demetrius had noticed Cody's behavior had changed over the last few months. He hadn't been on any dates, at least none he had told Demetrius about, and

Cody was an over-sharer in the worst possible way. And Demetrius had also noticed Cody acted differently around him. Where they'd always been comfortable together, Cody now seemed nervous in Demetrius's presence. And in some instances, he'd gone a bit too far and acted more than a little over-familiar. There no longer seemed to be a happy medium.

"Here we go," Cody said, and pulled out into the flow of traffic. "Finally."

"Good thing the storm hadn't damaged the airport," Demetrius said.

"We all got lucky."

"That we did."

Silence descended, and Demetrius watched the buildings go by outside his window.

"You've been quiet the last couple of days," Cody said.

"Oh?" Demetrius looked over at him.

"Not like you're mad at me or anything, just quiet." He gave him a quick smile. "You doing all right after everything that's happened?"

When Demetrius thought about it, he couldn't believe everything that had happened in the last two weeks. His mother's surgery and, two days ago, her return home. Helping his father interview and hire an in home caregiver to assist them a few times a week. Accompanying the police deep into the Everglades and, surprisingly, actually being able to direct them to the swamp monster's feeding ground. All in all, eighteen people and thirty-eight alligator remains had been recovered.

Hubert Potts's body had been among those found at the scene. Marshall had gone to the Potts's condo to pay his respects and said Hubert's wife, Eunice, didn't seem very upset about her husband's fate. Demetrius and Cody had seen her cruising down the street in a golf cart, dressed in a black track suit. She'd honked a ridiculous sounding horn and waved as she flashed a big smile.

The scratches on Cody's shoulders were well on the way to healing, as was the scrape on Demetrius's back from Abigail Barcelona's crawlspace. They were physically healing, but Demetrius wasn't so sure about the mental part of things. That would take more time.

With all that had happened in such a short amount of time, a lot seemed to be left undone. And all of that centered around what might lie at the core of his and Cody's relationship. But he wasn't ready to discuss that yet. He wasn't sure he'd ever be ready.

"Yeah, I'm doing okay. How about you?"

"Weird dreams a few times," Cody said. He moved his shoulders around. "The scratches feel better, that's for sure."

"Good."

Cody was quiet for a time, then said, "I still see it coming after me sometimes."

"Yeah? I do, too."

"The sounds are the worst part," Cody said. "I'll hear them, like really soft or something, you know, like maybe it's a real sound or maybe just my imagination. The squelch of the mud under its big feet. The roar it made. The sound of its stick fingers clicking together. It's happened a few times right as I'm about to fall asleep, and then my heart starts pounding and I lie awake for a while until I can finally nod off."

"It's like PTSD. You went through a lot."

"All three of us did."

"True."

Cody looked over and held his gaze a moment, finally turning his attention back to the road. Demetrius's brain felt scrambled, and all he could think to do was look out the window and say nothing. He had no idea what to say or how to say it or if he should suddenly decide to say anything at all. But if something was between him and Cody, and they never talked about it and never found out what it was or how deep it ran, would either of them be happy with someone else?

Demetrius rolled his eyes at the palm trees and buildings rushing past outside his window. What the hell was he doing even contemplating any of this? Cody was absolutely, unabashedly straight. He was just an emotive and demonstrative person when it came to the people he loved. And Demetrius knew Cody loved him; but as a friend and nothing more.

Even though he would never forget the sight of Cody masturbating in the guest room, he had to realize they would never be physically intimate with each other. Cody was his best friend — emphasis on *friend* — and the sooner Demetrius got that through his obviously love-starved brain, the better off things would be for the both of them.

"Sure you want to leave tomorrow morning?" Cody said. "We could stay another day or two."

"I think it's time we got back," Demetrius said. "Clark will be really helpful for Mom and Dad. He's got a lot of good references and training."

"Yeah, he was like the star pupil of all those interviews," Cody said.

"He was. Knowing he'll be stopping by three times a week makes me feel better about leaving. And we need to get back and get to work again. Jugs has been helpful, but, you know, I kind of miss it."

Cody snickered. "I'm going to remind you of that when we're crawling through mud and spiders and animal shit to pull some hissing raccoon out of someone's crawl space."

"You make it sound so glamorous," Demetrius said, and they both laughed.

For the rest of the drive back to the condo, they talked

about the business and ideas for future marketing. Cody brought up some previous clients they could ask to provide references, and Demetrius made notes using an app on his new phone. For the remainder of the drive, he didn't once ponder what Cody might be thinking or feeling or expecting. Instead, it was like old times, and it felt good.

His father was busy in the kitchen when they arrived, and dinner was almost ready. His mother was setting the table, and her smile was big and bright.

"There are my two handsome young men," Olivia said. "Ready for a good dinner?"

"I'm always ready," Cody said. "Let me wash up, and I'll help you out."

Olivia shook her head. "No help needed, Cody. Table's set and Marshall's almost finished with dinner. You boys clean up and open the wine."

"You're having wine?" Demetrius said.

Olivia shared a smile with Cody. "He's so protective."

Cody was still smiling as he looked at Demetrius. "Yeah, he is. You and Marshall did a good job."

Marshall entered the dining room with a bottle of wine and a corkscrew. "Actually, the surgeon told us a glass or two of wine a week has been shown to be beneficial following a bypass."

Demetrius and Cody washed up and joined the Singletons at the table. Marshall had broiled albacore tuna steaks and steamed rice and vegetables. The Riesling was a perfect pairing for the meal, and the conversation was easy and comfortable. Afterwards, Demetrius and Cody cleaned up the dishes then joined his parents in the living room to watch some television. Olivia nodded off in her recliner, and Marshall soon followed in his own. Demetrius and Cody smiled at each other where they sat on opposite ends of the couch.

"Think we should get them tucked in?" Cody said.

Demetrius nodded. "Yeah, then we can pack and get ready for the morning."

They gently woke Marshall and Olivia and escorted them to the master bedroom. Once his parents had brushed their teeth and changed into pajamas, Demetrius kissed them each on the cheek and switched off the light before closing the door behind him.

"They grow up so fast," Cody said and dabbed away imaginary tears.

"The role reversal is strange," Demetrius said. "I've read about this online, when a child becomes a caretaker, but it's really weird when it happens to you."

"Mine are probably going to live forever out there on that commune in Arizona."

"It's not a commune," Demetrius said with a laugh. He paused and looked over at Cody. "Is it?"

Cody shrugged as he folded a T-shirt. "From the descriptions I've heard, it sounds pretty commune-like to me."

"But your parents are in their fifties, aren't they?"

"They both turned fifty-eight this year," Cody said, giving him a tight smile. "And I don't want to talk about it. The less I think about my parents enjoying the art of free love, the happier I am."

"I see your point."

He had more to take home than he'd packed to bring with him, thanks to his father. Marshall had taken them all to the mall one night while Olivia was still in the hospital. He'd paid for dinner in the food court and bought each of the three of them two new pairs of shoes. They had protested as a group, but Marshall had insisted, pointing out all they had been through. He'd threatened to just buy them shoes online and have them delivered, and so they each gave in and picked out a pair of athletic shoes. Marshall had urged them to find a pair of casual dress shoes, claiming they all needed to be ready to attend a more formal function if required.

"Your dad really went all out on the thank you gifts," Cody said. "New phone, new clothes, and new shoes. We should come visit them more often."

"Or ask him for investment advice."

Cody laughed. "Leave it to you to take something fun like someone buying you gifts and turn it into a concern over money."

Demetrius shrugged as he packed away one of the new shirts his father had purchased. They were finished a short time later and decided to call it a night.

"What time did you want to hit the road tomorrow?" Cody asked after a jaw-stretching yawn.

"Let's wait until the morning rush hour is over," Demetrius said as he got into bed.

"Fine by me. You take first shift behind the wheel." Cody got into bed as well then switched off the lamp. "Good night, Lucy."

Demetrius chuckled. "Good night, Ricky."

It was just after ten p.m., and he didn't think he'd be able to fall asleep so early. Minutes later, however, he'd drifted off and right into a dream that he was driving Amelia's Explorer with Cody in the passenger seat. Something kept shifting in the back end, however, and he adjusted the rear view mirror to check the back seat. The glowing green eyes of the swamp monster filled the mirror and startled Demetrius awake. He laid very still on his side as his pounding heart slowed to a more normal pace, and he listened to Cody breathing heavily across the room.

He slipped quietly out of bed and left the room, being careful not to make any loud noises. A drink from the filtered water in the kitchen helped settle his nerves a bit. On his way back to the guest room, he was walking through the darkened living room and almost shouted when he saw someone sitting in his mother's recliner.

"It's just me, dear," his mother said. "I didn't say anything because I didn't want to scare you."

"Holy crap, Mom, you nearly killed me," Demetrius said with a hand on his chest. "Why are you up? Are you feeling okay?"

"Oh, I'm fine. The doctor said I may have some sleepless nights. What a time for a doctor to be right."

Demetrius chuckled as he sat in his father's recliner on the other side of an end table from her. "Cody and I are going to wait for rush hour traffic to clear out before we leave."

"I'm really glad you came down, Demetrius. You made your father feel so much better."

"Of course I would come down. And hopefully I made you feel a little better, too."

"Well, of course," Olivia said. "You always make me feel good."

They fell silent and sat in the dark for a time without saying anything. Demetrius was about to wish her a good night and return to bed when Olivia spoke again.

"There seems to be something strained between you and Cody. Everything okay with you two?"

Demetrius rolled his eyes. If one more person asked about their relationship, he might have to lose his temper. He kept his cool and said, "We're fine. It was a long week, what with the storm and Amelia getting taken and all."

In light of her heart condition, they'd told his mother the same story they'd told the police.

"I understand that part of it, but there seems to be something more. Cody watches you when you're not looking, you know."

"He watches me?"

Olivia chuckled. "Not in a stalker kind of way. He just can't seem to stop looking at you."

Demetrius was glad the lights were off because he felt his cheeks heat up with a blush. "Well, we've been friends for a long time."

"You know what they say about friendship and love," Olivia said.

"Yes, but Cody is straight, Mom."

"What does that really mean?"

Demetrius sighed. "It means he likes to sleep with women. I don't have the right equipment."

"It might not be a question of equipment," Olivia said. "It might be more of a question of the heart."

"I don't know what that means."

"It means that many times the heart does not recognize gender when it falls in love."

"Where did you hear that? Are you watching Dr. Phil these days?"

"Let's just say I've learned a few things as I'm approaching my seventy-fifth birthday."

"Oh yeah? Anything you care to share, or is this something I don't need to know about?"

"Oh, nothing that would change your father's and my relationship," Olivia said. "So you don't have to worry about that. Just something I've come to understand after all these years."

"Seems to be quite the consensus these days," Demetrius grumbled.

"Oh?"

"Forget it," he said. "I'll keep what you've said in mind. But Cody and I are pretty good where we're at. We own a business together, and we're best friends. I would hate to lose all of that."

"Why would you have to lose any of that?" Olivia asked. "Why couldn't you add a loving romantic partner to that mix?

Someone who knows you better than anyone else on this planet."

Demetrius's stomach tightened, and he wondered if this were another crazy dream that just felt real. He pinched his thigh and decided he was really awake. This conversation truly was happening, as awkward and painful as it might be.

"I don't know what to tell you, Mom," he said. "I know you like Cody, and I know you think it would be easy for me to just settle down with him, but he has some say in all of this, too, you know?"

"Have you asked him?"

Demetrius gave a startled laugh. "Asked him? No. Like I said, he's straight, okay? He sleeps with women. I'm not going to risk alienating him by telling him I'm attracted to him."

"So you do find him attractive," Olivia said.

"What? No! Well, yes, I think he's attractive, of course I do. Everyone thinks Cody is attractive. I mean, animals and insects all think he's attractive. But he's straight."

"He could be bisexual."

Demetrius widened his eyes in the dark. "Now I know you've been watching too much daytime TV. He's straight. If he were bisexual, I think I would know."

"You could tell?" Olivia asked.

"No, that's not what I… He would have told me. I mean, I came out to him, so I would assume he would have done the same. Besides, even if he was interested in men, who's to say he'd be attracted to me? I'm not really his type. I don't watch sports, I don't work out as often as he does, I just… I'm not…"

"You're good enough to be his best friend, but you're not good enough to be his romantic partner? Seems like you're not giving Cody much credit."

Demetrius put his head in his hands. How had this happened? He'd just come out here for a drink of water to calm his mind after that crazy dream, and now here he was with his thoughts spinning like a tornado. And his mother, of all people, was the one stirring up all of his emotions.

"I will say it again, Mom," Demetrius said, drawing out his words. "Cody. Is. Not. Gay. Why are you being so insistent about this?"

"I want what every mother wants, for my son to find love and be happy," Olivia said. "And I don't think you're happy, Demetrius. Certainly you have a good business that you share with your best friend. But what about love? I just want you to find that person who will complement all of your good qualities and make you laugh and make you feel what it's like to be safe and comfortable and happy. And I want you to have that soon so you can enjoy it for as long as possible. Is that such a horrible thing?"

Demetrius shook his head and wiped away a sudden and surprising tear. "No. It's not a horrible thing. It's a very, very good thing. But Cody..."

"Isn't gay," Olivia interrupted. "Yes, you've been saying that. But things change, Demetrius. People change. I don't want you to feel I'm pushing you into something that's going to get you hurt, but I want you to be aware of how he acts around you. I want you to be open to the possibility that Cody has finally come to his senses and realized who he's supposed to be with, no matter who he's been with in the past."

"I'll keep it in mind," Demetrius said. "I just... I can't imagine it. I've always tried to keep my thoughts about Cody safely anchored in the friend zone, you know? I didn't want to be one of those guys who was creeping on my straight best friend." He shook his head and stared off into the darkness. "And what if he was open to it? What if we got a shot at being together, and it didn't work out? Not only would I have lost a chance at love, but I would probably lose my business and my best friend. I don't think I could live through that, you know?"

"But what if it all worked out?" Olivia said, her voice quiet and soothing in the darkness. "What if you found that special someone who made you feel alive and deeply loved and made you laugh harder than you ever thought you would? What if you couldn't go to sleep without his arm around you and you never had to? What if the sound of his voice still gives you chills fifty years from now? What if every time he looks at you, you're able to see just how much he loves you? What if all of that and more is waiting just on the other side of that bedroom door, and you never took the chance?"

A tightness in his chest made it difficult to breathe. When he thought about his future, tried to picture the man he would, hopefully, spend many years with, Demetrius had to admit he had a lot of the same qualities as Cody. Which made sense because he and Cody had such a strong bond and a rich history of private jokes and experiences. Of course Demetrius would want the same for a romantic relationship. But what if Cody were to become that romantic partner? Putting aside the gender-defined roles of attraction, what would happen if he and Cody were to take their relationship over that sharp boundary line and into unexplored territory? Could they make it work? Could Cody handle the stress of switching teams after batting for the other all his life? And how did he know Cody had never had a go at playing for Demetrius's team? He didn't know all the details about his dating life. Well, to be honest, Cody liked to over share with Demetrius, but what if he had kept a night or two secret? What if none of this mattered because Cody was just being his affectionate self these days and Demetrius had read too much into it?

Did that mean, however, that those closest to them had also read too much into things?

His thoughts tumbled and ricocheted faster than

Demetrius could keep track of. He had too many questions and suppositions and "what ifs" to decide anything at that moment. The only thing he knew with one hundred percent of his heart, mind, and soul, was that his relationship with Cody as it stood at that point in time, was far too important to him to risk fucking it up by trying to take it even one step farther. Demetrius did not think he could handle losing the friendship he had with Cody.

"I've given you a lot to think about," Olivia said. "I can practically hear those wheels turning in your head."

Demetrius smiled, and it felt out of place on his face, sad instead of happy. "He takes up so much space in my life, I'm terrified of losing him. My whole world would collapse if I lost his friendship."

"That's your fear talking," Olivia said. "Put that aside and trust your instincts. Cody is your best friend. You two have been through so much together. He drove all night to come down here and be by your side because he was worried about you. Have faith in the strength of the foundation you two already have and build on that."

Demetrius nodded and was surprised by his sudden tears. He wiped them away, glad for the darkness in the room so his mother wouldn't see him cry. A deep, quiet breath helped him steady his nerves and he got to his feet.

"I should get some sleep since we're going to be on the road all day tomorrow."

"I hope I didn't upset you, Demetrius. I just want so much for you to be happy. I want you to experience what I have with your father."

"I know. I just don't think it's that easy."

"Maybe it's not as hard as you're making it out to be, either."

Demetrius chuckled quietly. "You've always tried to build up my self-esteem, haven't you?"

"I'm your mother." She pulled him in for a strong hug and whispered in his ear, "I love you, and I know you'll do the best thing for the both of you." When she stepped back, she took his hand and squeezed it. "And in case you haven't figured it out by now, I wholeheartedly approve of Cody."

Demetrius laughed, and it sounded loud in the quiet condo. He dropped his voice to a whisper. "I'm glad I have your blessing."

"Always. Now go back to bed. Hopefully you can get some sleep."

"Same goes for you. You need to rest."

"I know, I'm going."

Demetrius walked with her as far as the door to the guest bedroom where he leaned in to kiss her cheek. "Goodnight, Mom."

"Goodnight."

Demetrius entered the guest bedroom and eased the door shut. He walked slowly and carefully to his bed, being careful not to stub his toe on the bed frame or the dresser. A glance at his phone made him grimace: 3:19 a.m. The first part of the drive home was going to be tough. But that was what coffee was for. And maybe Cody would volunteer to take the first shift.

Certain he wouldn't be able to get back to sleep after the conversation with his mother, Demetrius was surprised by a yawn. He plumped the pillow into shape, settled into place, and was out in minutes

CHAPTER TWENTY-FOUR

Cody volunteered to take the first driving shift even though he'd had less sleep than Demmy. He'd heard Demmy get up in the night and lay awake waiting for him to return. When he hadn't come back right away, Cody had gotten up to go check on him, but when he opened the bedroom door, he'd heard Demmy talking with Olivia in the living room. He intended to listen only for a minute to make sure everything was okay with Olivia, but when he realized he was the topic of conversation, Cody remained in the door and eavesdropped. He heard every word Olivia and Demetrius shared in the dark, and although he felt like a sneaky rat for doing it, the reality of everything that could spring from what he'd overheard exploded inside his mind.

Demmy wanted him.

That was the gist of it all. But more than that, Demmy was afraid of ruining what they had, and that made Cody feel better. Well, somewhat better. It helped to know he and Demmy were on the same page when it came to the possibility of something more between them.

When he heard Demmy stand up and bid Olivia goodnight, Cody had eased the door shut and hurried back to bed. He'd contemplated broaching the subject right as Demetrius got into bed but decided to hold off. They would have plenty of time alone together on the road to talk about things. And, besides, he needed to think about everything.

So Cody had lain in bed, his mind churning through all he'd overheard, and it kept him awake the rest of the night. He'd held his tongue that morning while they'd eaten break-fast, loaded the car, showered, brushed their teeth, and said their goodbyes. Marshall made them thick deli sandwiches, and Olivia handed them energy drinks for the road.

Marshall had slipped Cody a few twenties while he hugged him, and whispered in his ear, "Buy yourselves a good meal when you stop for the night."

Cody knew he was being more quiet than usual as he drove along I95. The truth of the matter was he wasn't just tired. He was still trying to figure out how and when to broach the all important subject of their relationship with Demmy. He knew the discussion would be long, but they had to have it sometime soon or it would just eat away at each of them.

He was fortunate that Demmy seemed tired and preoccu-pied as well, so he hadn't picked up on Cody's unusual silence. That wouldn't last because Demmy was observant, especially where Cody was concerned. It was, however, a comfortable silence. All their years of friendship surrounded them like an unseen security blanket. Cody didn't want to break that silence, especially with such a life-changing topic, so he decided to hold his tongue for as long as he could.

He had been raised in a loud, boisterous household where his emotive, hippie parents had encouraged him and his four brothers to talk about everything they felt. Cody knew he would need to be the one to broach the subject because Demmy was more of a hoarder when it came to his feelings.

And from what Cody had overheard in the dark, Demmy was terrified of things between them changing. Cody was afraid of that as well, but he was also more than a little interested to see where these new feelings took them.

They were just south of Jacksonville, Florida, about five hours into the drive, when Demmy surprised him.

"How are you doing over there?"

"Right as rain and twice as wet," Cody said.

Demmy laughed. "What the hell does that mean?"

Cody shrugged and gave him a smile. "No idea. I heard Grandma Felicia say it once or twice, and it made me laugh."

"Sounds dirty."

"Well, coming from Felicia, I'm sure that's how it was intended." Cody flashed him another smile, and they fell silent. Just when Cody was about to start, Demmy cleared his throat and spoke up.

"I think there's something we should talk about."

Cody swore his heart actually jumped. His mouth went dry, and his stomach tightened. He decided not to play dumb about it all, however. He gave Demmy as long a look as he could manage while driving, trying to pass encouragement on to him through his gaze.

"I think so, too."

"You do?"

"I do." Cody wanted to make sure to keep their conversation on track and said, "And it's not about the business or the crazy paranormal cases we get involved in, or your parents, my parents, or Amelia."

Demmy blew out a shaky breath and looked away out his window. "I know."

"Who's going to start?" Cody said.

"I will." Demmy took a moment to look at his hands clasped tight in his lap as he gathered his thoughts. Cody let the silence stretch out, giving Demmy the time he needed.

Just when Cody was afraid he'd have to nudge him along, Demmy started talking.

"We've been friends for a long time now."

"A lifetime."

Demmy smiled. "It feels that way. Anyway, I've noticed some things lately that have me a little confused."

"Me too," Cody assured him.

"Yeah?"

"Absolutely."

"Okay. Well, I don't know what to do about it."

Cody smiled but kept his eyes on the road. "And by "it" do you mean us becoming more than just friends?"

Demmy laughed nervously. "Just hearing you say it out loud like that freaks me out."

"Freaks you out in a good way or a bad way?"

"I don't know if it's good or bad," Demmy said. "It just freaks me out. The fact that we're sitting here about to talk about something that will completely alter our relationship makes me feel like I'm going to throw up."

"Well, just so you know, it's freaking me out, too. I never thought I'd be sitting here with my best friend — my *male* best friend — and talking about these deeper feelings I've been having for him."

"Cody..." Demmy stopped and shook his head as he stared out the windshield.

"All right, this isn't going to work for me," Cody said. "I need to be able to look at you when we talk about this." He checked for traffic and changed lanes then slowed to take the next exit.

"What are you doing?"

"I'm pulling off the road. I'm going to find a parking lot, and we're going to talk about this."

"Okay." Demmy stared straight ahead. "My hands are cold. I think I'm going to throw up."

"Just keep it together for five more minutes," Cody said as he maneuvered through traffic to a McDonald's.

"You're getting food? How can you think about eating now?"

"Take it down a notch," Cody grumbled. "I'm going to park in the back."

"Oh. Good idea."

"I have them sometimes."

Cody pulled into the lot and eased the Explorer into a space in the back corner. He shifted into park, killed the engine, and turned in the seat to look at him.

"I'm saving gas so we have about fifteen minutes before it gets really wicked hot in here, and I have to start the engine again," Cody said. "So, where were we? Oh yeah, we were talking about how things have changed between us."

"But that's just it," Demmy nearly shouted. He turned to face Cody and waved his hands in the air. "I don't want them to change! Our friendship means too much to me. If I lost you... If we weren't friends anymore... Well, I don't want to think about it. You are my best friend. You know me better than anyone, and I can't lose that, Cody. I can't."

"Who's to say it has to end?"

Demmy sighed. He looked away a moment, and when he looked back his expression was so sad and devastated, Cody wanted to pull him into his arms and hold him tight.

"What if we try this and you meet a woman? What if she's the perfect woman for you, and you realize what we had was just a stepping stone to that? I wouldn't just lose a... a boyfriend. I'd lose my best friend."

"What if you meet a guy who's the perfect guy for you? That fear works both ways, you know?"

"Yeah, but, I can't compete with a woman," Demmy said.

"What's that mean?"

"It means that she'd have, you know, breasts and a vagina

and baby-making organs, and she'd be able to give you a normal life without judgment and whispers behind your back and smart ass comments." Demmy's shoulders slumped. "She'd give you every man's dream."

Cody's heart nearly broke at the sight of Demmy looking so beaten down. He took a moment to think how to respond, knowing he had to show empathy and kindness and patience. Finally, he let out a breath and said, "You're an idiot."

Demmy glared at him. "What?"

"You heard me," Cody said. "You're an idiot. Do you really think I would risk the best friend I've got in this entire shitty world for something you seem to think I'll consider a fling? No. After all of these years, after all the shit we've been through, all the times we've saved each others' lives, I would have thought you'd be able to give me more credit than that."

"Cody, I — "

Cody held up a finger. "No, not your turn to speak right now. I'm talking. This isn't easy for me, you know. It's a complete one eighty for me. I never thought I would be sitting in a car in the back of a McDonald's parking lot telling a guy that I would really like to date him. Not sleep with you, not fuck you, but date you. In the old-fashioned kind of way, you know? Court you the way you deserve, and treat you like the fucking prince of the city that you are but you're too fucking blind to see it.

"I'm sitting over here trying not to flip out because here I am throwing myself at your feet and asking you to feel more for me than you have any other guy you dated, any other guy who might come along after this. And I don't know what I'm doing. I don't have any experience in the gay world. I don't know what to expect with it all. I have too many questions and not enough answers, but I know one thing for sure, and that's when we're apart, I miss the hell out of you and look forward to when we can be together again. If that's not love, or at least the strong basis for love, then I don't know what is.

"Apparently I'm more open-minded than I ever thought I would be, and my heart and mind have decided I need to try to get you to see this is what's best for both of us. If I'm going to have these feelings for a man, then, goddammit, you're the only man I want to help me explore this side of myself."

They stared at each other. Silence stretched out between them. Cody noticed at that moment just how hot the interior of the car had become under the August sun, but he put that out of his mind. He didn't dare pull his gaze from Demmy's for fear of breaking the intensity of the moment and losing him forever. Finally, when he saw a ball of sweat run down the side of Demmy's face, he had to laugh, and Demmy followed suit.

"Can I start the engine and get the air going again?" Cody said.

Demmy smiled. "Yes, please."

Cody twisted the key and turned the fan to high. The air cooled down quickly, and they both breathed a sigh of relief.

"Okay, so where were we?" Cody said as he turned to face Demmy once again.

"An impasse."

Cody hung his head a moment. Then he met Demmy's gaze and said, "Out in the middle of the swamp — "

"Swamp*ish*," Demmy corrected in a quiet voice, and they shared a sad smile.

Cody thumped his fist over his heart and kissed two fingers then pointed up to the roof of the car. "Here's to you, Hubert Potts, you cranky old fuck. You will never be forgotten."

"Sorry I interrupted," Demmy said. "You were saying?"

"When the swamp monster had hold of my feet and you

were holding onto my hands, I looked at you and said 'I love you.' Do you remember that?"

"I can't stop thinking about it."

"I meant it, Demmy," Cody said in a quiet voice. "I really do love you. I think I've always loved you in some part of myself, but it wasn't until recently I've started to understand just what it means."

"But, it's just... It's me. And I'm, well, a guy. And you've always dated women." Demmy shook his head before frowning at him. "Have you been attracted to other guys over the years?"

Cody nodded. "I have. Not very often, but there have been some guys I've thought, 'You know, if things were different.'"

"Oh. My. God." Demmy's eyes went wide as he slowly shook his head. "All these years you've been having feelings for other men?"

"Not every other man," Cody clarified. "Just sometimes."

"But, for all this time? And you never once mentioned it?"

"Demmy, I—"

"I need some air."

Demmy fumbled with the handle and nearly fell out of the door. He slammed the car door shut and walked around the back of the car.

"This is stupid," Cody grumbled to himself.

He shut off the engine, stepped out of the car and caught up with Demmy in a few long strides. Cody grabbed him by the arm and spun him back around. He pulled Demmy in close and, in front of the long line of cars waiting to order at the drive through, he kissed him.

It was rushed, less perfect and much more public than Cody had hoped their first kiss would be. But despite all that, he felt the snap and crackle of their connection all through his body. Demmy pressed his hands against Cody's chest and tried to push away at first, but Cody held him fast and kept his lips pressed tight to Demmy's. In seconds, Demmy stopped resisting and leaned against him. The moment stretched out and everything seemed to stop around them. Cody's brain shorted out and rebooted itself, perhaps due to lack of blood flow as his cock hardened faster than he'd ever experienced from just a kiss.

But it wasn't just a kiss.

It was his first kiss with Demmy, and it was more than just *a* kiss. It was *the* kiss, the one and only first kiss he knew he would remember for the rest of his life. And he hoped to God Demmy was feeling the same thing or Cody feared he might not be able to stand it.

A horn blared, shattering the moment. Cody felt Demmy's muscles tighten beneath his hands, and they stepped apart. Demmy looked up at him, his gaze glassy and clouded with lust. He stared a moment and seemed to realize where they were standing. He stepped out of Cody's reach and looked around with a guilty expression.

Cody saw the expressions of the occupants waiting in line at the drive through: some shocked, some disgusted, and some with broad smiles. He looked away from the cars and back at Demmy, then reached out for him.

"Let's go, Demmy."

Demmy pulled out of his reach and avoided looking at him, but he nodded and headed back to the Explorer. Cody followed and got in on the driver's side. He started the engine and jumped when Demmy hit the door lock button. Cody sat with his hands on the steering wheel, just staring out the windshield as the air conditioning roared around them. Finally, he turned down the fan on the A/C and spoke without looking at Demmy.

"I'm not going to apologize for that. I'm glad I did it, and I'd do it all over again. It wasn't the most private place for a first kiss, but all of this talking around and around and around the subject was getting us nowhere. We just needed to see if there was any kind of spark there before we got ourselves all knotted up about it." He drew in a deep breath and let it out, then looked over at Demmy's profile. "I've never felt anything like that. How about you?"

Demmy didn't look at him for a moment, and a cold sense of fear started building up inside Cody's gut, like some kind of ice dam. Cody had misinterpreted Demmy's expression after the kiss. Instead of lust, he'd been feeling confusion and disappointment.

"It was good," Demmy whispered, still not looking at him. "It was really, really good."

Cody smiled as relief practically sang through his body. "Yeah?"

Demmy finally met his gaze and smiled. "Yeah."

He grabbed the front of Cody's shirt and pulled him over the console for another kiss. This time, Cody was the one surprised, and even more so when Demmy slid his tongue along the seam of his lips. Cody opened to him. Demmy's tongue felt familiar and right as it pushed into his mouth. Cody didn't hesitate. No warning bells went off inside his mind that he was kissing a dude and had to stop. He had absolutely no fear. He simply kissed Demmy back and enjoyed the taste of his mouth, even the feel of his light scruff scratching against his own.

Demmy pulled back and smiled at Cody. "Okay. Let's hit the road."

Cody blinked in surprise. "Hit the road?"

"We're going to get halfway home before we stop, remember?"

"But, that's Charleston, South Carolina," Cody said. "We're in Jacksonville. That's hours from now."

"That's why we need to get going," Demmy said with a grin. "The sooner begun, the sooner we're done."

Cody rolled his eyes and shook his head. He faced forward, buckled his seatbelt, and put his hands on the wheel. He paused a moment, then looked over at Demmy and cocked an eyebrow. "You know that's not how I do things in bed, right? The sooner begun, the sooner we're done?"

Demmy blushed a bright red and looked away as he buckled himself in. He refused to meet Cody's gaze, but a smile appeared to be permanently frozen in place.

"Did you hear me?"

"Yep," Demmy said, still not looking at him. "Noted."

Cody grinned with satisfaction. He backed out of the parking spot and headed for the highway, mentally calculating how long until they reached Charleston, then flinching when he realized it would be at least another four hours.

CHAPTER TWENTY-FIVE

Demetrius had no memory of the remainder of the drive. He was too inward focused to register anything about the world outside the car. He was torn between the potential to lose not just a boyfriend should something happen — and, with his dating history, things always ended — but also the possibility of losing his very best friend. Was that risk worth the apparently easy step he'd taken across the line separating platonic from romantic?

He and Cody managed to make some kind of conversation during that four hour drive, but Demetrius would never be able to remember what they talked about. The swamp monster, most likely, and maybe some stuff about the business. They avoided any discussion around relationship topics, most likely saving that for when they were off the road.

And so Demetrius pondered the situation. He tried to figure out all the possible outcomes of him and Cody getting together. He put aside thoughts of sex for the time being and focused on the relationship. Cody had been a serial dater all the years they'd grown up together. He had dated pretty much every type of girl over the years: jocks, cheerleaders, creative types, eggheads, and plenty of just normal girls. His longest relationship with a girl was maybe a month. How did Demetrius know Cody wouldn't decide being gay wasn't for him and switch back to women? And what if Cody enjoyed being with a guy, but found he needed more than Demetrius could provide?

But what if everything worked out, and they lived happily ever after? Could Cody ever truly be content with just one romantic partner? And if everything else in their relationship was perfect, including the sex, but Cody needed to see other people on occasion, including women, would Demetrius be able to live with that?

He sighed and shook his head as he stared out the windshield, completely lost within his own thoughts. No, that wasn't what he was looking for in a romantic relationship. He needed someone who would be monogamous. Could Cody rise to the occasion and be a monogamous partner?

"That was a pretty heavy sigh," Cody said.

"What?" Demetrius looked at him. "Oh, sorry. Just thinking."

"Yeah?" Cody nodded. "Me too."

"Good thoughts?"

Cody grinned at him. "Depends on your definition of good thoughts."

Demetrius blushed and looked away. "Oh."

Oh yeah, and there was the sex to contemplate, too. Demetrius was a versatile sex partner. He enjoyed being on the giving and receiving end of anal intercourse. How would Cody handle that aspect of their relationship? And how strange would it be to get to know Cody in such a physically intimate manner? They were already close emotionally, so would a physical intimacy strengthen that bond even more? Or would it be like having sex with a family member? After the spark Demetrius had felt during their kiss, however, he didn't think sex with Cody would feel creepy. At least he really hoped it didn't.

"Ten miles," Cody said.

"Huh?"

"Charleston, South Carolina is ten miles ahead. Did you have a hotel preference?"

"No. Something with a free breakfast would be nice."

"Mm, pancakes," Cody said.

"Oh yeah, no continental breakfast. Something hearty."

Demetrius decided he'd done enough heavy thinking for the moment and pushed aside all thoughts, concerns, and anticipations about his and Cody's relationship. Instead, he paid attention to roadside signs for hotel options. They passed by the main exits for downtown Charleston and, a few miles north, Demetrius saw a billboard for a Hampton Inn.

"How about that one?"

"Gotta love a night in the Hamptons," Cody said. "Sold, to the monster catcher in the passenger seat."

Demetrius laughed. "Think we should change the name of our business?"

"Monster Catchers?" Cody made a face as he considered it. "Nah. Doesn't have the same pizzazz as Critter Catchers."

"Good point."

"Creature Catchers?"

Demetrius shook his head. "I don't like it. Could mean space aliens, and that's a little too out there, even for us."

Cody laughed as he exited the highway. A mile down the road he turned into the parking lot of the Hampton Inn. The lot was nearly full, but Cody found a space around the side of the hotel as Demetrius worried there might not be any rooms available. He reached for the door handle, but stopped and looked over when Cody touched his arm.

"I really want to talk about things between us," Cody said. "Honestly and openly."

Demetrius nodded. "Me too."

"Okay. With that being said, let's get two queen beds."

Demetrius didn't know he'd been stressed about the sleeping arrangements until he felt the sense of relief wash through him. "Yeah, that's a good idea."

But the Hampton Inn had other ideas. Only two rooms were available, both with a single king-sized bed. Demetrius looked at Cody who shrugged in response.

"I can stay on my side if you can stay on yours," Cody said.

The girl behind the counter laughed, most likely thinking they were just two straight guys traveling together. Oh, if she only knew, Demetrius thought.

"I think I can contain myself," Demetrius said drily.

He stood to the side and watched as the girl flirted with Cody, and he flirted right back. It was the standard flirtation: Cody being coy and smirking and the girl laughing too loud at his jokes and comments. Demetrius had seen it happen hundreds, if not thousands of times. Only this time he was watching it from a totally different point of view.

The flirting itself was less interesting than Cody's role in it. And Demetrius didn't know how to feel about it. It was just innocent flirting, so he wasn't going to be a jerk and call him out on it, but he was going to have to learn to live with it because this was Cody. Flirting was a part of his personal make up.

The girl handed Cody two key cards and told him to enjoy his stay. Cody told her he would, as long as they had scrambled eggs and pancakes in the morning, and she assured him they would. Demetrius grabbed his bag and followed Cody around the corner to the elevator. They were silent on the ride up to their floor and as they walked down the hall in search of their room. But when the door swung shut behind them, they stood side-by-side and stared at the wide expanse of the bed, perfectly made up with a white duvet and plump white pillows.

"It looks smaller in person," Cody said.

"It does."

"Want me to get my own room?"

Demetrius took a breath and held it as he thought about everything. He slowly let the air out of his lungs and imagined every doubt and insecurity trailing along with it. The action seemed to work because his mind felt clearer for what felt like the first time in months.

He faced Cody and took his hand, noting how warm and damp Cody's palm felt. It helped to remind him Cody was just as nervous and scared about all of this as he was himself. If they could both keep that in mind, they just might get through this awkward transition in one piece.

Demetrius kept coming back to the memory of that first kiss and the shockwave it had sent through his system. No matter the outcome, he knew he had to take this risk.

Demetrius grabbed the front of Cody's shirt and pulled him down for a kiss. It was soft and sweet, and though it didn't last more than a few seconds, the feeling of it lingered long after they'd parted.

"No, I don't want you to get your own room," Demetrius said. "I want us to go get something to eat, together, and have some drinks with dinner. Then I want us to come back to our room, together, and go to bed. Together."

Cody pulled him in close and smiled down at him, his six more inches of height suddenly making him seem so much larger in Demetrius's eyes.

"I want that, too," Cody said, kissing him again, taking just long enough to slip his tongue between Demetrius's lips. "All of that and more."

"Well, let's go ask perky desk girl where a good place to

eat is around here," Demetrius said, trying not to sound too bitchy about it, but knowing he failed.

Cody laughed and gave him a quick kiss. "I can't seem to stop kissing you, even when you're being kind of a bitch."

"Keep rewarding me like that, and it will just encourage me to keep acting that way," Demetrius said.

Cody kissed him once more. "Duly noted. Come on, let's eat."

The perky desk girl was more than happy to provide Cody a recommendation for a reasonable place with good food. It just so happened to be within walking distance and had cheap margaritas, and her shift was over in a couple of hours. From a few feet away, Demetrius listened with interest as Cody said he was so tired from driving all day he'd probably be asleep by then. Cody wished the girl a good evening and turned away to deliver a wink to him.

"Smooth," Demetrius said as they stepped out of the hotel.

"Well, no need to break her heart," Cody said with a grin.

The El Dorado Steakhouse was everything the perky desk girl had promised. They ordered tall margaritas and steaks and started picking at the cheesy garlic rolls the waitress delivered. Demetrius was amazed at how normal the whole scenario felt. He'd sat across from Cody in restaurant booths so many times over the more than twenty years of their friendship, he had to keep reminding himself that tonight was different. While it all looked the same – just two friends having dinner together – everything on the inside had changed.

He tried not to think too far ahead, like what was going to happen once they returned to the room. He wanted to enjoy the anticipation, but a large part of his brain seemed to think the decades of friendship and his quiet crush on Cody had been anticipation enough, and it played hot scenarios on an endless loop. Cody braced above him, their gazes locked as he slid inside. Cody pounding into him, close to release. Even Cody sitting on Demetrius's cock, slowly impaling himself as Demetrius stroked his erection.

"Penny for your thoughts."

Cody's voice burst through the current sex scenario projected inside Demetrius's brain. He blinked then blushed at the sight of Cody's knowing smirk. He was totally busted.

"Um..." Demetrius's brain locked up, permanently frozen on the image of Cody sitting on his cock.

Cody leaned in over the table. "Why do you think I'm carb loading over here? I'm equal parts nervous and excited to get back to the room myself."

Demetrius let out a breath, and then he sat back when the waitress dropped off their margaritas.

"Oh, look," Demetrius said, "tequila." He held up his drink and Cody did the same so their glasses clinked in the center.

"To our long and impossible to describe friendship," Cody said.

Demetrius nodded. "To us."

He moved the straw to the other side of the glass and took a hearty gulp of his drink. The tequila flowed into him, smoothing over a few of the rough spots inside, and he sighed and closed his eyes.

"Better?"

Demetrius smiled at him. "It will be."

Cody nodded, glanced around, then leaned forward and lowered his voice. "I have to be honest with you, Demmy, I've got a huge case of performance anxiety going on right now."

Demetrius widened his eyes in surprise. "You do?"

"Of course I do!" Cody said in an urgent whisper. "I mean, not only is it... you know, *you*, or, I mean, *us*. But it's my first time with a guy. Ever."

Demetrius leaned in as well, taking the opportunity to sip from the straw of his drink. "You've really never been with another guy? Not even one of those drunk nights with the soccer team in college?"

Cody blushed and shrugged. "Well, I kissed a couple of guys, but nothing more than that."

Demetrius raised his eyebrows. "You kissed a couple of guys? Who?"

"You didn't know them."

"Not soccer guys?"

"Oh, no. If one of them had made a move on me, I probably would have gone for it." Cody sipped his drink. "Especially Brett Stemper."

"Brett Stemper?" Demetrius was quiet as he thought back on Brett Stemper. When he had a picture of him in his head, Demetrius nodded. "Good taste." Then he smirked. "Cody Bower, afraid to make the first move. Never thought I'd live to see the day."

Cody waved his words away. "Yeah, yeah."

Demetrius sipped his drink again and told himself to slow down as the tequila buzzed through his brain. He sat back and pushed his drink a little farther away.

"I don't know what to say. I'm honored and now a little terrified."

"I didn't tell you that to freak you out," Cody said. "I just wanted you to know you're not the only one who's nervous. And I'd like our first time together to be enjoyable for both of us, so easy on that margarita there, lightweight."

Demetrius smiled. "This is terrifying, all of this talk and contemplation. But, oh my God, Cody, this is the most fun and intensely erotic date I've ever been on."

Cody's smile was equal parts charm and sex. "I'm really glad you said that, because I feel the same way."

Their food arrived, and the waitress asked if they wanted another round of drinks. Demetrius was surprised to discover he had finished his. Cody's was nearly empty as well. They shared a look and both shrugged at the same time, nodding up at her.

"We're walking, why not?" Cody said.

As if on some kind of unspoken agreement, their conversation during dinner remained neutral. When the check arrived, Cody surprised Demetrius by laying down cash.

"Dinner's on your Dad."

Demetrius smiled and shook his head. "He spent a lot of money on us."

"He did," Cody said. "Your parents have always made me feel like a part of your family. I like them a lot."

"Yeah, they like you, too," Demetrius said. "What a strange trip it was. Well, still is, actually."

Cody nodded with wide eyes. The waitress returned with change and Cody counted out a tip. He sat back in the booth and they stared at each other a moment in silence.

"Think you're ready?" Cody said.

Demetrius's stomach was in so many knots he had no idea how he'd managed to eat. But the knots weren't all anxiety. A good helping of eagerness was in the mix as well. He nodded and they slid out of the booth and headed toward the door.

Outside, the hotel sign glowed like a beacon in the summer night as they walked in silence along the edge of the road. Demetrius could hear the steady drone of traffic on the nearby highway as well as an airplane coming in to land at the Charleston airport. He tried not to think about the fact that tonight everything he knew, pretty much everything about his life, was about to change.

He felt as if he were floating instead of walking as he followed Cody through the hotel's automatic doors into the lobby. The perky desk girl was gone, replaced now by a full figured black woman who gave them a big smile and called, "Good evening, gentlemen."

Demetrius knew he and Cody both responded, but he had

no idea what either of them said. They were silent on the elevator, unable to look at each other. Children's voices shrieked from behind the doors they passed, and Demetrius was glad their room was at the end of the hall away from the traveling families.

Cody opened the door, and Demetrius stepped inside after him. He glanced at the bed but decided to play things casual and leaned his butt against the edge of the work desk, watching as Cody put his wallet and keycard on the top of the dresser. Cody approached and stood close, looking into Demetrius's eyes. Without a word, he placed a palm against the side of his head, fingers parted around Demetrius's ear. Very slowly, Cody leaned down, eyes slipping closed as he moved closer. His lips were soft and the light scruff of his two-day beard scratched pleasantly against Demetrius's own as they kissed.

The moment drew out as their kiss deepened, tongues curling together. Demetrius pressed himself against Cody. He felt the long, hard line of Cody's erection against his hip and groaned. Cody slid his free hand between them and cupped Demetrius's crotch, squeezing gently as he kissed him harder.

Several minutes later, Cody broke the kiss but remained close to Demetrius, one hand cradling his head, the other massaging his cock through his shorts.

"I'm running pretty hot right now," Cody said, his voice a lust-fueled whisper.

"I can feel that," Demetrius said, putting his hands on Cody's ass to pull him up closer. He ground his hip against Cody's cock as he pressed Cody's hand more firmly against his crotch.

Cody closed his eyes and moaned. "Why did we wait this long to do this?"

"Let's hold off on questions like that until afterwards,"

Demetrius said with a nervous laugh. "We may not be compatible."

"Oh, we're compatible." Cody kissed him again, tongue slipping quickly in and then out of his mouth. "Is it okay if I get a quick shower?"

"Yeah, go ahead. I'll get in after you."

Cody stepped back and smiled. "Want to shower together?"

Demetrius considered it but shook his head. "Not just yet."

Cody nodded. "I get it. I'll be quick."

"You'd better be."

Demetrius watched him dig through his bag to grab his shaving kit. Cody kicked off his shoes and hurried into the bathroom where he shut the door. Demetrius paced a bit, shaking out his hands as he took deep breaths and let them out. This was it. This was happening. Holy hell on shit mountain, he was going to have sex with Cody.

He switched on the TV and skipped around the channels. News anchors shouted about the latest tragedy, and some reality show participants whispered nasty insults about a team member. He found HBO and rolled his eyes at the explicit sex scene with a handsome actor and beautiful actress. He shut the TV off. No need to remind Cody of what he was missing.

When the shower stopped, Demetrius realized he needed to get ready for his own and found his shaving kit and zip top bag of body wash and shampoo. The bathroom door opened, and Cody stepped out amid a cloud of steam, wearing a towel around his waist. His dark hair was damp and slightly curled and drops of water shimmered on his collarbone and in a few dark wisps of chest hair. His nipples were hard brown points and beneath the flat plane of his hairy belly, the outline of his erection was plainly visible beneath the towel.

"I'm all squeaky clean," Cody said with a grin. "Care to check?"

"In a minute." Demetrius hurried past him into the bathroom, calling over his shoulder, "Don't turn on HBO."

Demetrius stared at his reflection in the steam shrouded mirror. He was about to do the very thing he thought he'd never in his life get to do. Was he ready for this? He smiled at himself and nodded. Oh yeah, he was more than fucking ready for this.

He brushed his teeth, peed, then got in the shower and washed. He cleaned every crack and crevice thoroughly and carefully shaved his balls. He'd only had a few seconds to drink in the sight of Cody jerking off, but it had looked like Cody shaved his balls as well, and Demetrius wondered when Cody had started doing that. As he dried off, Demetrius was amazed he was still hard. Had he ever been this turned on while anticipating sex with anyone else? He could not remember it if he had been, and he was sure he would.

With a towel around his waist, Demetrius looked at his reflection one last time, drew in a deep breath, then opened the door and stepped out of the bathroom.

CHAPTER TWENTY-SIX

Cody sat in bed, pillows propped behind his back and the sheet pulled up just high enough to cover his crotch. He'd been hard pretty much all through dinner and on the walk back from the restaurant, and his erection was very visible beneath the sheet. He was tempted to check out what was playing on HBO that Demmy didn't want him to see, but decided not to push his luck or Demmy's temper, so he left the TV off.

The shower shut off, and Cody's dick jumped like an excited child. A wet spot had already formed from the pre-cum he was leaking, and he grabbed the washcloth he'd brought out of the bathroom and dabbed himself clean. He could not remember a time when he'd been this hard for this long. Well, not when waiting for a partner to come to bed. Maybe back when he'd been a teenager and had walked around with an erection pretty much twenty-four hours a day, but nothing like this.

What was it about Demmy that had gotten so deep under his skin? Obviously they had a stellar connection, otherwise they wouldn't have been best friends for so long. But if Cody were asked to point to the single thing that had changed that friendship to a sexual attraction, he'd be hard pressed to name it.

It was just Demmy, and in some way, Cody thought he might have known all along this was where they would end up. But he had to go through some women — okay, *a lot* of women — first.

Cody adjusted his position then wondered if he had chosen Demmy's side of the bed. For all the sleepovers and time they'd spent together, they still had a lot to learn about each other. What if Demmy preferred the same side of the bed? Or what if Demmy were more of a cuddler when he slept? Cody's core temperature always ran hot, so he liked to stretch out on his own side to keep from overheating. It didn't mean he didn't appreciate a brief snuggle before sleep, but he wasn't one to spend an entire night all entangled with a bed partner. And beyond that, and even worse, what if they weren't sexually compatible? Could they just abandon a sexual part of the relationship and carry on their friendship without a blip in the radar?

The bathroom door opened, and Cody's heart thumped hard, the beat echoing in his cock. Demmy walked out amid a cloud of steam with a nervous expression and a towel around his waist. At the sight of Demmy standing there with the soft curls of his chest hair catching the light from the bedside lamp, his hair slicked back, and his golden brown scruff of beard, Cody's mouth went dry and he had to swallow hard.

"You're on my side of the bed," Demmy said.

Cody grinned, and a sense of peace blew through him like a summer breeze. He might have been standing there in just a towel, ready to take a step off the precipice from friendship to sex-ship, but he was the same familiar smart-ass Demmy. Yeah, things were going to be just fine.

"Well get over here and make me move."

Demmy laughed and walked up to the side of the bed next to him. They looked at each other for a moment, then Demmy placed a hand over the outline of Cody's erection. His movements were quick and deliberate, as if he had to convince his hand it was permitted to touch him there.

"Did you smuggle a bratwurst out of that restaurant?" Demmy said.

"Possibly. As a matter of national security, I'll have to search your garment for other smuggled meats."

Cody gave the towel a gentle tug, and it fell to the floor. Demmy sucked in a breath as he stood nude before him. His cock stood straight out toward Cody, a clear drop of pre-cum glistening on the tip. He'd seen Demmy naked before, while they'd changed before and after gym class or even during sleepovers, so he knew he was circumcised and had a brown bush. But he had never seen Demmy aroused, and had never imagined he was so big and so fucking hard.

He slid to the middle of the king-sized mattress and pulled back the sheet, exposing himself and making room for Demmy.

"Come on," Cody said. "Get in."

Demmy got in bed, and Cody gathered him close. Their bodies were an odd fit at first since Cody was half a foot taller, but he was used to height differences as he'd dated a wide range of women. He hooked a leg over Demmy's and pulled him closer as he tightened his arms around Demmy's torso. They kissed, tongues winding together and dicks rubbing. Cody thought he'd have trouble adjusting to the feel of a dick against his own, but it felt surprisingly natural. He slid a hand across Demmy's chest and tweaked a nipple then rubbed his thumb back and forth across the other until it hardened like a pebble.

Cody rolled Demmy on his back and moved on top of

him. Demmy winced and helped him adjust his hips until he was able to lay without crushing Demmy's dick.

"Sorry," Cody whispered.

"It's okay," Demmy whispered back.

They kissed some more until Demmy pushed Cody off and on his back. He moved his mouth to Cody's neck and ran his tongue down to the hollow of his throat where he placed a gentle kiss. Shifting his attention to Cody's nipples, he took each one between his teeth and sucked them hard. Cody groaned and squirmed beneath Demmy, anxious for him to slide even lower but determined to wait for Demmy to move on his own.

As if he'd read Cody's thoughts, Demmy shifted position, running his tongue through the hair in the center of his chest and down over his belly. He dipped the tip into Cody's navel and the sensation sent a shiver through him. Girls had done the same thing to him before, but Cody had never fucking shivered when it happened. His pulse throbbed in his cock, and Cody feared he might come way too soon. Each inhalation made his thoughts seem to explode only to come back together on the exhalation. He couldn't form a coherent thought at that moment if he'd had a gun pointed to his head.

When Demmy gripped his cock, Cody couldn't suppress a groan. Demmy lifted it slowly and they both watched a string of pre-cum stretch between the puddle on his belly to the slick tip of his cock head. Demmy looked his dick over as he slowly stroked it, as if he were inspecting it, then he met Cody's gaze.

"Well, it's definitely not a bratwurst."

Cody grinned. "I tried to tell you."

Demmy smiled and looked between the cock in his hand and Cody's eyes. "I've thought about doing this for so long," Demmy said. "It's hard to believe I'm not dreaming."

Cody sat up and pulled him close for a tongue heavy kiss.

"It's hard for me to believe it, too. I didn't know I wanted you until this past year. And I know we haven't done anything yet, at least nothing too intimate, but now I wish I'd realized it years ago."

Demmy kissed him again, then placed a hand on his chest and pushed him back down. He slowly ran his tongue up and down his shaft, then took him in his mouth and swallowed his entire length in one swift move.

"Oh fucking hell," Cody said with a gasp. He gripped the bottom sheet in both fists and arched his back. He was big, Cody knew this for a fact. It wasn't bragging because it was the truth and, like most men, he'd measured himself. He was just about nine inches when hard, and only a few of the girls he'd dated had been able to deep throat him. And none of them had gone all the way down on him like Demmy just had.

Why the ever-loving fuck hadn't Cody seriously pursued Demmy before this?

Demmy moved up and down his shaft like a hungry beast, groaning and slurping. Cody was a verbal lover. He really got off on groans and moans and dirty talk, and, it appeared, so was Demmy.

Again, why the hell hadn't Cody done this before now?

Cody was about to tell Demmy to stop because he was getting close, but Demmy already seemed to realize it and pulled back on his own. He stroked him as he smiled.

"That okay?"

"You fucking well know it was better than okay," Cody said with a growl.

He pulled Demmy up and kissed him hard. The taste of his pre-cum still lingered on Demmy's tongue, and it surprised Cody. He'd tasted his pre-cum and even his own spunk before, just to see what all the fuss was about. Maybe it had been the first clue that he might be interested in guys, too, because he hadn't been grossed out about it. He hadn't craved the taste of it, but he didn't mind it.

Now, he wanted to get a taste of Demmy's pre-cum and see if it had a similar flavor. He rolled Demmy on his back and moved down his body, trailing kisses. He paused to suck and nip at Demmy's nipples, not at all bothered by the brush of chest hair against his face. As he moved lower, Cody felt Demmy's dick tap against the underside of his jaw, and he couldn't hold back any longer, he needed to see if he could actually suck a dick.

He slid down in the bed and took Demmy's cock in his hand. Cody looked it over, trying to put it all together in his mind that not only was he in bed with a man, but he was in bed with Demmy. He was about to suck his first cock, and it was attached to the only person on the planet who really, truly knew him.

"You okay?" Demmy said, his voice gentle.

Cody looked up at him and tried to smile, but it felt wrong so he knew he must look nervous. Even as he lay there with Demmy's dick in his hand, he was still nervous.

"Never done this before," Cody said. "Just want to make sure I get it right."

"I think you'll do fine," Demmy said. "I just want to make sure you really want to do this."

Cody crawled up the bed and, still on all fours, gave him a soft kiss. "I've never wanted anything, or any*one*, more."

Demmy let out a quiet breath as he looked into his eyes. "You really do know the right things to say, Cody Bower."

"Some times." Cody kissed him again, then moved down and once more took hold of Demmy's cock. Without further hesitation, he ran his tongue up the length of it. It was salty and dry, not really what he'd expected, but not terrible. Basically he was just licking skin. When he put his lips around the plump head slick with pre-cum, the bitter, briny taste burst across his tongue. He paused to suck gently on the tip then slowly took Demmy into his mouth until he had to stop halfway down. Cody moved up and tried again, glad that this time he was able to take him deeper into his throat.

"Oh God, Cody," Demmy said. "Yeah, just like that."

Cody wanted some more action for himself, so he shifted around to a sixty-nine position. Demmy was ready and started sucking him immediately and Cody went back to work on Demmy's cock. He fondled Demmy's balls, not surprised to find they were shaved and glad he'd been shaving his own for a few years.

When Demmy moved down to take Cody's balls in his mouth, Cody copied the move. He ran his tongue over the smooth skin of Demmy's nuts, took each one in his mouth and gently sucked it. By now he was about ready to blow, and as much as he wanted this to last, he knew he had to get off soon. Demmy's hand on his cock was keeping him close to the edge so it wasn't going to take much.

And then Demmy moved lower still. He pushed Cody's legs open wider and grazed his asshole with the tip of his tongue. Cody let out a surprised gasp. An ex-girlfriend had given him a rim job once, and he'd even returned the favor. But this felt entirely different. This was not only Demmy running his tongue across Cody's asshole, but a man, and Cody wasn't sure about the power in the relationship. Was the one receiving the rim job supposed to be on the receiving end of anal intercourse? He wasn't sure he was ready for that tonight. But would he ever be ready for Demmy to fuck him?

The question was temporarily shunted aside as Demmy shifted position, his balls falling out of Cody's mouth as he moved to the head of the bed. Cody rolled onto his back with his head at the foot of the bed. Demmy pushed Cody's legs up to expose his asshole and leaned down to press his tongue against, and then into his anus.

"Oh, fuck," Cody said with a gasp.

Demmy spread Cody's ass cheeks apart and worked his tongue over, into, and around Cody's hole. Cody stroked his cock slowly and carefully, willing himself not to come. He really wanted to come with or inside Demmy, and the thought of being inside him as he unloaded nearly made him come. Dammit, he needed to shut off his dirty-minded brain.

"God you're so fucking hot," Demmy said. "I can't believe this is happening."

"Oh, it's happening baby," Cody said. "And it's going to get even hotter."

Demmy moved up to suck Cody's balls, then his cock. He trailed his tongue up Cody's torso and kissed him hard on the mouth.

"I want you inside me," Demmy said between kisses.

Cody groaned into his mouth. "Are you sure?"

"Really sure."

Cody kissed him once more, not even caring that Demmy had just been tonguing his asshole. He slid out of bed and hurried to his shaving kit. He produced a small bottle of lube and some condoms and turned with a smile. "I bought these when we stopped for gas after our kiss."

Demmy laughed as he leaned back on his elbows. "Guess you were pretty sure of yourself, eh?"

Cody shrugged as he approached the bed. "Let's say I was hopeful and wanted to be prepared."

Demmy took the lube and condoms from him and checked the labels. He made a face and looked up at him. "We can't use these."

"What? Why not? Did they expire?" Cody took the items back and inspected them. "That fucking guy at the gas station, I knew there was something shifty about him."

Demmy laughed. "They're not expired. They have nonoxynol in them, and I'm allergic to it."

"Oh?" Cody read the labels of the condoms and the lube. Sure enough, both contained the chemical. "Well fuck."

"Or not," Demmy said with a chuckle.

He swung his feet over the edge of the bed and pulled Cody forward between his legs. Demmy slowly sucked his cock a few times then sat back and stroked him. He looked up at Cody and smiled.

"Have you been tested?"

"Tested? Like HIV and all of that?"

"Yeah, all of that," Demmy said.

Cody nodded. "A few months ago during my physical. All negative."

"I was tested, too, just last month. All negative."

Cody tossed the lube and condoms over his shoulder and leaned down to give Demmy a kiss. "What are you suggesting?"

"I'm suggesting you fuck me bareback."

Demmy's frank statement sent a surge of adrenaline and lust through Cody. His cock throbbed, and he felt a little dizzy. How had they managed to wait this long?

"What do we use for lube?"

"I have some lube in my bag," Demmy said.

"Do I want to know why?"

"For when I spent the night with Oliver. And, yes, we always used condoms. Unfortunately, we used the last of the condoms."

Cody put his hands over his ears and closed his eyes. "Nah nah nah nah nah. Not hearing that."

He got off the bed and hurried over to Demmy's shaving kit where he rifled through it. He found the lube and made a mental note of the brand so he could buy some for his apartment. That thought stopped him in his tracks for a moment and made him smile as he realized the expectation and anticipation that it signified. Once they got back home, he was hoping Demmy would spend nights with him at his apartment.

"Find it?"

Cody looked at the pale length of Demmy's body, taking in the details. The anticipation of what was about to happen lay coiled low within his belly, just above his crotch. He wanted to fix this moment in his mind and remember it for the rest of his life. He met Demmy's gaze and smiled. "Oh yeah, I found it."

"Well, then get over here with it."

Cody flipped open the cap and squirted some lube along his prick as he approached the bed. Demmy watched him, wide eyes fixed on his cock as he lifted his legs to expose his asshole. Cody was really in the groove at that point and dropped to his knees. Before he could think about it too much, he ran his tongue up the length of Demmy's crack and over the rough surface of his anus.

"Oh, fuck Cody," Demmy said. "I never imagined you as a rimmer."

"Baby, you've got no idea how fucking dirty I want to get with you."

"You nearly made me come just saying that," Demmy said.

Cody spread Demmy's cheeks wide and drilled his tongue deep into the hot center of his hole. He lapped at it, getting it slick with his spit. Then, with a final kiss right in the middle, he got to his feet. He slid a lubed finger around the outer ring and eased it inside. Demmy's muscles tightened around him, and Cody bit his lip as he shook his head.

"Pretty fucking tight, Demmy." He squirted more lube onto his fingers and spread it around. Using two fingers, he pushed lube inside. "Sure you can take me?"

"Don't worry, I can handle it."

"If you say Ollie is bigger than me, I'm leaving," Cody said with a scowl.

Demmy laughed and shook his head. "You've got no competition from Oliver, or from Clint for that matter."

Cody grinned. "I'll go slow."

He leaned forward to give him a gentle kiss on the mouth, then straightened up and aimed his slick and glistening cock. With slow, sure movements, Cody eased inside Demmy.

Cody hadn't had unprotected sex in years, not since he'd been an idiotic sexed up teenager in high school. A couple of girls he'd dated a few years ago had enjoyed anal sex, however, and so he had experience with the differences in sensation. But he'd never had unprotected anal sex, and never had anal sex with a man. The wet heat of Demmy's muscles closed around him like a warm velvet fist. Cody tightened his grip on Demmy's ankles and closed his eyes. He stopped halfway in and pulled back then eased in a little deeper. When at last he stood balls deep between Demmy's legs, Cody leaned down for a long kiss.

"You ready?" Cody asked between kisses.

"I've been ready for about twenty years."

Cody kissed him again. "Smooth talker."

"Learned it all from you," Demmy said. "Now fuck me."

Cody groaned. "If you start talking dirty, I'm not going to last long."

"You're the one that encouraged me to order a second margarita," Demmy said.

Straightening up, Cody pumped his hips, steadily building tempo. Demmy egged him on, asking for it harder and faster. Cody obliged until he was covered in sweat and pounding into Demmy. His sweat-tacky skin slapped against Demmy's ass cheeks, and he realized just how much he loved that sound. He was close, really close, and he wanted to finish inside Demmy, but didn't know if he should.

"I'm close," Cody said.

Demmy stroked himself faster. "Me too. Come inside me."

"I was hoping you'd say that."

A few more thrusts was all it took, and he buried himself in Demmy as he came with a deep grunt. Demmy's muscles clamped down around him, and Cody moaned as he watched Demmy come onto his belly. He kissed Demmy's sweaty calf and stood looking down at where they were still joined, loving the sight of Demmy's anus spread around his shaft. As he eased out of him, Cody smeared the thick cum into Demmy's skin then leaned in to kiss him.

"I have no words," Cody said.

Demmy smiled. "Cody Bower at a loss for words? Wow, I must be a good lay."

Cody kissed him again. "You're more than that, and you know it."

Demmy got up and stood before him. He took Cody's hand and led him to the bathroom. Demmy started the shower, and they stepped into the tub and pulled the curtain. Cody cleaned Demmy off and kissed him as he gently slid a soapy finger into his anus. Demmy surprised him by returning the favor, slipping his own soapy finger into Cody's anus up to the first knuckle.

"Easy there, sport," Cody said around a kiss.

"Just making sure you're really squeaky clean," Demmy said. "Don't worry, I don't expect anything like that."

Cody turned away to rinse off, and when he faced Demmy again, said, "It's not that I'm not open to it. I just need a little bit of time with some stuff."

Demmy kissed him and gently tugged on his cock. "I get it. Don't worry."

They exchanged glances and smiles as they dried off and wrapped towels around themselves before leaving the bathroom. Demmy let out a big yawn and gave Cody a sheepish smile.

"Sorry. I didn't sleep very well last night."

"Oh?" Cody decided to keep to himself the fact that he'd overheard Demmy talking with Olivia. "Well, since we both like the same side of the bed, how about — "

Demmy dropped his towel and crossed the room in two steps, jumping into bed and claiming that side.

"You little sneak," Cody said with a laugh.

"Snooze you lose," Demmy said, and yawned again.

"Fine, you can have that side." Cody tossed both towels into the bathroom and got in bed where he pulled Demmy closer to the middle then right up against him. "Just tell me one thing: are you an all night snuggler?"

"All night? No. I like my space."

Cody kissed him softly and smiled. "I think we're going to get along just fine."

"This is still going to feel this way when we wake up, right? It's not going to be weird in the morning?"

"Oh, it'll be weird off an on for a while," Cody said. "But we'll get through it. We both just need to be patient."

"Great," Demmy said. "Something we've never been good at with each other."

"Never too old to learn, right?" Cody hugged him close a moment and released him. "Get some sleep, Demmy. Your turn to drive tomorrow."

"Good night, Cody," Demmy said through another yawn.

"Good night, Demmy."

Cody listened to Demmy's breathing deepen into sleep. He didn't know if he'd be able to sleep, though he knew he needed to. He was a little afraid to go to sleep, if he was honest with himself. Afraid that when he awoke, things between them would be different, just like Demmy said. Well, he would just have to make sure everything was the same as ever. No, that wouldn't work. It needed to be better.

Cody switched off the light and got comfortable. Demmy shifted position in his sleep, and his leg pressed up against

Cody's. Instead of moving away, Cody stayed where he was, savoring the contact. He had no idea what would happen once they got home, but he was damn sure not going to let anything ruin what he'd just discovered.

With that thought fixed firmly in mind, Cody turned on his side and, surprisingly, fell right to sleep.

CHAPTER TWENTY-SEVEN

Demetrius awoke slowly and lay still. A sliver of space in the blackout curtains allowed a blade of sunlight to cut the darkness in the room and reveal scarce details of the furniture. He was in a hotel room. No, he was in *the* hotel room where the night before he'd had sex with Cody.

Once he realized where he was, Demetrius became aware of deep, heavy breathing and, keeping his back to Cody, slowly turned his head. Cody lay on his back, one arm raised and crooked behind his head, exposing the dark, furry hollow of his armpit. Demmy studied his profile, amazed that even now, with his hair mussed up and his mouth hanging open, Cody looked more handsome than a man had any right to. It required some level of self-convincing to make himself believe the night before had actually happened and hadn't been just some hot and crazy dream.

He turned fully onto his side to face Cody and watched him sleep for a few minutes, thinking back over their years of friendship. This step they'd taken could either go really well or blow up in their faces, and it made him feel nervous and unsettled. But when he thought about the night before, remembered how it had felt to kiss Cody, the taste of his cock, the feeling when he had pushed inside of him, Demetrius had to admit it had all felt good and right and meant to be.

Maybe the other men he'd been with had just been distractions until Cody had figured out they belonged together.

Demetrius only hoped Cody felt the same way, too.

He was nervous over how Cody would treat him when he awoke. Would he feel guilty about what had happened and act cool and aloof? He'd certainly seemed into things the night before, and had especially shocked Demetrius when he'd given him a hell of a rim job. Demetrius's cock stirred at the memory, and he decided it might be a good time to get out of bed and use the bathroom.

While he was in the bathroom, Demetrius heard Cody's breathing deepen into a loud snort that would undoubtedly have woken him up. He listened to the rustle of the sheet as Cody rolled over, and decided to make some noise to try and wake him up a bit more before he returned to the room. Demetrius turned on the faucet stronger than needed and splashed water on his face. He brushed his teeth then peed, making sure his stream hit the center of the water to make the loudest sound.

When he stepped out of the bathroom, he scurried across the room to grab his white briefs off the floor and pulled them on.

"You know my cock was in your ass last night, right?" Cody said, his voice deep and scratchy and sexy. "You don't have to be self-conscious about letting your dick hang out."

Demetrius laughed and glared at him with his hands on his hips. "Good morning to you, too."

Cody rolled to face Demetrius's side of the bed and pulled back the sheet. "Come back to bed."

"We have a lot of driving to do today," Demetrius said, suddenly nervous.

"The road will still be there waiting in an hour," Cody said. "Or two."

Demetrius's stomach felt like it did a loop the loop. He got back into bed still wearing his underwear and pulled the sheet up over himself. Stretching out on his back, he smiled as casually as he could manage at Cody.

"Good morning," Demetrius said. "How'd you sleep?"

Cody smiled and slid closer. He slipped an arm behind Demetrius's head and pulled him up against his body. Demetrius felt the hardened heat of Cody's dick press against his hip and a loud buzzing sound started up inside his skull. Holy hell, Cody was up and raring to go already, with apparently no feelings of remorse about what they'd done the night before. Was this a dream now?

"You seem nervous," Cody said into Demetrius's ear. "Are you feeling all right about last night?"

"Yeah," Demetrius said, his voice rising unintentionally into squeak territory.

Cody eased back a bit and looked at him. "The tone of your voice indicates otherwise. What's up?"

"Nothing," Demetrius said. He let out a breath and turned his head to look away from Cody and up at the ceiling. "Okay, I'm terrified."

"Yeah?" Cody pulled his arm free and rolled onto his back as well so they both stared at the ceiling. "I'm glad we're at this point, I really am."

"But?" Demetrius said.

"But... I'm worried about us, too. I mean, you're pretty much the most important person in my life."

Demetrius turned his head to look at him. "Really?"

Cody frowned at him. "Of course. You're my best friend. I spend almost every hour of every day with you, and I like doing it. I don't think there's any other person on the planet I'd want to be with that much. I know it makes sense that this is our next step, but I gotta tell you, Demmy, I am a little scared here."

"Yeah?" Demetrius swallowed hard.

"Yeah." Cody met his gaze and held it. "I've never felt this way about anyone, no matter their gender. And now that we've..."

"Been intimate?"

Cody grinned. "I was going to say fucked hard and deep and I came inside you, but I'll take yours."

Demetrius's stomach did a slow flip as his cock hardened. Jesus, Cody could really hit those pressure points, even with just his words and tone of voice.

"Anyway," Cody continued, "we both know my track record with sexual relationships, which is less than stellar. And now that we've done the dirty deed, there's a part of me that's counting down the days until this all blows up on me."

"Oh," Demetrius said as a chill went through him.

"But there's another part of me, a stronger part, that's jumping around in excitement like a kid on a snow day, you know? I mean, it's you, and it's us, and how much better could it get, right?"

"Do you think there's added pressure because I'm a man?"

Cody thought about it. He was quiet for so long, Demetrius started to worry that the answer would be yes.

Then Cody looked at him and smiled. "No, I gotta say it doesn't matter." He pulled Demetrius close again and kissed him hard on the mouth, then pulled back and frowned. "Sorry, that was probably pretty gross. I haven't brushed my teeth yet."

Demetrius smiled. "I don't care." He pulled him in for another kiss, then they lay facing each other. "I know this is going to be tough sometimes, for both of us. We'll get a lot of shit from people back home."

Cody winced. "Lucia Durant."

Demetrius nodded as he thought of the sheriff's deputy and one of Cody's many ex-girlfriends who still lived in Parson's Hollow. "Not to mention Zenona."

Cody nodded and sighed. "I know I'll get a lot of shit from them, and I deserve it. I just don't want you to get the brunt of it."

"I think I'll be okay," Demetrius said. "And if not, I have a big, strong boyfriend I can sic on them."

"Boyfriend, eh?" Cody grinned. "I like the sound of that."

"Really?" Demetrius kissed him. "That means you have a boyfriend, too."

"Yeah? Sounds dirty." Cody kissed him and slipped out of bed, his erection bobbing before him. "Hold that thought. I need to pee and brush my teeth."

Demmy shucked off his underwear and pulled the sheet up over himself again. There was a lot of shit they were going to have to get through until this relationship smoothed out, but he intended to enjoy the newlywed feeling of it all until that point.

Cody emerged from the bathroom, his half erect cock lazily brushing against his thigh. Demetrius watched him approach the bed, eyes fixed on that thick slab of meat as it swayed back and forth.

"Be careful," Cody said. "If you stare at it too long you could fall under its spell."

Demetrius laughed and then shouted when Cody yanked the sheet off him.

"Well, someone else is up and at 'em this morning," Cody said at the sight of Demetrius's hard-on.

"Yeah, he's still pretty interested in what you have to offer," Demetrius said.

Cody stretched out alongside Demetrius and gave him a slow, deep kiss. As they kissed, Cody stroked Demetrius's dick, his palm warm and damp. Demetrius cupped Cody's heavy balls before moving up to stroke him as well.

"You really get me hot, Demmy," Cody said between kisses. "I've been wondering how this would feel, but I never imagined it like this." More kisses and faster stroking. "I can't stop kissing you."

"I don't want you to."

Demetrius pushed Cody on his back and straddled his thighs. He grabbed the lube off the nightstand, slicked up a hand, then took hold of both of them at once. Cody closed his eyes and dropped his mouth open, hands gripping Demetrius's thighs.

"Oh, fuck yeah," Cody said. "That feels really good. A little higher."

Demetrius adjusted his grip, and the new position earned him a groan.

"You really know how to work a dick," Cody said. "How's that feel for you?"

"Amazing."

Demetrius increased his speed and closed his eyes. The feeling of Cody's dick against his own and his fingers tight around them both was bringing him to the edge faster than he'd expected. He looked down at Cody's face, watching his expression as he stroked them even faster and tightened his grip just a bit more.

"I'm getting close." Cody opened his eyes. "Are you?"

Demetrius nodded. "Really close."

"I'm almost there."

"Me, too," Demetrius said.

Cody shuddered and lifted his hips. His cock bucked against Demetrius's and, as Cody sprayed semen across his own belly, Demetrius hit the edge and tumbled over. His cock pulsed, and his cum splashed over Cody's skin, mixing with

Cody's semen. Demetrius kept both of them in his grip a little longer, strokes slowing as he milked the last few drops of cum from each. He could feel his balls resting on top of Cody's, and he marveled at the intimacy of it all: stroking their dicks together, their combined semen covering Cody's skin, and Cody's balls shifting and loosening beneath his own.

"That was amazing," Cody said.

Demetrius kissed him before he climbed off. He leaned down to kiss the tip of Cody's softening cock, then stood beside the bed.

"Okay, time to shower," Demetrius said.

Cody widened his eyes in surprise. "What? We just came together. No snuggling in the afterglow?"

"Nope." Demetrius shook his head. "I know you very well, and if I lay down with you again we'll fall asleep together, then wake up and have another quickie and then fall asleep again and we'll never get home."

Cody grinned. "Nothing wrong with that."

"No, nothing at all," Demetrius said. "But not when we're driving Amelia's car back to her. Let's get home and then we can spend the day in bed."

Cody swung his feet over the side of the bed and pulled Demetrius between his legs, hugging him around the waist. "Promise?"

Demetrius kissed him. "I promise. Now let's get a move on, Bower. We're burning daylight." He took Cody's hand and pulled him to his feet, then into the bathroom with him. Demetrius positioned Cody in front of the shower and darted out of the room.

"Hey!" Cody leaned out the bathroom door. "You're not going to shower with me?"

"Not this time," Demetrius said and made a shooing motion. "Go on. Clean up."

"Spoilsport."

"Shouldn't be a surprise to you," Demetrius said.

"Yeah, it's not."

The water started, and Demetrius busied himself packing and getting ready for his own shower. When Cody finally left the bathroom, Demetrius took a quick shower and got dressed. Within thirty minutes, they were out the door with their bags, which they stowed in the car before returning to the hotel for the breakfast buffet.

Demetrius thought everything looked the same as it always had between them on the outside. He sat across from Cody and they ate and talked about their business and wondered what Jugs had been up to. Demetrius watched Cody devour a heaping plate of food and guzzle cups of coffee. All of it looked the same, but everything had changed. Demetrius's stomach was a tangle of knots, but he couldn't tell if it was excitement or nervousness or a combination of the two. All he knew was that every time Cody's dark brown eyes met his and he smirked that sexy smirk, something low in his belly grew very, very warm.

"Doing okay over there?"

Demetrius nodded. "Doing great. How about you?"

Cody leaned in over the table and lowered his voice to say, "I worked up a hell of an appetite."

Demetrius blushed and had to look away. "Well, yeah."

Silence stretched out between them, and when Demetrius finally managed to look across the table again, he was surprised to find Cody watching him. "What?"

"It's going to be okay, Demmy. *We're* going to be okay."

"Yeah?"

"Yeah."

Demetrius let out a breath he didn't know he'd been holding. "Okay."

"I'm serious."

"I know."

Cody raised his eyebrows. "No, I really mean it. We're going to be okay."

"All right, I get it." Demetrius couldn't help smiling as he pushed his plate away. "I'm pretty much done."

"You'll be hungry in two hours," Cody said, using his last piece of toast to mop up some leftover yolk.

"Yeah, I know. But you'll have to use the bathroom by then anyway."

Cody laughed and nodded. "Guilty."

They looked at each other for a moment, the years of their friendship lying between them and the unknown future of where their relationship was headed waiting to be discovered. Although he was nervous about what upheavals the changes would bring, Demetrius was glad to realize he was more excited than scared. Along with the excitement was the comforting knowledge that he trusted Cody more than anyone outside of his family, and he could not imagine taking this drastic of a step with any other person.

"Ready?" Cody said.

Demetrius nodded and smiled. "I'm ready."

Cody smiled back. "Me, too."

They dodged some scampering children, dropped their dishes in the dish bin, and stepped out of the hotel into the bright sun of mid-morning. Demetrius unlocked the Explorer and got in behind the wheel.

"Hey," Cody said after Demetrius had started the engine and turned up the air conditioning.

Demetrius looked over to see Cody leaning toward him. He smiled and moved in for a soft kiss.

"What was that for?"

"Just because." Cody reclined his seat and closed his eyes. "Home, James."

"Home it is, sir," Demetrius said with a smile.

Cody opened one eye. "I like the 'sir' part."

"Don't get used to it."

"Maybe only in bed?"

Demetrius made a face. "Probably not."

"Maybe only when I'm hard?"

Demetrius laughed as he backed out of the parking space. "That would be pretty much all day."

"So you have been checking me out all these years," Cody said.

Demetrius shrugged. "Once or twice, maybe."

"Perv."

"Totally."

They chuckled together and Demetrius aimed the Explorer toward the highway and home.

THE END

TRADEMARK ACKNOWLEDGMENTS

The author acknowledges the trademark status and trademark owners of the following places and items mentioned in this work of fiction:

Lincoln MKS: Ford Motor Co.
Old Spice: Shulton, Inc.
Ben Gay: Pfizer, Inc.
Costco: Costco Wholesale Membership, Inc.
Superman: D.C. Comics/E.C. Publications, Inc.
Ford Explorer: Ford Motor Co.
Ray-Bans: Luxottica Group
McDonald's: McDonald's Corp.
HBO: Home Box Office, Inc.
Hampton Inn: Hilton Hospitality, Inc.

THE DEVIL OF PINESVILLE
CRITTER CATCHERS BOOK FOUR

Demetrius and Cody return for an all new adventure in THE DEVIL OF PINESVILLE: Critter Catchers Book Four, available now!

THE DEVIL OF PINESVILLE

An old friendship shifting to a new romance. An ex-boyfriend extending an invitation. An urban legend in the flesh.

Critter Catchers and amateur monster hunters Cody and Demetrius are building their friendship into something hotter and deeper. Both are way out of their comfort zones, but willing to work at things. It will just take a little time until Cody feels comfortable "coming out" to their friends, family, and the rest of Parson's Hollow. Demetrius is trying to be patient and understanding about Cody's position, and focuses on their business. Or, rather, the lack thereof.

When Demetrius's ex, Oliver Berridge, invites him to come to Pinesville, New Jersey for a case that might be right up their alley, Demetrius is intrigued. Sensing not just physical but romantic danger as well, Cody makes certain to accompany Demmy on the trip. Things in Pinesville are quickly complicated by a competing animal control company and a group of monster trackers from a low-budget TV show. The case quickly intensifies, leading to short tempers and tested loyalties, and forcing Demmy and Cody to decide if they're willing to save their business, their friendship, or their romance.

The Devil of Pinesville is available in digital, print, and audio from these retailers: https://books2read.com/crittercatchers4

ABOUT THE AUTHOR

Hank Edwards (he/him) has been writing gay fiction for more than twenty years. He has published over forty novels and novellas and dozens of short stories. His writing crosses many sub-genres, including contemporary romance, rom-com, paranormal, suspense, mystery, wacky comedy, and erotica. He has written a number of series such as the funny and spooky Critter Catchers, Old West historical horror of Venom Valley, suspenseful FBI and civilian Up to Trouble, and the erotic and funny Fluffers, Inc. Under the pen name R. G. Thomas, he has written a young adult urban fantasy gay romance series called The Town of Superstition. He was born and still lives in a northwest suburb of the Motor City, Detroit, Michigan.

For more information:
www.hankedwardsbooks.com
hankedwardsbooks@gmail.com
www.facebook.com/groups/hankshangout

ALSO BY HANK EDWARDS

<u>Critter Catchers Series</u>

Terror by Moonlight

Chasing the Chupacabra

Swamped by Fear

The Devil of Pinesville

Screams of the Season

Horror at Hideaway Cove

Dread of Night

Critter Catchers Box Set 1

Critter Catchers Box Set 2

<u>Critter Catchers Universe Stories</u>

The Mystery of the Morelock Motel

<u>Critter Catchers: Level Up Series</u>

Grave Danger

Wet Screams

<u>Williamsville Inn Gay Romance:</u>

Snowflakes and Song Lyrics

The Cupid Crawl

Fake Date Flip-Flop

Star-Spangled Showdown

<u>Lacetown Murder Mysteries</u>

(co-written with Deanna Wadsworth)

Murder Most Lovely

Murder Most Deserving

<u>Venom Valley Series</u>

Cowboys & Vampires

Stakes & Spurs

Blood & Stone

<u>Up to Trouble Series</u>

Holed Up

Shacked Up

Roughed Up

Choked Up

<u>Fluffers, Inc. Series</u>

Fluffers, Inc.

A Carnal Cruise

Vancouver Nights

<u>Standalone Gay Romance</u>

Buried Secrets

Destiny's Bastard

Hired Muscle

Plus Ones

Repossession is 9/10ths of the Law

Wicked Reflection

<u>Holiday Gay Romance:</u>

A Gift for Greg (A Story Orgy Single)

Mistletoe at Midnight (A Story Orgy Single)

The Christmas Accomplice

<u>Story Orgy Singles Gay Romance</u>:

A Gift for Greg

By the Book

Cross Country Foreplay

Mistletoe at Midnight

The Cheapskate: Bad Boyfriends

With This Ring

The Story Orgy Singles Boxed Set

<u>The Town of Superstition (YA urban fantasy series)</u>
<u>Published under pen name R. G. Thomas</u>

The Midnight Gardener

The Well of Tears

The Battle of Iron Gulch

A Tangle of Secrets

<u>Gay Erotic Short Story Collections</u>:

A Very Dirty Dozen

Another Very Dirty Dozen

A Third Very Dirty Dozen

A Fourth Very Dirty Dozen

<u>Salacious Singles Gay Erotic Short Stories</u>:

Bear Market

Convoy

Double Down

Exchange Rate

Finding North

Hotel Dick

Kindred Spirits

Sacked

Stroking Midnight

Vanity Loves Company

Wet Lands

www.ingramcontent.com/pod-product-compliance
Lightning Source LLC
Chambersburg PA
CBHW061429150726
47987CB00001B/150